PRAISE FOR DUBRAVKA UGRESIC

"Ugresic's wit is bound by no preconceived purposes, and once the story takes off, a wild freedom of association and adventurous discernment is set in motion. Open to the absurdity of all pretensions of rationality, Ugresic dissects the social world, especially the endless nuances of gender and sexuality."

—*World Literature Today*

"As long as some, like Ugresic, who can write well, do, there will be hope for literature."

—*New Criterion*

"A madcap wit and a lively sense of the absurd. . . . Filled with ingenious invention and surreal incident."

—Marina Warner

"Ugresic must be numbered among what Jacques Maritain called the dreamers of the true; she draws us into the dream."

—Richard Eder, *New York Times*

"Like Nabokov, Ugresic affirms our ability to remember as a source for saving our moral and compassionate identity."

—John Balaban, *Washington Post*

"Dubravka Ugresic is the philosopher of evil and exile, and the storyteller of many shattered lives the wars in the former Yugoslavia produced. . . . This is an utterly original, beautiful, and supremely intelligent novel."

—Charles Simic

DUBRAVKA UGRESIC

Lend Me Your Character

TRANSLATION BY CELIA HAWKESWORTH AND MICHAEL HENRY HEIM,
REVISED BY DAMION SEARLS

Dalkey Archive Press
Normal · London

Štefica Cvek u raljama života ("Steffie Cvek in the Jaws of Life") was first
published in Zagreb in 1981.

Život je bajka ("Life Is a Fairy Tale") was first published in Zagreb in 1983.
An additional story, "The Kharms Case," was taken from Nule I ništice,
first published in Zagreb in 1987.

First edition, 2005

Library of Congress Cataloging-in-Publication Data:

Ugrešić, Dubravka.
    [Short stories. English. Selections]
    Lend me your character / by Dubravka Ugrešić ; translation by Celia
Hawkesworth and Michael Henry Heim ; as revised by Damion Searls.
       p. cm.
    Contents: Steffie Cvek in the jaws of life — Life is a fairy tale.
    ISBN 1-56478-375-8 (alk. paper)
    1. Ugrešić, Dubravka—Translations into English. I. Hawkesworth,
Celia, 1942– II. Heim, Michael Henry. III. Searls, Damion. IV. Title.

PG1619.31.G7A25 2005
898.8'23—dc22
                                                        2004063477

Partially funded by grants from the National Endowment for the Arts,
a federal agency, and the Illinois Arts Council, a state agency.

Dalkey Archive Press is a nonprofit organization located at Milner Library
(Illinois State University) and distributed in the UK by
Turnaround Publisher Services Ltd. (London).

www.dalkeyarchive.com

Printed on permanent/durable acid-free paper and bound in
the United States of America.

CONTENTS

STEFFIE CVEK
IN THE JAWS OF LIFE
(*a little patchwork novel*)

KEY TO SYMBOLS

······✄   *Cut* the text as desired along the dotted line.

- · - · - · -   *Stretch*: The text may be resized in any direction in case of unfulfilled expectations, after moistening it with an ordinary damp imagination.

·········   *Take in*: The text may be taken in as required with critical darts.

/////////   *Gather*: Make large thematic stitches on either side of the author's seam. Then pull the lower threads a little and arrange the fabric evenly.

" " " " "   *Smocking*: Accordion-fold from seam to seam and make small sentimental stitches across the folds. Smooth down gently.

= = = =   *Knot*: Make a metatextual knot and pull tight as needed.

+ + + +   *Slits* for the co-author's ribbons, cords, etc.

THE PATTERN

Designing the garment
a) Technique
b) Material
c) Style

While shelling peas, Steffie Cvek* is overcome by a feeling that something is wrong (*basting*)

Steffie consults Anuška, an expert in questions of depression (*pleating*)

At the office, Steffie gets advice from her friend Marianna (*padding*)

Steffie takes her friend Marianna's advice (*hemming*)
A) Clothes
B) Figure
C) Makeup

Steffie meets some men (*concealed button fastenings*)
A) Steffie and the Truck Driver
B) Steffie and the He-Man
C) Steffie and the Intellectual

Steffie Cvek's dream (*interfacing*)

Topstitching by the author

---

* English-speaking readers may find it helpful to know that "Cvek" is pronounced "Tsvek."

Emancipated Ela gives Steffie Cvek some advice
(*kick pleating*)

Steffie Cvek takes Emancipated Ela's advice (*pinning*)
A) Steffie Cvek at the theater
B) Steffie Cvek reads *Madame Bovary* by Gustave Flaubert
C) Steffie Cvek reads at the museum, or, Some unexpected overstitching of S. C. with the author's own zigzag stitch

Steffie Cvek sleeps with a pig's head, or, A new attack of depression (*concealed plackets*)

Anuška, an expert in questions of depression, gives Steffie some news (*lapped seams*)

Steffie Cvek and the parakeet, or, Nursing a monster (*pinked hems*)

Steffie Cvek contemplates the man who took her virginity, the second man who took her virginity, and suicide (*toggle fastenings*)

Steffie Cvek remembers another piece of Emancipated Ela's advice (*gussets*)

Head over heels in a happy ending, or, The appearance of Monsieur Frndic (*finishing*)

Scraps of romance for appliqué work (*supplement*)

The author's darts

The author's mother, Aunt Seka, their neighbor Maja, Lence from Macedonia, and Yarmila from the Czech Republic continue the story of our heroine

Finishing touches

DESIGNING THE GARMENT

A) Technique

People kept suggesting I should write a representative piece of women's writing. Something, you know, feminine! My girlfriends said so (*Write about us! About us!*); my tailor said so (*There's so much material, if you only knew!*); my hairdresser said so (*I've styled a lot of 'em in my time, let me tell you!*); and my neurotic male friend said so too, the one who doesn't acknowledge any difference between the sexes and is always complaining about cramps (*I keep getting these pains in my belly, I must be pregnant*).

So I sat down at the typewriter to write such a story, a women's story made to order. I write very slowly, because I always get carried away by the sound of the typewriter, and the sound of the typing reminds me of a sewing machine. I'm fascinated by the clattering (plump fingertips squirming in the little, contoured seats of the letters), the sounds slipping by so steadily. But not the time—all typists and seamstresses (dressmakers, spinners, weavers, embroiderers) are flies in amber, as in Vermeer's paintings.

I'm fascinated by chatter, that passionate conquest of emptiness. People chattering, typing (weaving, embroidering) are almost as engrossed as whoever observes or watches them. The observer feels that they are in a different world, condemned to the same eternal movements. And illuminated from within, as in Vermeer's paintings.

So that's how I'll do it—textual textiles. The typist as
seamstress, the sewing machine as typing machine:
Typewriting, seamstressing, hemming, and hawing . . .
I'll sew as I go.

B) Material

*"I'm 18 years old and I think I'm at a major turning point,
but I can't figure out what to do. I'm pretty, smart, people
like me, I have good values and know how to live my life.
I'm not scared or insecure, I don't usually go looking for
shoulders to cry on, I'm independent enough to find my
own answers to things. I've been in love with all kinds of
boys, and I know how to see the best in them and love them
for that. And they loved me too but still they dumped me,
and all they said was that I'm a nice girl and a really great
person. It just happened again. A year ago I started going
out with a guy my own age, I really loved him and gave
him everything a girl can give, but he dumped me and told
me what a really great person I am. I want to go back to
him, but I think I've lost him forever and this has turned
my whole value system upside down. I can't decide whether
I'm expecting too much from life or too little. Is there any
hope?"*
Ana

*"I'm 18. I don't think I'm any different from most girls my
age. I'm friendly, average looking, and active in sports and
school clubs. But I can't find anyone to be in love with. I've
always been true to myself, my feelings and principles, and
that's cost me a lot. For more than two years now I've loved
a boy who's got someone else and I'm just a convenient
shoulder to cry on when things get rough for him, a helping*

hand when he's in trouble. Still, even though it's hopeless, I love him more than I can say. What should I do?"
Prometheus

. . . . ✂

"I'm 23 and divorced, with a three-year-old daughter. I've got a job, people say I'm attractive. I got married when I was 17 and divorced at 20. We lived with my parents, but they disapproved of our relationship and our marriage. They kept criticizing him, but I loved him nonetheless. In the end my parents were happy when their daughter got rid of that "lazy bastard." I was disillusioned and hurt, and I looked for comfort in a series of love affairs, trying to forget. I'm always dating married men—I'm no homewrecker, but something keeps drawing me to them. Maybe I'm looking for security. They're all the same, all liars. Some are good lovers, some are bad lovers—that's the only difference between them. But I can't go on like this. All they want is my body. I've been going round in circles for three years. Maybe my choices have deeper roots. My parents always argued, always neglected me. I've always had money, but never parents. And I was raped at 13. There's still something wrong with the way I talk, but no one ever asked me why. Maybe I'm just trying to escape into a dream world of empty pleasures. What should I do?"
Only a Shadow

. . . . ✂

"I am 25 years old and a typist by profession. I live with my aunt. I don't think I'm very attractive, but some people tell me I am. I'm different from everybody my age: they're all married or have boyfriends, and I have no one. I'm lonely and sad, and don't know what to do. Do you have any advice?"
Steffie

. . . . ✂

Here, at the melancholy typist, something brings me up short. This feels like the ideal fabric under my fingers. Remaindered, discount, your basic cotton weave. Humble cotton! A cotton tale like Peter Cottontail, and sweet as cotton candy.

So Steffie, you'll be my fabric, my fabrication. Last but not least, you need a last but not least name—where should I look? How about in the phone book: A, B, C . . . Cottontail . . . Cvek . . . Cvek? That's it—a perfect fit!

C) Style

Now the fabric is taken care of, but the author must admit, with no small amount of dismay, an almost complete ignorance of embroidering, weaving, crocheting, and tapestry-making. All she has is a textile typewriter. So she needs a simple style: patchwork! (She does like to cobble things together . . .) Patchwork quilt, patchwork shirt, patchwork skirt—no matter what the garment, patchwork is universal, democratic. It's not just a style, it's an attitude! And, fortunately for the author, imperfections and irregularities in the garment are inherent and desirable characteristics of this handcrafted item, which only add to its unique personality and style.

I keep typing, guiding the fabric along the machine. I'm sewing a prose dress, no more no less. Length and breadth, diagonal too, weaving straw into gold for you, I'm a butterfly seeking a lacewing king, and to start my stitches without a hitch I'll make a cut high and I'll make a cut low. Snippety-snip and away we go!

WHILE SHELLING PEAS,
STEFFIE CVEK IS OVERCOME BY
A FEELING THAT SOMETHING IS WRONG

(*basting*)

....✄

Garlic about to sprout? Put the bulbs head down in a can or other container and cover them with sea salt.

....✄

"Have you theen my teeth?" asked Steffie's aunt, coming into the kitchen.

"No."

"I mutht have put them down thomewhere again!" she sighed.

Steffie's aunt waddled in, mumbling and opening and closing the drawers. Then she stopped, as though thinking about something very important, and sighed again, opened the door of the pantry, took out a bag of peas, and shook them onto the table.

"Here, you shell the peath," she said, "I'll look for my teeth."

"Try the bed—last time we found them in the pillowcase."

Steffie's aunt smiled sadly, sucked her lips back into her toothless mouth, and shuffled out of the kitchen.

"Like a fig!" thought Steffie. "Figs suck their little tails into themselves when they dry out."

Steffie took out a plate and started shelling peas. -·-·-·-
The kitchen, bathed in sunlight, pulsated rhythmically.

From the courtyard came the sound of children playing and pigeons cooing. Steffie shelled the peas, slowly,
lazily, as if in slow motion, and she thought about
how she might be stuck in that pose forever if the film
stopped, or if someone—who knows who—turned off
the projector.

"You know," said Steffie's aunt, coming back into
the kitchen, "thomeone in Bothanthka Krupa, you don't
know her, lotht her teeth jutht like thith and never did
find them. She wath done for in thixth monthth!"

"Dead?"

"Dead."

"Ah," Steffie shrugged.

"Yeth!" And her aunt added: "Peel the potatoeth
when you're done."

-.-.-.- She shuffled out of the kitchen. Steffie separated the
pods, pressed along the bulges, pulled the little green
strings, undid the pockets, and the little green balls fell
out. They wriggled around on the plate, soaking up the
sunlight. Steffie picked up a handful and they slid down
her fingers and drummed out a sound on the bottom of
the plate like rain.

"Baby peas!" sighed Steffie tenderly, putting one in
her mouth.

"Don't eat thothe peath!" said her aunt, coming into
the kitchen.

"Why not?"

"Thomeone in Bothanthka Krupa, they called him
crazy Mirko, ate all the raw peath he could, jutht like
thith, for a bet, and he died."

"Of raw peas?"

"Yeth," said Steffie's aunt. "Alwayth thimmer peath
properly, with onionth." She flapped around the kitchen,

opening and closing the drawers. "Are you almotht done?" she asked.

"Almost . . . "

Her aunt left the room and Steffie continued to fiddle with the little pockets, pulling the threads as though unstitching them.

Suddenly she felt a warm mist gather and solidify around her, like cotton wool. She felt she had shelled peas like this before, at the same time of day, in the same kitchen, at the same table. "Maybe I've been sitting in this kitchen shelling peas my whole life, without noticing it . . ." " " " " "

The wool slowly wound itself round Steffie Cvek, encasing her like a cocoon. "I'm like a caterpillar," thought Steffie, wriggling. "Like a little green caterpillar . . ." She spun more daydreams. She tugged the last thread and four chubby peas rolled out of the pod. " " " " "

Steffie picked up the plate but it slipped out of her hands and clattered onto the floor. The peas flew in all directions. Steffie bent down and began to pick up the peas, on her knees, one by one. In the rays of sunlight spreading over the floor, as under a magnifying glass, Steffie could see dust, scratches, peas . . . She was overcome by an incomprehensible despair.

Oh my God, I'm going to be stuck in this kitchen forever, picking up peas, one by one, Steffie sniffled, my whole life, Steffie thought, with my aunt, Steffie wept, she'll keep losing her teeth, the tears fell to the floor, I'll keep picking up peas, Steffie sniffled, everyone's doing better than me, Steffie thought, Marianna, Ela, Anuška, the peas rolled away, at least they've got someone, the peas escaped, a husband, children, friends, Steffie sniffed, I'm the only one who's all alone, Steffie thought, I go to work, " " " " "

= = = =

" " " " "

go home, go to work, the tears poured down Steffie's face, nothing, nothing ever changes, the tears rolled on, I'll drop plates and be here forever, picking up peas, one by one, the peas swam in her tears, like a bad dream, Steffie sniffed, why isn't Ela in a bad dream, Steffie asked herself, why doesn't Marianna drop any plates, the floor shimmered through her tears, why doesn't Anuška have to pick up any peas, Steffie fingered her green rosary, why me, I have to do something, her fingers moved along the thread pea by pea, as soon as I've picked up these peas I have to do something, her hand like blotting paper wiped up the tears on her cheek.

= = = =   Two white doves alighted on the windowsill, nodding their heads and watching Steffie Cvek. Her aunt shuffled into the kitchen.

"Shoo, you nathty thingth!" she cried and the doves flew away. Suddenly she beamed: "My teeth!"

Steffie saw her aunt's teeth right next to the table leg. She picked them up with two fingers and handed them to her aunt.

As Steffie's aunt stood there, looking with pity at the young woman kneeling on the floor in tears, the film of old age vanished from her eyes and she seemed like she wanted to say something. But she changed her mind and, shaking her head, shuffled out the door.

There were only a few peas left on the floor.

STEFFIE CONSULTS ANUŠKA, AN EXPERT IN QUESTIONS OF DEPRESSION

(pleating)

....✂

If you stand on your head for just five minutes a day, you'll have clearer skin and better circulation. To start, try propping yourself against a wall for two to three minutes whenever you feel tired or out of sorts.

Keep your makeup pencils in the fridge and they will be easier to sharpen.

....✂

"Anuška?"

"Yes?"

"It's me, Steffie."

"Oh, Steffie! How are you doing, honey?"

"Um, not bad . . . What are you doing?"

"I'm ironing. I've got a whole mountain here . . . What have you been up to? I haven't seen you for ages."

"I'm okay . . . um . . . I wanted to ask you something. Remember you told me once you were depressed? I think you said you went to the doctor's. Remember?"

"I don't remember, but it doesn't matter. I'm depressed every day. Why?"

"I think I am too."

"Depressed?"

"I'm not sure. I think so . . ."

"Hm . . . wait a sec, honey, I've got it all written down here somewhere, don't hang up, I'll be right back . . ."

"Steffie, are you still there?"

"Yes."

"I found it. 'Major symptoms. Depression can be recognized by such interrelated symptoms as indecisiveness . . .' Are you listening?"

"Yes."

" 'Indecisiveness, insomnia, loss of interest in things that are important to you . . .' Are you listening?"

"Yes."

"Well?"

"What?"

"Have you got those symptoms or not?"

"Indecisiveness and loss of interest yes. Not insomnia."

"There's more: 'Fatigue, anxiety, aversive affect . . .' "

"Aversive aah-affect? What's that?"

"I don't know, being shy, being scared of life, something like that."

"That's me all right. Keep going."

" 'Hopelessness, feelings of guilt, low self-confidence, negativity, and gastro-intestinal troubles.' That's it."

"I've got them all! But what were those last two things?"

"Negativity—that's when everything seems bad. The other one's something to do with your stomach, when you lose your appetite and so on."

"Oh."

"What do you mean 'oh'? Are you depressed or not?"

"I'm not sure. I've got almost all of the symptoms . . ."

"Then you are, but only partially. That's not so bad, honey."

"Yes it is."

"Steffie, are you there? Say something!"

"I'm still here . . ."

"What is it now? Probably crying your eyes out!"

"Yes, I mean no, not any more . . ."

"Crying and indecisiveness, that's two symptoms right there!"

"What should I do?"

"I don't know, honey. If I knew I'd do it myself. Got a boyfriend?"

"No."

"That's what I thought. You need to get one, it's the best cure there is for depression. Didn't you know that?"

"No."

"Steffie, listen, when I'm done with this mountain of + + + + ironing I'll call you back, okay?"

"Okay."

"And don't worry about it. Everyone's depressed, more or less. I get depressed every day, ten minutes a day at least. Are you listening, honey?"

"Okay."

"I'll call you later, all right?"

"All right."

"Okay then."

"Okay."

"Hey, don't hang up! I forgot to tell you. You know Matilda? She's gone off with a tour group to Mallorca. A whole week! Can you believe it?"

"Really?"

"Even getting killed wouldn't make Matilda depressed."

"Yeah, um, why is the phone crackling like that?"

"It's not the phone, it's a parakeet. I bought myself a parakeet, didn't you know that? No, how could you. A couple days ago. He's great, but he's got a filthy mouth."

"Really?"

"Uh huh."

"Alright . . . Call me."

"I will. As soon as I finish this ironing."

"Okay . . ."

AT THE OFFICE, STEFFIE GETS ADVICE FROM HER FRIEND MARIANNA

(*padding*)

⋯⋯⋯⋯⋯⋯⋯⋯⋯⋯⋯⋯⋯⋯⋯⋯⋯⋯⋯⋯⋯⋯✄

You can use little balls of soft fresh bread for wiping finger-prints from light surfaces, wood, wallpaper, and playing cards. Change the balls as soon as they get dirty.

⋯⋯⋯⋯⋯⋯⋯⋯⋯⋯⋯⋯⋯⋯⋯⋯⋯⋯⋯⋯⋯⋯✄

"Guys today are real losers, I'm lucky I got myself a good one in time," sighed Marianna, biting into a ham sandwich. A little piece of ham sprung out of the middle of the sandwich like a jack-in-the-box and Marianna skillfully thrust it back with her finger. "After all," Marianna went on, her mouth full, "maybe I've got a one-track mind, but a guy's the most important thing in a girl's life. So come on, get a hold of yourself, you're not stupid!"

Marianna swallowed the last mouthful, then took another sandwich out of a plastic bag, checked to make sure the ham was neat and tidy, and went on:

"Come on now, tell me, what's your life like? You sit at home with that old aunt of yours waiting for a guy to drop into your lap—it doesn't work that way! You have to make more of an effort, you know?"

Marianna pulled a paper plate toward her and turned it around to the side with the chocolate pastry.

"Here, I'll have this one, you take the apricot. Okay? Let's forget the diet today, we can start with the hard-boiled eggs tomorrow. Okay?

++++   "Look, Steffie, let me tell you straight out, you have no sex appeal at all. Diddly-squat. That's the way it is." Marianna stabbed her plastic spoon into her pastry. "But don't worry, we can take care of that," she added briskly, licking her spoon. "First you need to lose a few pounds. I'll see to that, I've got a great diet. Second, get yourself a good haircut. Then buy yourself some nice things to wear. You don't have to spend tons of money, you know, there are some great second-hand places and thrift-store clothes are in these days. Flip through some magazines. But the main thing," she said, pulling her coffee cup towards her, "how can I put it, you're too uptight, too goody-two-shoes somehow, I don't know . . ." Marianna shook her head, and then lit a cigarette, blew out the smoke and went on energetically:

"You just can't let it get to you." Marianna slurped some coffee. "The coffee's really good today! What I'm trying to say is, when you make a face and clam up the way you always do it's enough to scare anyone, even me! Guys like girls who smile, and you always look, I don't know, offended. Like someone just slapped you. That'd make any guy feel guilty, and who wants to go around feeling guilty all the time? Think about it.

"And another thing." Marianna took the plastic spoon again and scraped up the remains of the pastry. "You must have some girlfriends. Go out with them, go wild once in a while! It's not a bar of soap that'll disappear if you get it wet, if you know what I mean! Look around—there are guys on every corner, every single one." Marianna cracked her fingers with passion.

"If I were you," said Marianna, exhaling a cloud of smoke, "I'd even go out with married men. Only they never marry you, and sometimes they can't get it up because of the motel prices! God, what a dirty mouth I have, don't listen to me. Anyway, I'm sorry for you, you're a good kid, and life is passing you by, just passing you by."

Marianna paused, picked up the crumbs from the table with the tip of her finger, and nibbled them, then frowned, deep in thought, and said, "Listen, I'll ask around about our new delivery truck driver. He's hot. Maybe he's single . . . Okay, okay, I won't . . . Well," she added, "maybe I'll ask around just a little."

Marianna got up, picked up the plastic bag and paper plate and dropped them into the trash. Then she looked at her watch and said, "Let's have one more smoke, okay?"

Marianna looked compassionately at Steffie, blew out a puff of smoke, and said conspiratorially, "Steffie, there are a million ways to catch a guy. Don't hook up   + + + +
with anyone at work, unless he marries you on the spot, but there are bars, clubs . . . Well maybe that's not your scene . . . But take Kika, for instance. D'you hear about her? No? Well, you know Kika couldn't get any guys for ages, so finally she gave up and bought a dog. With a pedigree and everything. One day she's taking it for a walk when this guy with a dog comes up and says, 'How's your dog?' and she says, 'Fine, how's your dog?' and blah, blah, blah. Next thing you know they were married. A real fairy tale."

Marianna stopped, took some chocolate out of her bag, broke off a piece, offered it to Steffie, and went on.

"And Ankica? Did you hear about Ankica? The one   + + + +
with the beautiful teeth. She got married in the dentist's chair! One day she had toothache and that was that—a dashing young dentist. Unbelievable! Go on, go on, have some," Marianna said, pushing some of her chocolate

toward Steffie. "We'll start our diet on Monday . . . Yes
. . . And Lela? You won't believe that either! You didn't
hear? Well, you know her folks left her a house, right? She
decided to sell it. What would a single girl do all alone in
that great big place? All right, you haven't got a house,
I'm just telling you this to show you how many ways there
are to meet people. Anyway, she puts an ad in the paper,
and this dreamboat rings the bell and says he wants to
buy the house for himself and his folks. An architect.
They haggled over the house for a month and finally got
married, now they're all living happily together, the two
of them and his family . . . I'm telling you, you never know
when you'll run into Mr. Right."

Marianna looked at her watch, quickly turned back
to her typewriter, and said, "It's one o'clock, time to get
back to work!"

She pressed a few keys on the typewriter and sighed.
"Now why don't *I* ever get depressed?"

STEFFIE TAKES HER FRIEND MARIANNA'S ADVICE

(*hemming*)

A) Clothes

··✄

Did you know? Water you've cooked spinach in makes a great detergent for black clothes.

··✄

Steffie read:

Here are our favorite ways to wear the season's hottest styles. Pair a satin baseball jacket with a pencil skirt and add pointy-toe pumps. The result is fun, '50s inspired, and full of attitude. The full-skirt silhouette, harkening back to an earlier era, has made a comeback and is pretty as ever. The picnic skirt: A full, flouncy shape that's as flattering as it is feminine. Keep spring chills in check with one of these undeniably feminine, vintage-influenced pieces. This packable dress is so lightweight—it folds down to T-shirt size—and so hard to wrinkle that it'll go everywhere with us this summer. The airy weave, black-ribbon lacing, and sweet rosette are enough to transform an all-black evening ensemble into something even more special. Ironically, the trick to wearing a tennis dress is to make it look like you don't intend to play the game. Add accessories that play off the preppiness of the dress, like retro-looking wedges and a slightly hippie bag. We like the way the bright straps of this swimwear-inspired bra peek out from a tank and tone down the buttoned-up feel of a blazer—giving the whole look a laid-back, beach-girl vibe. Espadrilles: Why? A jute sole epitomizes laid-back, warm-weather chic. Wear them with? Circle skirts, minis, or any cropped pant, all the better to show off their cute details. Pleats that start at the waist look much more modern than ones that begin at the hips. Fancy and elephant, not over-the-top dressy. Chiffon always books best with thumbsing thimble so try it over a plain tank in keeping with the soft femininine looks so popular this season these ballet-inspired cheaters are a sweet alchurnative try one of these playful print-sover a lightweight cottondress aupaired withatank auntamini pry a colorful pelt over a neutral plazer—it's unexpected but sill stafe. Weather tangerineortaxiyellow a burst of collar adds funto function grommeted straps takepink toawhole new-place silverstuds conveyinstantattitude magentagives-you—andyourwardrobe—alift a floatyflop flows alongflay evenifit's just fleekingoutofajacketlookingcomfortableisthe-mostimportantthingandaslightlydrapeyjerseydressiseasytowe arandfeelgoodin (it'sstylishbutdoesn'tlooklikeyou'retryingtoo hard) . . .

Steffie's eyelids grew heavy, the fashion magazine slipped onto the floor, and Steffie turned onto her side and fell asleep.

Meanwhile her aunt was sitting in a rocking chair, mut-tering softly: "It'th not true that drethmakerth all die by the needle. We had one in Bothanthka Krupa who died of ithe cream. In thothe dayth ithe cream wath thold by ithe cream vendorth, from a little cart, and they shouted like thith: Ithe cream! Ithe creeeeeam! I thtill remember how the drethmaker went the window with a tape measure round her neck and her mouth full of pinth, and shouted: Ithe creeeeam! Over heeere, over heeeere! She put away bowl after bowl, it was awful. Died of pneumonia, all becauthe of the ithe cream. The pinth had nothing to do with it . . ."

B) Figure

....✄

Does the meat you just bought look hard and tough? Put it in a bowl of milk and let it soak for half an hour—it doesn't matter how you plan to cook it, it will come out tender and tasty.

....✄

On the morning of the fifth day Steffie Cvek stood on the scale. Marianna had said, "You can't go wrong! I've tried it myself, eight pounds in four days! It's a great diet."

On the morning of the fifth day Steffie stood on the scale, but the needle had not moved even a fraction of an inch to the left. "Not an ounce!" thought Steffie.

On the fifth day at seven minutes past five Steffie walked out of the office and headed for the pastry shop, where she bought five apple strudels and a pound of small cakes. Then she went to the supermarket and bought a quarter pound of cold cuts, a jar of mayonnaise, two pounds of tomatoes, a pound of strawberries, a loaf of French bread, a bottle of red wine, and half a roast chicken.

On the late afternoon of the fifth day Steffie Cvek made her way home like someone about to slink into the first available doorway.

On the fifth day Steffie Cvek's aunt was away, in Bosanska Krupa, which was very convenient.

On the late afternoon of the fifth day Steffie Cvek reached home and locked the door behind her.

She locked the door behind her and drew the cur-   //////// tains. Then she turned on the TV. There was a kid's show on, with the cartoon version of *Snow White and the Seven Dwarves*. Steffie went into the kitchen and took her groceries out of the bag. First she washed the strawberries, sprinkled them with sugar, and put them in the fridge. Then she put the cold cuts, mayonnaise, and tomatoes on a plate, the chicken on another plate, the apple strudels on a third plate, and the small cakes in a dish. Finally she opened the wine and took it all into the living room.

Steffie spread some mayonnaise on a piece of bread and added several slices of sausage. On TV the wicked stepmother was asking the mirror who the fairest of them all was. Steffie moved on to the roast chicken, broke off a wing, and concluded as usual that the wing was the best part because the skin crackled so splendidly.

"You know," her aunt used to say, "in Bothanthka Krupa there uthed to be a man named Marko who jutht loved everything crithpy. Everything that crunched when you ate it and everything that wath a little burnt. I uthed to be like that mythelf, alwayth thcraping panth. But that Marko thcraped panth and crunched away until he got thick, and latht month he died."

Steffie tore the skin off the roast chicken and crunched it. On TV a hunter was about to kill Snow White, but his heart was wrung with pity and he refrained, and killed a deer instead. Steffie cut up a tomato. Snow White met the dwarves, who were singing a cheerful little song about digging. Steffie gnawed the last chicken bone.

Suddenly it occurred to Steffie that her aunt might come home from Bosanska Krupa. She hurried to collect the bones and throw them out. Then she cleared the table and laid out the apple strudels, the small cakes, and the wine and had another look to make sure the door was locked.

While the dwarves were digging, the wicked step-mother came and gave Snow White an apple. To start with Steffie ate one apple strudel and drank a glass of wine. The dwarves came back from their digging and found Snow White dead. Steffie remembered her aunt's friend Mara who had drowned in a marsh. "The rusheth got caught round her feet and dragged her down to the bottom. Rusheth are terrible thingth." Steffie ate another apple strudel and poured herself some more wine. Snow White lay in her coffin, and the dwarves and the animals of the forest were crying. Steffie tried one of the small cakes. It wasn't bad. The prince kissed Snow White. Steffie drank a glass of wine. The prince and Snow White rode on a white horse into the sunset and a beautiful castle on a mountaintop. The dwarves and animals waved.

"What if Snow White was ugly?" Steffie wondered as she started in on another apple strudel. "Maybe there wouldn't have been a story," Steffie thought, sipping her wine. "The whole problem was that she was prettier than her wicked stepmother." Steffie had trouble swallowing the apple strudel. "That's it. There wouldn't have been a story," Steffie thought and suddenly burst into tears. Her tears dripped onto the confectioner's sugar sprinkled on the top of the bun and left marks there. Plop! Plop! Plop! fell the tears, dissolving the sugar. "Not an ounce!" Steffie thought, crying, as she polished off the apple strudel. "Not an ounce!" Steffie thought, sobbing, as she took the strawberries out of the fridge.

Through her tears Steffie saw the strawberries peeping out from under their white blanket of sugar. She grabbed a spoon. At first she felt like she was swallowing her fate, her unhappy little fate, spoonful by spoonful, that she was chewing up her loneliness, that she was slurping down Mallorca where Matilda was and where she, Steffie, would never be . . . Faster, faster, faster, the life out there waiting for her, faster, the open spaces, faster, before the lovers she was meant to kiss grew old, faster, before the trains she was meant to catch stopped, faster, before the seas dried up, faster, before the dresses turned to dust, faster, before life dissolved like the sugar on the strudel, faster, Steffie shuttled her spoon back and forth, faster, Steffie licked the spoon as though it were her fate itself, faster, typed Steffie's thoughts, faster, Steffie Cvek took her terrible revenge.

+ + + +   She felt a delicious sense of fatigue come over her, her head spun and hummed, she felt she was drowning, her legs entangled in rushes dragging her down to the bottom. It was scary but intoxicating, and she let herself go.

C) Makeup

....✄

If you smudge a little makeup under your eyelid, you can remove the excess mascara with a corner of a kleenex. Or, you can put the tissue under your eyelashes when you apply the mascara.

....✄

....   Steffie Cvek's finger mechanically tapped under her chin as she read the following:

Skin: You have radiant skin, you just haven't discovered it yet. Now you can look like your *complexion* is perfect—not your makeup! By working with your own natural skin tones, you can't miss. You're perfect! And perfectly you.

Eyes: When you shape your eyebrows, don't go too thin. Eyeshadow with a subtle shimmer makes for a sexy glam effect.

Don't stick to the safe, superwearable pinks and browns; green *is* the color of the season, and we can't get enough of it.

Cheeks: A daily face scrub cleans below the surface, yet is gentle enough to use every day. Or, you can exfoliate and deep-clean your pores with a thick cleansing cloth. A rich, sexy rouge that brightens up your face is essential for a big night out.

Lips: Red lips with fair skin look gorgeous. But stay away from reds with an orangey or berry tinge, and opt for truer reds with bluish undertones. If a particular shade seems too dramatic for you, put clear gloss on top to de-intensify it ever so slightly.

Hair: Everyone knows you're supposed to choose a hairstyle based on your hair type and the shape of your face—but what matters is whether it makes you feel good! If you're dying for a pixie cut but you're afraid of those crazy cowlicks, you can always twist the strands near your ears and on the crown to add spikes and ringlets. At night, straight-iron your bangs, sides, and ends to make them seem longer, and slick them back for a dramatic, polished look.

Steffie Cvek stopped reading, opened her mouth, and drew her upper and lower lips over her teeth as though she wanted to hide them. She held her lips in this position for fifteen seconds. Then she pulled her upper lip over the lower one but kept them apart by half a little finger width. Then she "whistled" silently for three seconds, then pulled her lips into a "smile" and held it for five seconds. Then she puckered her lips into a "kiss" and held them there for three seconds. She repeated the exercise regimen ten times.

Steffie's aunt said: "There wath a woman in Bothan-thka Krupa who alwayth made herthelf up with the charcoal from matcheth. She would light a match, like thith . . . then she would uthe the burnt end to make herthelf up. Onthe she poked the match into her eye and went completely blind. Maybe she'th thtill alive, I don't know, but I do know she never got married . . ."

STEFFIE MEETS SOME MEN

(concealed button fastenings)

A) Steffie and the Truck Driver

....✂

You've been careless and sat on the grass in light clothes. Don't worry, you can get those grass stains out! Dissolve a little rubbing alcohol in some bottled water and dab lightly.

....✂

("What if the old lady comes back from Bosanska Krupa early?" the Truck Driver thought as he rang the bell.)

"Oh, it's you" said Steffie, flustered.

"Yes," the Truck Driver said modestly.

"Come in, sit down, I'll be there in a second," said Steffie, slipping into the kitchen. "He's handsome, oh gosh, he's so handsome!" the words tapped out in Steffie's head. "First a drink, then lunch, and if he's not interested a cup of coffee," thought Steffie, taking down two glasses, a bottle, and a tray. "Alwayth put a cloth or a clean napkin on the tray. It lookth nither," her aunt used to say, so Steffie put a clean napkin on the tray.

For some reason the Truck Driver had chosen the edge of the bed as the most suitable place to sit. He put down a largish black bag by his feet. Steffie poured drinks.

"Steffie, Steffie . . ." said the Truck Driver. "Pretty name. Nice and simple, everyone's calling themselves something fancy these days."

"Thanks . . ." said Steffie because she couldn't think what else to say.

"Call me Ivo," said the Truck Driver, clinking his glass against hers.

"OK," said Steffie.

("Maybe he won't want lunch. And maybe I shouldn't ask him to lunch so soon, he'll think I like him . . . Lunch can wait until a second date, for now we can just have a drink . . .")

"This is great brandy!" said the Truck Driver and smiled. ("What a sexy smile! He sure is handsome," thought Steffie.)

"So Steffie, how well do you know Marianna?" asked the Truck Driver.

"We're pretty good friends . . ." ("Why is he asking about Marianna? What did she tell him about me anyway? Maybe he doesn't know what else to talk about? If he's thinking about staying for lunch I better take the meat out of the fridge." She poured him some more brandy.)

"Steffie, do you have a boyfriend?" the Truck Driver suddenly asked. He cast a piercing glance at her.

"No!" she said quickly, and blushed. ("I shouldn't have said that. What an idiot I am!")

"A pretty girl like you, and no boyfriend?" the Truck Driver cast another piercing glance. Steffie didn't know how to answer so she got up and went to the kitchen. ("What's going to happen now? Will he try and kiss me? What should I do?" she thought and went back into the room carrying a glass of water.)

The Truck Driver was sitting on the edge of the bed, turning the glass of brandy around in his hand. The piercing glance remained stuck on his face.

"Hey, come over here for a minute. Sit next to me," he said in a deep, rumbling voice.

Steffie obediently sat down next to the Truck Driver. He stroked her hair and then kissed her. Steffie's head spun.

"Steffie, Steffie . . . !" panted the Truck Driver, pulling her forcefully onto the bed.

("God, he'll take off my clothes and we haven't even finished our drinks! Maybe I really should have taken the meat out of the fridge . . . ?")

"Steffie, Steffie . . . !" panted the Truck Driver.

("God, does he mean just like this, I didn't even change the sheets . . . Should I stop him? I'm letting him go too far, I ought to resist . . . It's too soon, it's all too fast . . . we haven't even finished our drinks, maybe we should wait . . .")

"Wait," whispered the Truck Driver. He sat up and /////////
emptied his glass. As he was about to throw himself back onto the bed, his foot bumped into his black bag.

Something started barking. It came from the bag, which was shaking back and forth.

"Bow-wow-wow-wow-wow-wow!" barked the bag.

"What's that?" asked Steffie, confused. She tugged the hem of her skirt back down.

"Nothing!" the Truck Driver answered, tucking in his shirt.

"Bow-wow-wow-wow-wow-wow!" barked the bag · · · · · · · · ·
stubbornly.

"Dammit!" the Truck Driver said angrily and opened the bag. Steffie saw two white mechanical dogs; the Truck Driver took one and quickly shut the bag. The dog in his hand ferociously snapped its sharp metal teeth. "Bow-wow-wow-wow!" it barked.

"Fuck! What the hell's the matter with it?" the Truck Driver shoved a key into its side. The dog went on barking. "Damn machines!" raged the Truck Driver, shaking the dog. "The motor must have broken! Franjo brought it from Germany for me. The crap those Germans make, total crap!"

Steffie was cowering in confusion at the end of the bed and picking at the hem of her skirt. The Truck Driver groaned helplessly: "Fucking dog! I thought you might like it. It's a nice dog. I thought a nice little toy would be better than flowers . . ."

The Truck Driver pulled himself together, poured a little brandy for himself, a little for Steffie, clinked his glass against hers and said, "Well, Steffie, I really should get going . . . I've got plans to meet Franjo. Known him since we were kids. He's going back tomorrow. You know how it is. Don't feel bad. I'll call you. Let's drink to it!"

The Truck Driver got up in a formal kind of way, tossed back his brandy, picked up his bag, and left. The toy dog was still barking.

Steffie closed the door and put away the bottle and glasses. The dog kept barking. Steffie picked it up cautiously with two fingers and threw it into the garbage can. "Bow-wow-wow-wow!" the garbage can rumbled. Steffie took the dog out of the garbage and shook it. The dog ferociously snapped its mechanical teeth. Steffie put the dog on the floor and jumped on it with her whole weight. The dog went quiet.

" " " " "   Then she went back to her room and saw that a wallet had slipped down between the bed and the wall. Steffie opened the wallet. A driver's license, some money, some receipts, and a photograph fell out. The picture was of a woman hugging two little boys. "Twins," thought Steffie. "I'll ask Marianna to give it back," she decided, and went back into the kitchen.

B) Steffie and the He-Man

....✄

Constructing a front opening: Place closed zipper face up under right turned-in edge. Baste. Bring left front over zipper, matching centers along the teeth. On inside, open out left fly. Baste zipper in place, keeping garment free. Stitch zipper to left fly, close to teeth and again at tape edge. Pin. Baste through all layers. Sew.

....✄

"Where's your aunt?" asked the He-Man, slipping through the door.

"In Bosanska Krupa," said Steffie.

"Good!" said the He-Man. "I don't like aunts roaming around the apartment while I'm on the job."

As soon as they entered the room, the He-Man threw himself straight onto the bed and cased out the furniture, the walls, the books.

"You in school?"

"No," said Steffie quietly.

"Good. I don't like girls in school."

The He-Man cased out Steffie.

"You're not bad. Let's screw! I'll give it to you good. I'm the real deal, don't you worry! Two hours nonstop. What am I talking about? I can keep it up all night, until that aunt of yours comes back from Bosanska Krupa. Alright?"

"Alright," said Steffie humbly, looking at the He-Man with some trepidation. ("We'll never both fit in the bed," she thought.) One of the He-Man's arms, one shoulder, and a leg were already slipping towards the floor.

"Don't you worry," said the He-Man. He stretched out the piece of gum he was chewing and put the long string back in his mouth.

The room was quiet. All Steffie could hear was the He-Man's persistent, rhythmic chewing. Steffie glanced at him and their eyes met; she quickly lowered her gaze and the He-Man looked away too, scanning the walls of the room as if looking for something interesting, like a safe to crack.

Steffie lit a cigarette. The He-Man took the gum out of his mouth and stuck it on the headboard.

"Toss me one too," he said.

They smoked. Steffie wondered what time it was. She thought it must be getting late, and then thought that they ought to be talking about something, anything.

"There," said the He-Man suddenly, putting out his cigarette. "Now it's time to get busy! Take your clothes off."

"No, no . . ." Steffie hesitated, her face red.

"Okay," said the He-Man, agreeing at once. "Maybe you're scared. Look, I'm not a violent guy; I understand women perfectly. Soon you'll be saying yes, yes! YES! You'll faint, you'll beg me never to stop. I'll take my clothes off first, to make you feel better."

The He-Man took off his clothes. Huge, swollen chunks of body burst out of them.

"There," said the He-Man, taking his gum off the headboard and putting it back in his mouth. "Now I'll take a little walk around the room," said the He-Man, walking up and down in front of Steffie and criss-crossing the room with its vast gray shadows. "There. And now it's time to get busy!" The He-Man headed toward Steffie.

Breathing heavily, he began to take Steffie's clothes off. He fumbled with her buttons, panting, until at last she was naked. ("We'll never both fit in this bed," Steffie thought, and found herself on the floor.)

Chewing away, the He-Man flung and tossed Steffie this way and that, squeezing her, pummelling her, rolling her over the floor like a piece of dough; Steffie rocked, sank, and rose up on the He-Man's smooth muscles and thought in some alarm, "This must be the way you do it."

"There!" said the He-Man. "That was the foreplay. Now it's really time to get busy! Nonstop till morning."

"Alright," Steffie whispered into the He-Man's huge ear. The He-Man lay on his side with his head propped on one hand. He used the other to pull the gum out of his mouth and put it back in, out and in.

Steffie looked inquiringly at the He-Man.

"We're not in any hurry," he answered. "We've got all night. Relax!"

"OK," said Steffie with a blush, still lying submissively next to him on the floor. There was another long silence.

"Hey, you don't have anything to eat, do you?" it suddenly occurred to the He-Man.

Steffie hurried to the kitchen, glad that something was happening, and opened the fridge. She found a quart of milk in a cardboard carton, some salami, and a jar of mayonnaise. ("I'll make a few sandwiches," she thought, and made—seven. Then she changed her mind and made three more. "Ten ought to be enough," she decided, and went back to the bedroom.)

The He-Man was lying in the same position, pulling out his gum and shoving it back into his mouth, while looking around for the imagined safe.

"Great!" said the He-Man, taking the first sandwich. "This is how I'll kiss you, like this and like this! This is how I'll screw you the first time!" He devoured the first sandwich.

" " " " "   It was getting dark, and for the first time Steffie felt comfortable in her room. She wrapped herself in a blanket and lay down on the floor. The blanket tickled her naked body. ("I should sleep like this all the time," she thought, and felt her eyelids closing.)

"This is how I'll screw you, crunch, crunch, grind, grind, this is how I'll do it the tenth time," mumbled the He-Man, and through her lashes Steffie saw him finish sandwich number ten. Then he tipped the carton of milk into his mouth. A gray morning light slowly started to come in through the window.

"There," said the He-Man, wiping his mouth decisively with his hand. "C'mere!"

Steffie wriggled over to the He-Man, still wrapped in her blanket. the He-Man squeezed her tight, put a hand under the blanket, and distractedly ran it over her hips.

"It's getting light," he said, with gentle melancholy.

"Yes," said Steffie.

/////////   Suddenly the He-Man gave a start and anxiously
+ + + +   slapped his hand to his forehead.

"Hey! Where did I leave my gum?"

"I don't know," said Steffie.

"It must be here somewhere!" he said, feeling his way across the headboard. "It's not here," he fretted. "Maybe I swallowed it. But that never happens to me, never!"

Steffie sighed sympathetically.

The He-Man looked distractedly at Steffie.

"What do you think?"

"Maybe you swallowed it."

"Ah well, what's done is done," sighed the He-Man. "But hey, I'm off. It's morning. Your aunt could come back from Bosanska Krupa any minute, and I don't like aunts roaming around the apartment when I'm on the job."

"Okay," said Steffie. She wanted to add that her aunt would be gone for several days, but the He-Man was already energetically pulling on his clothes.

"There!" he said. "Got any cigarettes?"

"Yes."

"Let's have one for the road!" He lit one and put another behind his ear, with a waggish grin. "Chin up, kid!"

At the door the He-Man stopped for a moment.

"Hey, what's your name anyway?"

"Steffie," said Steffie softly.

"Good! I don't like girls who aren't named Steffie!" He pulled his face into another waggish grin. "You're a good kid," the He-Man said, pinching Steffie's cheek. The smile on his face slipped abruptly downwards, followed by his head and then his shoulders.

The He-Man slowly descended the front stairs.

C) Steffie and the Intellectual

....✂

If you don't have anything to use for sprains or bruises, soak a cotton ball in olive oil and apply it to the sore area.

....✂

"Didn't you tell me you lived with your aunt?" asked the Intellectual, coming into the room.

"Yes, but she's not here."

"Where is she?"

"Bosanska Krupa."

"Too bad," said the Intellectual. "I adore old aunts!"

He staggered a bit, sat down on the floor, and took a bottle of cheap brandy out of his coat pocket. He took a drink, then offered the bottle to Steffie.

"Want some?"

"Maybe a little," said Steffie and went into the kitchen for some glasses.

"One 'maybe a little' for you," muttered the Intellectual, pouring some out for Steffie, "and one 'maybe not so little' for me!" he added, drinking from the bottle himself and wiping his mouth with his hand.

He looked indifferently around the room, evidently finding nothing to attract his attention. He took off his coat, threw it on the floor, took a handkerchief out of his pocket and clumsily wiped his glasses.

"What do you do?"

"Oh, nothing. I work in an office. I'm a typist."

"Oh," the Intellectual said absentmindedly, putting his glasses back on and taking another swig from the bottle. "What were the two of you doing there that day?"

"Nothing. We'd gone for coffee."

"What's her name, the other one?"

"Anuška."

"And what made you choose that place for coffee?"

"No reason. Anuška said it was nice."

"Were you looking for men?"

"No!" Steffie said quickly, and turned red. "Anuška goes there for coffee all the time."

"That's no café, it's a pick-up joint," said the Intellectual irritably. "And what does she do?"

"The same as me in another office."

"So the two of you went for a coffee, on the hunt for some men!"

"No we did not," said Steffie, offended.

The Intellectual tipped up the bottle and drained it.

"All gone! All—gone!" said the Intellectual, rolling the bottle across the floor. "Got anything else to drink?"

Steffie went into the kitchen and brought back an open bottle of brandy.

"You're terrific!"

The Intellectual poured some brandy into a glass and drained it in one long swallow. Then he pulled at his beard thoughtfully for a while, squinting vaguely, as though confirming some unspoken reply to himself, and suddenly he started waving his arms.

"They all want love. All of them! All they want is love. They feed on other people's love like vampires. More, more! Oh, the braying, the yelping, the yowling disgusts me. Spawning! Revolting egotism! Ugh!"

The Intellectual downed another swig with an expression of disgust and lit a cigarette.

"You, for example," the Intellectual pointed his finger at Steffie, "you're always going to be on the losing end in that department!"

"Why?" Steffie asked dejectedly. She believed him.

"Because that's how it is. There's nothing you can do about it!" He waved his hand abruptly and knocked over his glass.

("Why, he's drunk!" thought Steffie.)

"What, why are you staring at me? So I'm drunk! I've been boozing for days. I have an excellent, and what's more, o-ri-gi-nal reason—my wife ran off with someone! A plumber, an electrician, a waiter, who cares, they all run off sooner or later with someone like that, a typist, whatever."

"Then what happened?" asked Steffie.

"He left her. The plumber and I have both left my wife! I moved out and the bus driver went back to his own wife."

The Intellectual drained another glass and slapped Steffie on the shoulder with a drunken grimace.

"Get it, Stef? Eh, Stef, get it?"

Steffie was suddenly offended and tried to hide it by lighting a cigarette. They sat in silence. Then the Intellectual asked in a conciliatory tone, as though apologizing, "Do you have any music?"

"No I don't," said Steffie, still offended.

They sat in silence. Steffie twisted her cigarette between her fingers and stared fixedly at the floor. Then she asked, "Why am I always going to be on the losing end?"

The Intellectual gave his full attention to Steffie and looked at her for a long time. She thought she was going to cry.

==== "There's a story by Hašek," he said slowly, "and in the story there's a Mr. Kalina who smokes a pipe. To make it smell nice, he puts dried rose petals in the tobacco. And the petals come from roses that suitors bring to his daughter Klara. Every time he smokes, Mr. Kalina smokes up a suitor. 'Now I've smoked Mr. Mařík, now Mr. Ninger, now Mr. Ruzicka or Hubicka'—or something, I don't remember. It doesn't matter."

The Intellectual brought his face right up to Steffie's.

"See what I mean? Someone or something is always going to smoke up your loves. Some invisible Kalina! It's terrible, but that's how it is. Like they did my wife! Like they did my trip to Paris! I've been all set to go to Paris hundreds of times, and every time something smokes it up. There's a hole on the map where Paris is supposed to be, a burnt hole! To hell with everything, including Paris."

Steffie's chin trembled. He was right! He understood perfectly. And, drunk as he was, he too would be smoked up by morning. A little heap of ashes would be all that was left. He had offended her, she thought, "I have to get back at him!"

"Well, actually, I'm . . . on my way to Mallorca!" she said out loud, blushing.

The Intellectual didn't hear her. He was playing with the empty bottle, rolling it back and forth on the floor. Suddenly he slid the bottle into a corner and curled up like a baby.

"What you need is to be loved," he mumbled drunkenly. "You! You, Stef, because you are what you are. Just as you are. I'll love you!"

Steffie tried to pick him up off the floor, but without success. She did manage to drag him closer to the bed and raise him to his knees. The Intellectual stood up abruptly, staggered, and collapsed on the bed, dragging Steffie with him.

"Look, a breast! You've got a breast!" he mumbled, grabbing Steffie firmly by the breast. "You've got a breast! Breasts bite! It'll bite me! Let me shut its mouth. There! I'm going to . . . breeaast . . . !"

He fell asleep, breathing heavily.

For a while Steffie listened to his breathing, then she tried to move his hand. She couldn't—the Intellectual's fingers were firmly clamped onto her breast. She resigned herself to staying in that position until morning. Looking at the Intellectual, she felt herself fill with tenderness, she didn't mind at all that he was there, beside her. He wriggled and leaned his head on her shoulder. Now she was entirely captive. She felt their breath mingling and her breast swelling in his hand. Soon the warmth of his sleep sent her to sleep as well.

Steffie woke up at six. The Intellectual was still asleep. She tugged gently at his beard. He stirred. She tried again.

The Intellectual half opened his eyes, squinting at her. She saw the film of sleep in his eyes. He didn't recognize her. Then he muttered, "Oh, Stef . . ."

"Move over, I've got to go to work."

In the bathroom, under the shower, Steffie tried in vain to rinse off the tender sediment of their common sleep. When she went back into the bedroom, the Intellectual was asleep again. Steffie liked pulling his beard. She tugged at it tenderly again.

"Uh," the Intellectual mumbled sleepily.

Steffie made coffee in the kitchen. The Intellectual dragged himself in after her and laid his hand on her shoulder.

"Listen, did anything happen . . . I mean, you know what I mean?"

"Nothing," Steffie blushed.

"I was really plastered . . . I'm sorry . . . You're making coffee? Great!"

" " " " "   Steffie made coffee: softly she placed the teaspoons of sugar and coffee in the water, softly she stirred the coffee, softly she picked up the cups, softly laid a cloth on a tray, softly placed two cups and the pot on the cloth. She was all soft with inner warmth.

She went into the room and put the coffee on the table. She opened the windows. Soft morning light filled the room.

The Intellectual sat there quietly, stroking his beard. He drank a mouthful of coffee, lit a cigarette, and gazed sadly at Steffie for a long time. Steffie said nothing. ("I'm going to melt," she thought.)

+ + + +   Then the Intellectual broke the silence.

"So, Stef," he said, "what do you think? Is there any point in calling Mrs. Plumber?"

STEFFIE CVEK'S DREAM
(interfacing)

··✄

When you wake up in the middle of the night and can't get back
to sleep, don't just count sheep. Air out the room if you're hot
and straighten out your bed. If the room is cold, pull on some
thick, comfy socks. If that doesn't help, make some chamomile
tea and sweeten it with honey.

··✄

Marianna was lying completely naked on a gigantic cake,
lazily licking all around her and saying: "Steffie, look
around for God's sake! There are guys everywhere, in the
water, in the air . . ."

Steffie went up to the cake but Marianna sank into
the thick layers of icing. The cake dissolved at miraculous
speed, and Marianna with it.

Steffie found herself underwater. She felt sand be-   /////////
neath her feet, slippery weeds on her body. "Rusheth are
terrible thingth!" said her aunt. She poured a plate of
peas over Steffie and disappeared. Steffie knelt down to
pick up the peas, but they kept slipping away. Then she
saw that they weren't peas but the little round shells of
green crabs that scuttled away across the sand.

Steffie saw an enormous carp swimming toward her.
She waved and called out, "Hey, He-Man!" But only
little bubbles came out of her mouth and the He-Man
didn't hear her. His smooth scales scraped indifferently
against Steffie as he swam sluggishly past.

"Look out, Steffie," whispered Marianna's voice from somewhere. Steffie ducked and saw the Truck Driver above her. He was a white, mechanical dog and he was having trouble swimming; he kept sinking, surfacing, sinking again. Steffie wanted to tell him that it might be better if he turned onto his back, but when she opened her mouth no sounds came out. The Truck Driver disappeared.

Steffie dragged herself deeper into the sand and weeds and noticed a massive turtle. It was the Intellectual. She was happy to see him, even in that state. But the turtle just bobbed his head, drew his neck into his shell, and lurched slowly away.

"You see," rustled the weed, "men are animals, most of them aquatic!" Suddenly Steffie felt herself growing unstoppably, becoming smooth and full of water. "Steffie," Marianna's voice hissed through the slime and weeds, "you're not a bar of soap that can melt away, elt away, away, way, aaaayyy . . ." Her voice slowly dissolved and vanished into the sand, leaving a narrow hole behind it.

Steffie felt herself lathering like a giant piece of soap. "Gosh, I'm going to make it all soapy," she thought. There were more and more bubbles, more and more and more . . . "I've dissolved, I guess," she thought. She saw herself on the palm of her hand as a smooth, oval, last piece of soap, and then nothing.

TOPSTITCHING BY THE AUTHOR

Poor Steffie Cvek! One slap in the face after another! If I ++++
were a real writer I'd come rushing to your defense, poor
thing, and introduce you to the man of your dreams at
last.

You would take a goup tour to Mallorca, like Matilda.
In Mallorca, at the hotel swimming pool, while sipping
fruit juice with ice cubes shaped like little hearts, you
would meet your neighbor on the lounge chair next to
you, a famous director (he speaks your language because
his mother is from the same country as you, an immi-
grant who married an American and was widowed a
few months ago). He is divine, simply and indescribably
divine, dear Steffie, and you have no choice but to fall
in love with him at first sight. He is handsome, gentle,
thoughtful, and intelligent, though somewhat subdued.
You notice that right away, of course, but you don't want
to ask him what's troubling him. You are afraid. After
all, this one week (you are aware of it, all too painfully
aware) is your whole life. And you will never forget it. You
will never forget swimming in the hotel pool at night or
riding the silver waves of the sea at noon; or the day when
it poured with rain, and you ran like children, and kissed,
wet and happy, in quiet doorways; or the morning when
you had champagne for breakfast and a tiny golden snake
sparkled in the fragile crystal glass—a delicate necklace
which he gave you in such a shy and original way. You
will never forget the afternoon when you waited for him

//////// in a charming café and suddenly an olive-skinned boy
came over and thrust into your hands the biggest bouquet
of white roses you had ever seen (you knew they were
from him); or that madcap night of music when you wore
++++ a black silk dress, translucent as a breath of air (it too
had arrived in a mysterious package with a little spray
of orchids from an "unknown" admirer). Ah, that crazy
night, those crazy nights! While the others lazed around
the pool, watching you with envious eyes, you lived a
whole lifetime.

On the last day, you are in despair as you pack your
bags to return home with the rest of the tour group, and
he knocks on the door of your room ("Who is it?" you
ask, flustered, but you know—your heart tells you) and
he says he loves you, he has loved you his whole life, only
he didn't know it, and you tell him you love him and
that he is the one, the one and only man you have always
dreamed of. Here his face clouds over. You ask him the
matter. "What's the matter?" you ask. What are these
cares and worries ceaselessly circling his heart? Why is
he always so melancholy? He tells you, with a look of
abject misery, that he is married (he was afraid to tell
you, he was afraid of losing you!), his wife is a famous ac-
tress (you know her, you have seen her in lots of movies).
The eyes of the public are fixed on them, but those eyes
do not know the truth that he has been hiding all these
unhappy years: for as long as he can remember that
fiendish woman has been in the jaws of drugs, alcohol,
and debauchery. And the children (there are four: two
boys and two little girls) hardly know their mother. In
short, Steffie dear, he asks you to go to Hollywood with
him, where he will immediately seek a divorce because
things can't go on like this any longer. Standing at the

door, he adds that you don't need to decide right away. He'll be back in five minutes.

Your heart beats madly, and suddenly you become brave and decisive, you tell someone in the tour group to go by your office and tell them you quit, and also to let Marianna know that you have found the man of your dreams and will write to her as soon as you can to tell her all about it.

You both fly to Hollywood and you will never forget   /////////
that flight—it is a flight into a new life, unknown but deliriously happy. He takes you straight from the airport to his mother. His mother bursts into tears when she sees   + + + +
you and immediately tells you her life story, how she was widowed, and mentions that she was born in Bosanska Krupa. "Bosanska Krupa!" you say, "my aunt's from Bosanska Krupa!" "What's her name?" his mother asks. You tell her your aunt's name, Maria Matić. "Maria!" cries his mother, "we were at school together, we sat at the same desk!" Here you burst into tears as well, and you hug each other sobbing.

Then he tells you that, alas, he has to leave right away to shoot a major motion picture. He asks you to take his children to Hawaii—so the children can get used to you, over the summer, on vacation—and meanwhile he will arrange for the divorce. For a moment you hesitate, wondering if this is a dream: is it possible that he has really chosen you over a beautiful, famous woman like his wife, and over so many other glamorous Hollywood stars? He tells you that he loves your good heart, and love is blind, and you shouldn't worry (in other words, not to trouble your pretty little head with such nonsense). And off he goes to shoot his major motion picture.

You fly to Hawaii with the children but one of the wings of the airplane explodes and you crash into the jungle. All the passengers are killed, except you and, thank God, all four children. Untold dangers beset you! But you display superhuman courage in the jungle, and fight with ferocious strength to keep the children alive (and yourself too). My dear Steffie, if only you knew everything I would put into the descriptions of your heartrending struggle to preserve the lives of his children in those unspeakably savage conditions! The whole world learns of your fate, including him, and follows it anxiously on the news. At last he flies into the jungle with a special rescue team and I give a truly touching description of your reunion.

////////   You take a private jet to Hollywood. There, of course, the reporters are waiting for you. A man, someone you
+ + + +   have never seen before, comes up to your future husband and whispers something in his ear. During the dramatic events in the jungle his wife has died of a galloping leukemia. You are naturally sorry for the unfortunate woman, but you also know that now nothing stands in the way of your love.

You marry, dear Steffie (it is a breathtaking wedding, the kind you have only ever seen in the movies!), and you not only become a wonderful wife, lover, and mother of four, soon five children (yes, my dear Steffie, yes!), but you also lose twenty pounds and become so beautiful that your very own aunt doesn't recognize you when she comes to visit you, your husband, and her old friend from Bosanska Krupa. She sobs and says "After thith I can die happy!" But of course she doesn't die, on the contrary: your husband pays for a two-week stay in a famous clinic, where she receives a dental transplant from an unfortunate fifteen-year-old girl who has just died in a car crash.

All of you—your mother-in-law, your aunt, your five, soon six, children who all adore you, your husband, who has just won an Academy Award for his major motion picture, and you—live happily ever after and beyond!

That's how I'd have happyended you, Steffie dear, if I were a real writer. But I'm afraid I'm one of those pitiless "true to life" writers. Or worse. I have to keep sewing, Steffie, your loose ends can't be tied up just yet. I'm so sorry, but don't worry, we'll soon get to the end of your story—when I put down my needle and thread after all, you will have the most beautiful dress at the ball!

EMANCIPATED ELA GIVES
STEFFIE CVEK SOME ADVICE
(kick pleating)

···>✂

If you want your nail polish to last longer, brush your nails with egg-white as soon as the polish dries.

···>✂

"I can't stand typical women!" Emancipated Ela shouted, tossing her hair vigorously and placing a cigarette into an ivory holder.

"Oh?" said Steffie absently, her head tilted to one side.

A carved Buddha smiled out of Ela's cigarette holder.

"A present from Fred," Ela remarked, following Steffie's gaze.

++++ "What do you mean by a typical woman?" Steffie asked.

"Don't pretend you don't understand," said Emancipated Ela. "You're not far past it yourself! All those ninnies who snivel and whimper all the time, drape themselves all over a man, suffocate him, manipulate him, just because God gave them holes!"

("She's so crude!" Steffie thought. Ela waved her cigarette holder around agitatedly and ran a hand through her curly hair. "Her hair's so curly!" Steffie thought.)

"Good thing there are less and less of them around. What a woman really needs is to work, to breathe, to live life as deeply as she can and remember that men aren't the only thing in the world."

"Marianna thinks they are," said Steffie quietly.

"Marianna's an idiot. She thinks marrying some jerk ++++ takes you straight to seventh heaven."

"Yes, but . . ."

"No *yes but*s!" Ela snapped, shaking her curls angrily. "I can see that she's stuffed you full of her ideas about life like a stuffed goose!"

"Marianna's nice. When I got depressed, she was there for me," said Steffie, trying to smooth things over.

"Ha!" Emancipated Ela snorted, raising her cigarette holder like a flag. "I can just imagine! She told you to find a man, and it didn't work, and now you're in worse shit than before."

"How do you know?"

"I know everything! I know your souls, the way you breathe. Of course it didn't work. It couldn't have."

"What do you mean?"

"You latched onto the idea of a man as your last hope. It's written all over your face. You're the kind of woman who falls in love at the drop of a hat, all a guy has to do is stop on the street and ask you the time."

"Then what should I do?" said Steffie, drooping.

"Live, for God's sake! Work! Read! When's the last time you read a book?"

Steffie said nothing.

"When's the last time you went to a museum?" Eman- ++++ cipated Ela asked, pointing her ivory cigarette holder at Steffie. Steffie was about to say that she never went to museums at all, but Ela went on mercilessly. "And the theater? Admit it! You haven't been to a play for ages. ++++ Oh you stupid, limited, sexual slaves, all you can think about is catching a man. You're a bunch of hens, scratching around, making your nests. There's another world out there, you know. Go for a walk, read a book, make friends, take a course, travel . . . Learn a language. Why not learn French? Life is so interesting!"

Emancipated Ela talked and talked. Steffie blushed and blushed. How right she was! How clever she was!

Steffie and Ela ordered two more coffees. Ela sighed, drank a mouthful, pushed her hand through her curly hair, looked imperiously around the room, and punctuated the air with her cigarette holder. Steffie breathed a sigh of relief, though she didn't know why.

"Did you know I'm getting married?" said Ela.

"Again?" Steffie was shocked. She quickly added, "To who?"

"Fred." Ela offered no details.

According to Steffie's calculations, Fred was number five. ("Incredible!" she thought, with envy.)

"Gotta go," said Emancipated Ela, getting up. "Give me a call sometime. Don't look so shocked! So he's my fifth husband! Men have been chewing us up and spitting us out for thousands of years, now it's our turn. Total equality," she smiled.

("What a lot of teeth she's got!" thought Steffie. "And how right she is!")

After sitting there for a while, Steffie suddenly seemed to reach a decision. Then she called the waitress over and paid for the coffees.

STEFFIE CVEK TAKES EMANCIPATED ELA'S ADVICE
(pinning)

A) Steffie Cvek at the theater

....✂

You can't boil eggs with cracked or crushed shells without the white leaking out, or sometimes even the yolk. But if you have to use them, you can wrap them in tin foil and plunge them into the water with confidence!

....✂

It was very stuffy in the auditorium. At first Steffie followed everything on stage with rapt attention: the king, the queen, and young Ophelia in love. Steffie liked her the best and was sorry when she drowned herself. Then the grave diggers came on. For a while they stood in the pit talking about something; then they tossed spadefuls of real live earth out of the pit, which surprised Steffie a lot because not much else on the stage was real.

But soon the stuffy air made Steffie feel sick. She got up and stumbled her way along the row of seats. People grumbled. She headed toward a red light, felt thick plush curtains, left the auditorium, and hurried down the stairs and into the restroom. She went into the first stall, locked the door, lowered the seat, and sat down.

Steffie pictured the theater as a large box with the auditorium as a smaller one inside it, the restroom as a smaller one, and the stall as an even smaller one with no way out. ("A grave . . ." thought Steffie, breathing heavily.)

= = = =   Suddenly she heard voices.

"I didn't tell you," said the first voice, "they took it all out. She's got nothing left down there."

"Not a thing?" asked the second voice.

"Nothing. And when it spread to her breast, they had to get rid of that too."

"Really?"

. . . .   "Really. You can't fool around with these things. When I had my last abortion they told me I had to be careful because I've got a cyst . . ."

"You do?"

"Yeah. Big as a quarter."

"They can burn it or freeze it. That's what they did to mine, only mine was smaller."

"Yeah, they told me to go and have that done, before it's too late."

"You really should, it's no big deal. Just stings a little. It's better than having your womb dry up."

"Whose womb is drying up?"

"Mine. They told me it's getting smaller. They say it's because I'm skinny."

"Really! I didn't know . . . Well, Ankica, you know her, hers is falling out."

"What do you mean, falling out?"

"How should I know? Falling out . . ."

"It sure is hard for us women!"

"Yeah, but what can you do? Look, someone forgot their comb."

"Take it and let's go."

"I'll just lock up the mops and bucket."

" " " " "   The voices fell silent. Steffie was overcome with pity, without knowing exactly why or for what, and she burst into tears. It occurred to her that someone might hear her so she flushed the toilet, which only made her cry harder, so she flushed it again.

Wiping away her tears, she thought of the cyst the size of a quarter and without thinking bent her thumb and index finger into a little loop. She sat frozen in that position for a while, then gave a start and caught sight of her hand with the fingers bent into a sign whose meaning she had forgotten. The senseless ring remained frozen in midair for another second or two until her hand fell by her side. Steffie flushed the toilet again and left.

There was no one in the hall but Steffie made her way to the exit on tiptoe. The grave diggers must be gone by now, she thought, they've buried Ophelia, I'll have to see the play again, the prince wasn't bad, an excellent actor really, and just right for a prince . . .

B) Steffie Cvek reads *Madame Bovary* by Gustave Flaubert

....✄

A simple way to keep your place in a book without folding down the corner of the page is to slip a rubber band vertically through the middle of the book at the place where you stop reading.

....✄

Steffie Cvek was reading *Madame Bovary* by Gustave Flaubert and underlining certain passages. On p. 50, Steffie Cvek underlined:

But *her* life was as cold as an attic facing north; and boredom, like a silent spider, was weaving its web in the shadows, in every corner of her heart.

Next Steffie Cvek underlined two passages on p. 70:

Deep down, all the while, she was waiting for something to happen. Like a sailor in distress, she kept casting desperate glances over the solitary waste of her life, seeking some white sail in the distant mists of the horizon. She had no idea by what wind it would reach her, toward what shore it would bear her, or what kind of craft it would be—tiny boat or towering vessel, laden with heartbreaks or filled to the gunwales with rapture. But every morning when she awoke she hoped that today would be the day; she listened for every sound, gave sudden starts, was surprised when nothing happened; and then, sadder with each succeeding sunset, she longed for tomorrow.

So from now on they were going to continue one after the other like this, always the same, innumerable, bringing nothing! Other people's lives, drab though they might be, held at least the possibility of an event. One unexpected happening often set in motion a whole chain of change: the entire setting of one's life could be transformed. But to her nothing happened. It was God's will. The future was a pitch-black tunnel, ending in a locked door.

On p. 73, Steffie Cvek put a squiggle in the margin:

All the bitterness of life seemed to be served up to her on her plate; and the steam rising from the boiled meat brought gusts of revulsion from the depths of her soul.

On p. 75, Steffie Cvek just put an X:

She began to drink vinegar to lose weight, acquired a little dry cough, and lost her appetite completely.

On p. 101, Steffie Cvek put a long question mark:

A man is free, at least—free to range the passions and the world, to surmount obstacles, to taste the rarest pleasures. Whereas a woman is continually thwarted. Inert, compliant, she has to struggle against her physical weakness and legal subjection.

Her will, like the veil tied to her hat, quivers with every breeze: there is always a desire that entices, always a convention that restrains.

On p. 139, Steffie Cvek underlined:

Everything appeared to her as though shrouded in vague, hovering blackness; and grief swirled through her soul, moaning softly like the winter wind in a deserted castle. She was prey to the brooding brought on by irrevocable partings, to the weariness that follows every consummation, to the pain caused by the breaking off of a confirmed habit or the brusque stopping of a prolonged vibration.

On p. 147, Steffie Cvek read:

Poor little thing! She's gasping for love like a carp on a kitchen table gasping for water.

and then closed the book and stared emptily out the window.

"Look at thith," said her aunt, shuffling into the room.   = = = =
"Aren't they beautiful!"

Her aunt was holding a plate of apricots in her hand. She looked at Steffie in surprise, put the plate on the table, sat down in the rocking chair, and took an apricot. Pecking slowly at the apricot, she said, "What ith it?   = = = =
Feeling low again? You theem to do nothing but read thethe dayth. There wath a girl in Bothanthka Krupa named Petra, her father wath the parish prietht. She wath alwayth tho mitherable that when I thaw her thtanding on the front thtepth of her houthe, I thought she looked like a shroud thtretched out in front of the door. It theemth she thuffered from a kind of fog in the head, and neither the doctorth nor the prietht could do

anything to help her. When the attackth got really bad, she would go off all by herthelf into the woodth and the forethter would find her there, lying on her thtomach on the grath, crying her eyeth out. But later she got married and people thaid it all went away . . . Too bad," her aunt said all of a sudden, and put the apricot she had started down on the table, "it'th too bad I can't eat them, bec-authe of my teeth."

She stood up, went over to Steffie, and turned the book over to see the title.

= = = = "What'th thith? Oh, *Madame Bovary*! Ith she the one who killth herthelf for love? That'th tho boring. The only novelth I like are the oneth that thcare you out of your witth." Shuffling out of the room, she added, "Eat thome apricoth!"

Steffie sighed, picked up an apricot, turned it thoughtfully between her fingers, and bit into it.

C) Steffie Cvek reads at the museum, or, Some unexpected overstitching of S. C. with the author's own zigzag stitch

Unexpected? Like hell it is. The reader must surely have perceived by now the inviolability of the number three: Marianna's three pieces of advice, the three men, Ela's three suggestions. Which only goes to show that writers are an unnaturally frivolous, irresponsible, and cruel breed! The reader must have known that the author would send Steffie Cvek to a museum. Well, here are the author's working notes:

S. C. at the museum. Walks past an exhibit—mechanical penis. Penis (the exhibit) rises. S. C. frozen to spot. Electric

*eye. Alarm goes off. Handsome bearded painter (the man of
her dreams?) comes up, embraces her, kisses her passionately
for a full 5 mins. It turns out alarm system reacts to every
10th visitor, and painter randomly kisses whoever sets it
off. Jerk painter goes back to his beautiful art babe (curly
haired). S. C. leaves discouraged and humiliated.*

The author was convinced that this would be a moving
episode, nothing short of brilliant. Then the author
read around and was disappointed to learn that another
writer had already used a mechanical penis/electric eye
incident. It's not enough to have a brilliant idea, you have
to have it first!

So the author searched high and low for something   ++++
else in the artistico-erotic line that would be suitable
for S. C. The only thing worth considering was Jesús
Raphael Soto with his wonderful plastic noodles. S. C.
would wade through them, the plastic noodles would
wobble and vibrate, S. C. would keep parting them with
her hands. The author could do a wonderful job with
that, definitely. S. C. would get hopelessly lost in the
forest of vibrating plastic noodles (a touch of symbolism)
and burst into tears.

But then the author abandoned the museum episode
altogether. She was mad at herself: whenever she doesn't
know what to do, she makes poor S. C. burst into tears.
Instead, the author satisfied her childish desire to do
everything in threes but left S. C. at home watching TV
with her aunt.

She failed to find a suitable patch on this occasion. To
salvage something from it all, the best she can do is offer
a handy hint that fits in admirably with the proposed
theme:

---✄

To keep your pictures from slipping, stick a piece of double-sided tape to the back of the frame.

---✄

STEFFIE CVEK SLEEPS WITH A PIG'S HEAD, OR, A NEW ATTACK OF DEPRESSION

(concealed plackets)

··>✂

Never use a hairdryer while you're in the tub.

··>✂

Apparently none of Emancipated Ela's four ex-husbands   /////////
had left her an apartment. Emancipated Ela had refused
alimony on feminist grounds and abandoned the expensive square-footage to them. So, since Fred and Ela only
had a room in someone else's apartment, Steffie thought
that the use of her own for the reception would be the
best wedding present she could give them. Her aunt went
to Bosanska Krupa and Fred and Ela brought all the food
and drink. Steffie was a little anxious when she saw the
roast pig, the cakes, and the bottles, but somehow they
managed to fit it all into her apartment.

It was the first time Steffie had been to one of Ela's
weddings. "When we leave the Justice of the Peace's
office," Ela said warmly, "stand in a good spot so I can
throw you the bouquet."

Steffie found a suitable spot, on the bottom step,
and Ela could have easily thrown her the bouquet if she
wanted to, but she kept stubborn hold of it. She must have
forgotten her promise.

The guests arranged themselves as best as they could   -·-·-·-
in Steffie's room, some on the bed, others on the floor.
The food and drink were on the table by the window.

Steffie settled down on the end of the bed, the most comfortable place.

Ela's wedding wasn't much fun for Steffie. To cheer herself up she drank a glass of wine and ate some crispy pig's skin. Ela was in high spirits. Her innumerable teeth kept flashing into view ("She's got so many," Steffie kept repeating to herself, "so many!") and Ela's new husband, Fred, was quiet and unassuming. The fifth little chunk on the shish kebab of Ela's marriages! He acted like he was waiting for the next one, the sixth, who would shove him down the skewer up against the fourth. And Ela? She kept training her sights on whoever was around, out of habit.

Steffie drank a second glass of wine, nibbled at the roast pork, and let her eyes roam over the guests. There was a married couple—Ela's curly haired friend and her husband, a hippie who had had quite a lot to drink and kept pedaling his feet up and down as though working a sewing machine—and another couple, very nice, a friend of Fred's who was only interested in the alcohol and a really nice fat girl who was sitting in a corner quietly eating her fifth piece of cake. Moving onto her third glass of wine and a plate of potato salad, Steffie wondered why she didn't feel sick.

Then Ela came back into Steffie's field of vision. She was the only one laughing, and she laughed as if there were a hundred people at the wedding. She appeared to Steffie as a giant blender, ready to puree everyone in the room if someone switched her on.

On her way to work every day Steffie walked past a construction site and always stopped to watch. Her favorite thing was when the big steam shovel tore up layers of dirt with its metal teeth. There was something about it that reminded her of Ela. Ela's teeth sparkled and gleamed, she shone with a metallic glint. ("Horrible," thought Steffie, draining another glass.)

Then suddenly, from the corner where Steffie was sitting, an inhuman voice rang out: "Ela, you're a sexual steam shovel!"

Everyone stopped talking for a moment. Then Ela burst out laughing. Steffie felt dizzy, something was dragging her down into sleep, she stretched out, felt herself bump into someone's arms or legs, but what did it matter?

In the morning Steffie woke up but didn't open her eyes. She was lying on her stomach, head sunk in the pillow. Her eyelids were completely stuck together and she couldn't remember what had happened. She did not move; she listened. There were pigeons cooing outside. What time could it be? . . . She slowly and lazily started to set her thoughts in motion.

And then she cautiously unstuck one lid and squinted. She parted her eyelids a little more. *A pig's head!* Right next to her, cheek to cheek, lay a pig's head. No, it can't be! She quickly shut her eye. Then she cautiously peered out again. The pig's head was still lying right next to Steffie's cheek. She could clearly see its teeth and one of its eyes.

Steffie sat up in horror and saw the head of the roast pig on the pillow next to her. The room was in chaos, what was left of the food cluttered the table, and everything smelled of wine and cigarette butts. Steffie's bed was decorated with withered flowers, and next to the pig's head lay the promised wedding bouquet.

"Wasn't that nice of them!" Steffie thought, and shoved the pig's head onto the floor. Then she shook the flowers from the bedcovers, flung Ela's bouquet off too, and pulled the covers over her head.

In the darkness, under the covers, Steffie made up her mind to die.

ANUŠKA, AN EXPERT IN QUESTIONS OF DEPRESSION, GIVES STEFFIE SOME NEWS

(lapped seams)

─────────────────────────────✂

To keep cut daisies fresh, put them in warm water instead of cold.

─────────────────────────────✂

"Hello, Steffie? It's Anuška."

"Anuška! What are you up to? Where are you?"

"Here, where else? How are you, honey? Any news?"

"Nothing. Everything's the same."

"Not for me, honey, nothing's the same!"

"Really?"

"I'm in love!"

"For real? With who?"

"You'll meet him yourself and see. He's an astrologer. Well, not really, but that's how I met him. I went to him to have my horoscope done—"

"And then?—"

"That's it! I fell in love!"

"I'm really glad."

"I called because I've got something for you. I asked him about your horoscope too, honey."

"You did? What did he say?"

"You'll have to talk to him yourself. The main thing was that you've been going through your dark phase and that's why things haven't worked out. Now you're slowly moving into your light phase. Are you listening?"

"Yes."

"You don't seem very interested . . . "

"Oh, I am, I am. What else did he say?"

"He said you were about to reach a turning point in your life. A turn for the better, I mean. Oh, and also that your lucky number is thirteen. As in good luck."

"Really?"

"That's what he said."

"What else?"

"Nothing for now. But you'll meet him. I can't tell you how much he's predicted in my life!"

"What?"

"He predicted himself . . ."

"And you fell in love?"

"Uh huh."

"What about him?"

"He did too."

"Hey, what's wrong with the phone? The receiver's crackling."

"It's not the phone, it's the parakeet. I bought a para-keet, didn't I tell you?"

"Oh, I forgot. It's that loud?"

"Yes. And terribly rude! A dreadful bird."

"What's his name?"

"Who? The parakeet?"

"No, that astrologer of yours."

"Martin."

"Uh-huh. Well, that's great, Anuška. I'll come and see you both some time."

"Okay, honey, just give me a call . . ."

"Uh-huh."

STEFFIE CVEK AND THE PARAKEET, OR, NURSING A MONSTER

(*pinked hems*)

···✄

Uh oh! Spring brings bug bites. But simple onion juice works wonders. Rub a few drops onto the bite and the pain and swelling go right down.

···✄

Steffie decided definitively, absolutely definitively this time, to stay depressed. ("Even Anuška, even Anuška's in love!" she wept.)

At first Steffie didn't understand why Anuška's falling in love had thrown her into such despair. Then she realized it was because everyone needs someone who is worse off than they are. That's who Anuška was for Steffie. And now things were looking up for Anuška too.

Out of the blue it came to her: the parakeet! That's it! Anuška bought a parakeet because she was depressed all the time and that's when everything started to get better. That parakeet was obviously a subtle signal to life, " " " " a discreet call for help, a small sign to destiny—like a half-open curtain on a window or a bowl of flowers, like a dropped handkerchief or a light left burning in the room . . . And destiny had heeded Anuška's call.

After all, Steffie's thoughts went on, a parakeet is smaller than a dog, and cheaper, and it's not really an animal, it's just a bird, and a dog barks but not a parakeet, a parakeet only squawks and pecks seeds, it's definitely a lot perkier than a dog . . .

To make a long story short, Steffie bought a parakeet. Her aunt suggested they call it Miki. "Jutht ath long ath it doethn't die in thix monthth . . . !"

Miki was a perky and friendly bird. Steffie was glad it didn't know how to talk; Anuška's made it impossible to make a phone call in peace.

==== All at once, Steffie Cvek's life began to improve. The
" " " " " friendly little bird brought a certain cheer into the quiet home of Steffie and her aunt. Steffie simply stopped being so sad. One afternoon she was lazily turning the pages of a fashion magazine; her aunt was napping in the rocking chair. Rays of afternoon sun were streaming through the open window, making patterns on the walls. Steffie closed the magazine and looked blissfully around the room—at her aunt in the rocking chair, at the play of light—and she felt that her life was filled with warmth, it would soon be bringing her much more of everything . . .

Then Steffie heard an inhuman voice:

"Fatty, fatty, fat and batty . . ."

Steffie cried out in horror. From the cage the parakeet's little black eyes stared unblinkingly back at her.

"Fatty, fatty, fat and batty . . ." the parakeet repeated impassively, in its tinny, old man's voice.

Steffie turned pale, stood up, and sat down. She couldn't breathe. She looked at the parakeet. It didn't bat an eyelid. Then it opened its evil beak again, but Steffie leapt up, put the cage on the windowsill and opened it. The parakeet slowly stepped out of the cage and, without once looking at Steffie, flew away.

"You monster!" Steffie shouted after it.

" " " " " Her tears began to flow of their own accord. She stared at the empty cage. The tears streamed down her cheeks.

Goddamn bird! Her tears welled up uncontrollably. She had nursed a serpent in her lap, without realizing it. Her tears flowed in little streams. Her heart was unraveling. The tears poured on. Her whole being was unraveling. The tears flooded down her face in a torrent. Soon there would be nothing left of her but a thread.

"Thith is the thtory of Old Mother White," her aunt mumbled in her sleep. "She thtitcheth by day and unth-titcheth by night . . ." Then she squirmed in her rocking chair and began to snore.

STEFFIE CVEK CONTEMPLATES THE MAN WHO TOOK HER VIRGINITY, THE SECOND MAN WHO TOOK HER VIRGINITY, AND SUICIDE

(toggle fastenings)

···✂

It's easy to tell when your vegetables are cooked: as long as they float they're not ready, but when they sit on the bottom of the pan, they're done.

···✂

There really were two of them! Ela had said: "Don't be ridiculous! A deflowerer is a deflowerer—there's only the first." Steffie didn't like the word "deflowerer," but Ela had said that in this day and age you have to call things by their proper names. Ah, Ela! She was something else.

Steffie's first deflowerer was their new neighbors' son. He studied electrical engineering and was crazy about anything that could be taken apart and put together again, and also about anything that rhymed. The first time he saw her in the hallway, he said: "Hey little miss, how 'bout a kiss?" Later he started to drop by to visit, and he would say to her aunt: "How 'bout your niece, she's quite a piece!" Steffie's aunt would say "Moron! A real moron!" Then one day the TV broke and her aunt was in Bosanska Krupa; First spent a long time fiddling with the TV until finally it worked, and then spent a long time fiddling with Steffie. That was it. It happened, without her quite knowing how—the only thing she remembered was the sound of the TV talking to itself. Steffie didn't like it, but First did. After that day, Steffie often found scraps of paper in the mailbox with poems on them, rhyming "screen" with "has-been" ("I'm no star of the screen, but I'm not a has-been"), "lover" with "cover" ("I'm a manly lover, not a manhole cover"), and the like. "Moron!" Steffie's aunt repeated, and Steffie had to agree.

Second came soon after First. And again it was all quite shabby and accidental. Her chemistry teacher from middle school. His nickname was "Kinda," because he used the word "kinda" in every sentence. He loved experiments, all those bottles, powders, test tubes, bunsen burners. You kinda measure this much powder in here, you kinda boil this liquid over there . . . Steffie met him again at her typing course. He was working there as an administrator and was even shorter, shier, and stranger than Steffie remembered. He reminded her of a snail. The time came for her final typing test and the farewell party at a restaurant, and Second was there too, acting weird and embarrassed. He kept looking at Steffie the whole time and at the end he offered to drive her home. Steffie no longer remembered how it came about, she only remembered her decision to kinda do it with Second, kinda just like that. He was clumsy and pathetic and she was glad to help him along. Afterwards he said: "Forgive me, Miss Cvek, I have kinda deflowered you," then he fell asleep. "Okay," Steffie said. ("I guess if he says so," she thought.) Second fell asleep with his arms around Steffie and her ear uncomfortably pressed against his watch. In the terrible silence of the night, Steffie listened, hypnotized, to the endless ticking of the watch. And then she heard a bird twitter, then another, and kinda felt that at that very moment—while the watch hammered in her ear and the day's first bird sang outside, in that pure crystal morning fragment of time—it was then that she became a woman. Independently of First, independently of Second. On her own.

First left the sound of the TV, Second the ticking of a watch. Everything else about them had blurred together and turned mushy. "Like porridge!" thought Steffie, and she remembered that the rice had been waiting for a long time, she should turn on the stove, it was dark, and in fact she was starving.

While the rice bubbled, rose and fell, simmering in the little pot on the stove, Steffie took a melon out of the refrigerator. "No," thought Steffie, drumming on the melon, "things can't go on like this!" She absent-mindedly stroked the melon for a long time, thoughtfully tweaked its little dry stalk, and then grabbed a knife and cut the melon in two. "What would happen" she thought, picking up the knife again and slicing off a sliver of melon, "if I killed myself?"

Yes, thought Steffie, that would show them! She imagined the modest funeral. Everyone from the office would definitely be there. Marianna would cry an awful lot, she was sure of that, Marianna would be devastated. Anuška too. And Anuška's new boyfriend, even though they'd never met. What was his name again? Oh, Martin . . . Ela would be sorry, but she wouldn't show it. She'd be angry. "That idiot, that idiot! Why did she do it?" She'd be angry all right, but sorry too.

It was all very moving, and Steffie cut another slice of melon, tapping the knife thoughtfully against the green rind. The Truck Driver would hear about it from Marianna and maybe he would come. The He-Man wouldn't come, because there's no way he could find out about it, and as for the Intellectual . . . he read the papers, maybe he'd hear about it. She pictured him drunk with a rose in his hand. And her aunt? Her aunt would die of grief. Or maybe not. Her eyes filled with tears. She counted the people who would come to her funeral and was appalled at how low the number was. "I'll do it," thought Steffie. If someone has so few people to come to her funeral then she deserves to die!

"That's it," said Steffie half aloud and turned off the stove. The rice gave one last gurgle and subsided. Her aunt could eat it when she came home from Bosanska Krupa in the morning, Steffie thought, and put the lid on.

Then she began to think about how to do it. A rope hurt, it wasn't practical, and people look awful when they're hanged. Throwing herself under a train was not an option: she would be terrified. Besides, you never know: a person could survive and be crippled for life. Cutting her wrists, no not that! Her aunt would be furious. Pills were best . . . She found four bottles in her aunt's cupboard. Three were full of nasty-looking pills and Steffie emptied all of them into a cup. There were only three tablets in the fourth bottle. White. She poured them in too. There. If that didn't kill her, nothing would! Maybe she should leave a note for her aunt? No, it wouldn't matter afterward in any case . . .

Steffie walked through the apartment, put the rest of the melon in the fridge, and wiped the table. She checked the stove, lifted the lid of the pot, tried the rice—it was perfect, just needed some salt—put the lid back on, and went into the bathroom.

She spent a long time looking at herself in the mirror, and then filled the bath with hot water. She'd commit double suicide. She had seen it in the movies. A razor blade was messy, but it didn't hurt, they say.

= = = =

· · · · · · · · ·

" " " " "

" " " " "   In the bath, in clouds of steam, Steffie slowly swallowed her aunt's pills and when the cup was totally empty she slid into the water. She thought she could already feel the effect of the pills, so she decided against the razor. Soon she felt horribly sleepy. Death wasn't so bad really. Just like a deep sleep. In the distance, in her sleep, she could see them all gathered there: her aunt, Anuška, Marianna, Ela, the Truck Driver, the He-Man, the Intellectual, even First and Second and a few other people from the office. They were smiling and waving to her. "They like me, all of them!" She was touched, and she wanted to run toward them, but the water was strange and heavy, it stuck to her body and it took a great effort for her to come to the surface.

/////////   Steffie was awoken from death by a sneeze. Her own. She opened her eyes and saw a man in white; a tanned face was smiling at her, with deep blue eyes and pearly teeth.

"Steffie, are you all right?" asked a deep voice.

"Who are you?" whispered Steffie, closing her eyes.

"Look at me, Steffie!"

Steffie sank into the blue of the unknown eyes. ("I must be dreaming," she thought, and closed her eyes tight.)

"Everything will be fine. Call me if you need anything," said the deep voice.

Steffie opened one eye and saw her aunt's face.

"I don't underthtand!" said her aunt. "Why wath the bath full of water, why did you get into bed naked and wet, why did you take all my multivitamin pillth and three thleeping tableth?"

Steffie sneezed and snuggled under the covers.

"Why wath the rithe burned?" Steffie's aunt complained. Steffie pulled the covers over her head.

"Amateurth!" her aunt muttered. "It'th like that Pero from Bothanthka Krupa. He dethided to kill himthelf in the motht dreadful way. He thwallowed a knife. And nothing happened. He tried again with a fork. No luck. He wath furiouth, went betherk and thwallowed hith wife'th entire thilverware thet, for twelve people! Thtill nothing happened. He'th thtill alive and well, that moron! Too bad about the thilverware . . ."

STEFFIE CVEK REMEMBERS ANOTHER PIECE
OF EMANCIPATED ELA'S ADVICE

(*gussets*)

···✂

Even if your toothpaste tube looks empty, you can squeeze out some more if you soak the tube in hot water first.

···✂

HOW DO YOU SAY BLOOD TYPE IN FRENCH? threatening black letters asked Steffie Cvek. Steffie looked around her; no one was there. The question was directed solely at her. "I wonder," thought Steffie, "how *do* you say blood type in French?" She stepped cautiously up to the poster.

THERE IS NO EXCUSE FOR PEOPLE WHO SAY
THEY CAN'T LEARN A FOREIGN LANGUAGE!

"True!" Steffie Cvek agreed at once.

OUR COURSES PROVE THAT EVERYONE CAN LEARN
A FOREIGN LANGUAGE. AGE DOESN'T MATTER.
RESULTS GUARANTEED!

"How true!" thought Steffie.

A FOREIGN LANGUAGE IS YOUR WINDOW TO THE WORLD!
OPEN THAT WINDOW—LEARN A LANGUAGE!
MILLIONS OF PEOPLE ALL OVER THE WORLD KNOW HOW TO SAY
BLOOD TYPE IN FRENCH BUT YOU DON'T!
THE LANGUAGE COURSE KNOWS AND SO CAN YOU!

"Absolutely right," Steffie thought. She found a pencil and a piece of paper and wrote down the address and phone number at the bottom of the poster.

She went home and called to her aunt from the door:

"How do you say blood type in French?"

"Clasthement de sthang! Why do you athk?" her aunt shot back, and added, "Your blood type ith very important. I'm a B and I never forget it. It'th thomething you really thould know, in other languageth too. Jutht think how many people have died becauthe they didn't know their blood type!"

HEAD OVER HEELS IN A HAPPY ENDING, OR, THE APPEARANCE OF MONSIEUR FRNDIC

(*finishing*)

....✂

Can't get your whipped cream whipped? Put down that whisk and add an egg white first, then put it in the fridge for ten minutes. You'll be able to whip it firm and frothy in no time!

....✂

Steffie liked her French class from the start. The school wasn't far from her office, and on the top floor there was a little café where they drank tea or coffee and chatted during the break. Not only they, the French students, but the others learning German, Italian . . . People of all ages and occupations, all nice. Steffie felt that they all liked being out of the house, being there, together, more than they actually wanted to learn a foreign language.

Steffie decided that knowing another language would be very useful, if for no other reason than that when she went to Mallorca, like Matilda, she wouldn't feel like a complete fool. She would be able to chat happily with the locals, and with tourists from other countries.

The teacher was nice too, friendly with all the students. She knew French like a real live French person. What Steffie liked best was working in the language lab, because then she could put on the headphones, press Play, and think about other things while French rolled quietly around in her ears.

On the day they reached the thirteenth lesson, a young ////////
man came into the classroom and introduced himself as
Monsieur Frndic, from which one could deduce that he " " " " "
knew some French already. Monsieur Frndic sat down
next to Steffie and soon took an active part in the class.

The lesson seemed to fly by, and before Steffie knew it
she was on her way to the bus stop with her textbook and
three-ring binder under her arm. And who should turn
up at the same stop but Monsieur Frndic!

They didn't say anything, but just as the bus, number
fifteen, arrived and Steffie was about to get on, Monsieur
Frndic said softly: "Je m'appelle Vinko Frndic."

Steffie, in amazement, heard her own voice say: "Je
m'appelle Steffie Cvek."

"Enchanté," he said.

She looked cautiously at Monsieur Frndic. He was
smiling. She turned to see if another bus was coming.
There was one, a fifteen. Maybe he's in a hurry, she
thought, and he's being polite and waiting for me to leave
first? The bus arrived. Steffie looked at Monsieur Frndic.
In front of her a fat woman was clambering onto the bus,
breathing heavily. Steffie had already raised her foot to
step on when Monsieur Frndic said:

"Qu'est-ce que vous préférez, le café ou le thé?"

"Le café!" Steffie burst out so suddenly, breathlessly,
and loudly that instead of "café" she made a strange, incomprehensible squeak. And the bus pulled away.

They stood in silence. Steffie thought she was going
to die of embarrassment. Monsieur Frndic must want
to leave, and instead she kept stupidly missing the
busses and making him wait with her. She looked at
him again. He had gentle blue eyes and was polite and
shy, or at least that's how he seemed to her. In any case,

she didn't feel much like getting on a bus. Here came another one, a fifteen. Steffie firmly crushed a cigarette butt by her foot. That's it, she thought, I really have to leave!

She cast a last glance at Frndic, and then turned at last to get onto the bus. At that precise moment Monsieur Frndic said: "Alors, allons boire une tasse de café!"

"Oui," replied Steffie in confusion.

Steffie and Monsieur Frndic walked down the street without saying anything. Maybe I should stop speaking French and talk to him, she thought, and decided against it. It might spoil it, something between them might split apart, like a run in a stocking. Anyway, if two people meet on the moon they would have speak some new moon language, right? . . . Now why did such a silly example pop into her head? What did the moon have to do with it?

A vision of the thirteenth lesson floated slowly before her eyes. She suddenly felt it was vitally important that Monsieur Frndic had appeared at precisely the thirteenth lesson. Hadn't Anuška said something about lucky number thirteen? As in good luck?

When they stopped at a crosswalk, waiting for the light to turn green, Steffie quickly opened her book, found the treizième leçon and ran her eyes over the text.* It felt like

---

* The text Steffie ran her eyes over is given here in full:

TREIZIÈME LEÇON   A HUMBLE DWELLING

La famille était réunie dans le petit salon, où il y avait deux fauteuils, un piano, deux lampes coiffées de petits chapeaux verts et une petite étagère remplie de bibelots.

Par économie, on n'allumait pour la maison entière qu'un seul feu et qu'une lampe, autour de laquelle toutes les occupations, toutes les distractions se groupaient, une bonne grosse

reading a message from a fortune cookie meant just for her.

Oui, winked the green traffic light, *oui* typed out " " " " "
Steffie's thoughts, *oui* beat her heart, *oui* said the smiles of
the passersby, *oui* rang the busses, *oui* staggered a passing
drunk, *oui* the streets agreed, *et oui, mais oui, mais oui* . . .

All the cafés were closed, but Steffie Cvek and Monsieur Frndic kept walking. Steffie knew that her whole life
had changed and that it wouldn't stop changing, everything was moving onwards, upwards, moving forwards,
quatorzième leçon, quinzième leçon, seizième leçon . . .

(FIN)

---

lampe de famille dont le vieil abat-jour montrant des scènes de
nuit, semées de points brillants, avait été l'étonnement et la joie
de tous ces enfants.

Sortant doucement de l'ombre de la pièce, quatre jeunes
têtes se penchaient, blondes ou brunes, souriantes ou appli-
quées, sous ce rayon intime et réchauffant qui les éclairait à la
hauteur des yeux.

Ainsi serrée dans une petite pièce en haut de la maison
déserte, dans la chaleur, la sécurité de son intérieur, bien garni
et soigné, la famille Joyeuse a l'air d'un nid tout en haut d'un
grand arbre.

une étagère: a shelf; *des bibelots*: small ornaments; *un abat-jour*:
a lampshade

SCRAPS OF ROMANCE FOR APPLIQUÉ WORK

(supplement)

··❋

She had known Monsieur Frndic for less than an hour, and already she felt irresistibly drawn to him. She yearned to be with him every minute. She told herself she was being a fool, but already she couldn't help imagining a future by his side. She wanted passionately to be with him forever.

··❋

Steffie was truly overwhelmed with happiness. She kept telling herself, over and over again, how foolish she was to tie her life so firmly to a man she barely knew. Then again, she consoled herself, Monsieur Frndic was no ordinary man and surely anyone would love his astonishing mixture of childlike innocence and manly strength.

··❋

As they walked towards the traffic lights, it seemed to Steffie that the river of doubts and fears—her whole life up until then—had been imperceptibly crossed and now lay firmly behind her, all in the short time she had spent with him.

··❋

His words and the passionate sound of his voice were like caresses. Steffie felt her heart beating harder.

··❋

He was handsome, clever, sophisticated; he possessed all the qualities that Steffie valued in a man.

··❋

When he looked at her with his tender eyes, Steffie realized he would be able to offer her lasting love and not just a passing affair.

....✄

He raised her hand to his lips and kissed it. Steffie trembled at his touch. They said nothing, but the kiss was eloquent enough.

....✄

Monsieur Frndic aroused in her feelings that had long been buried. She knew that his presence would lead her into temptation.

....✄

When Steffie said nothing, he took her in his arms and pressed her to his chest. Steffie looked up at his face and felt a sudden urge to kiss him. She gazed into his deep eyes and they implored her for a kiss, telling her of his loneliness and his desire to conquer her heart, to keep her by his side forever.

....✄

He pressed her firmly to him and kissed her passionately. His galloping love swept aside every obstacle, every difficulty. Steffie realized at last that her heart was still capable of trembling with love.

....✄

If only that moment could last forever! She wanted them to be together until the end of time, she and Monsieur Frndic, in that little restaurant garden filled with flowers. When you love someone, the simplest things in life bring joy. You not only think of that person, of love, but also of a shared house, a garden, children . . . Perhaps her dreams were not idle fantasies, perhaps Monsieur Frndic really would make them come true!

....✄

THE AUTHOR'S DARTS

= = = = Well? What happened next? There's no more thread, I've stopped stitching, I'm holding the last strand of thread in my mouth and I don't know what to do with it. I chew on it and think sadly: they lived happily ever after, but what about me? I'm not going to live happily ever after.

Already I can hear them talking.

"I don't like it!" says a friend of mine. "The sleeves are too long. That Steffie's not a real character, she's nothing!"

+ + + + "I don't like it!" says another friend. "You haven't padded it evenly. You didn't give Steffie a chance!"

"I don't like it!" says a female acquaintance. "It's too flimsy. There's nothing about the plight of women—where's the gynecologist, the plot twist with the abortion, the illegitimate child?"

"I don't like it!" says my brother. "It's out of date. You should have sent Steffie to a club at the end."

"I don't like it!" says a male acquaintance. "Sloppy workmanship. You didn't make it clear whether that Frndic guy will marry her."

"I don't like it!" says my mother. "It's too tight. Let it out in a couple of places! The aunt is only a caricature, not a character."

"I don't like it!" says my hairdresser. "Airport reading. They're all clichés, your Steffies, Anuškas, Mariannas. I cut their hair every day! What you need is more imagination. The best thing for you to do is unpick the whole thing and start over."

I've run out of thread, *thread* I'm telling you . . . Okay, I'll unpick it. There. But now I hear another voice, familiar and hard.

"Too short!" my editor says.

"What?"

"Just too short!"

"Oh," I say.

My arms drop wearily. And then what do I see on my desk but three golden apples. They weren't the a minute ago! One, two, three—one for Steffie and one for me. One, two, three—and the third one . . . the third one for Steffie's aunt!

= = = =

THE AUTHOR'S MOTHER, AUNT SEKA, THEIR NEIGHBOR MAJA, LENCE FROM MACEDONIA, AND YARMILA FROM THE CZECH REPUBLIC CONTINUE THE STORY OF OUR HEROINE

....✂

The hem of a quotation: "They prattle together; out of the darkness they draw a long hopeless braid of conversation."
(Bruno Schulz)
....✂

"Do come," Mother had said, "your Aunt Seka and Maja will be here as usual, then Aunt Seka's friend Yarmila from Brno and Maja's cousin Lence from Strumica. They're all older and wiser, we'll come up with something if we put our heads together."

After a long silence my mother took a resolute sip of coffee, put her cup down on the saucer, shook her head a few times, sighed, and said:

"So that's what he said? It's too short?"

"Yes," I sighed too.

"What's that supposed to mean?" she asked in a quiet, threatening tone.

"Just that, it's too short."

"Oh," my mother said more mildly.

Maja, her cousin Lence, Aunt Seka, and Aunt Seka's friend Yarmila calmed down as well. I relaxed too and lit a cigarette.

"Hmm . . . ," my mother began, but then fell silent. Aunt Seka, Maja, Lence, and Yarmila made compassionate noises. There was a long silence. I rustled my cigarette packet nervously and waited.

"Well, if it's too short, we should make longer!" Lence from Strumica burst out.

"Yes, longer!" the others agreed.

"We are all here to help—?" said Yarmila kindly. Her lilting voice made everything she said sound like a question.

"Hmm . . ." my mother repeated, taking matters into ++++ her own hands. "How about adding a chapter to describe Steffie's married life? They have a nice, normal wedding, and she has her first child, a girl. They're both extremely busy at work. Oh, by the way, you never said what this Frndic does for a living. Anyway, she has a second child and, of course, starts to let herself go. So he finds himself a mistress, some young student, and Steffie finds out. She's devastated, and starts fighting to get him back."

"And the battle means going to the hairdresser," Aunt ++++ Seka joined in irritably, "and just when she's coming home from the hairdresser it begins to pour! She hasn't got an umbrella, of course! A passing car splatters her with mud! And everything falls apart, dissolves, bursts into flames, collapses, shatters into tiny little pieces! We've seen it all a hundred times in the movies!" Aunt Seka was growing increasingly furious. "Why do we women always come off so badly! Have Frndic run over by a car!" Choking with fury, Aunt Seka lit a cigarette.

Aunt Seka exhaled; my mother gulped; Lence rolled her eyes; and Maja, the neighbor, knitted rapidly.

"But why does it have to be so drastic—?" asked the ++++ delicate Yarmila in her sing-song voice. "Who am I to say, but maybe your Miss Steffie and her Mr. Frndic could inherit some money and just go buy a house on the Adriatic—? Heavens, the sea, it's so wonderfully blue there—?"

I was about to say that her idea about the wonderful blue sea wasn't bad at all, but my mother ignored Yarmila's suggestion and went on:

+ + + +   "Okay," she said, "if you think the marriage can't work then let them break up. The life of a divorced woman is interesting too, all the troubles she has."

"But we've seen it millions of times!" said Aunt Seka, getting angry again.

"I don't know, I don't know—?" Yarmila repeated, more to herself than anyone else.

Maja's knitting needles suddenly stopped clacking, + + + + and she said triumphantly: "And a few months after her divorce, Steffie's boss at work, a disgusting pig, tries to blackmail her!"

"For what?" spat Aunt Seka in a savage tone.

"Well . . . I mean . . . you know . . . to get her to sleep with him!" Maja was confused, but came up with something at last.

"So what? Let her sleep with him! Bosses they have needs too." Lence rolled her eyes.

"I don't know . . . I only thought . . . It always happens in novels. I mean, there's always a boss, and so on . . ."

"Maja's right in a way," said my mother, turning toward me. "You're not going to let your heroine sleep with just anyone, are you?"

"Who she sleeps with depends on the plot," I said bitterly. "It has nothing to do with morality! If the plot required it, I'd send her hopping from one bed to another!"

+ + + +   "Or perhaps you could send your Miss Steffie on a lovely trip—?" Yarmila pleaded. "A cruise around the Mediterranean, with her two children—? On deck, Miss

Steffie meets a gentleman who has lost his wife—? And, please, everything turns out for the best, I mean for Miss Steffie—?"

"How about we send her on a safari?" Aunt Seka suggested maliciously.

"Oooh good idea!" Lence exclaimed.

"The story doesn't have to go forward, we can go ++++ backward! For example, we have no idea who the girl's parents were. Where does her aunt fit in? See what I mean? It's all so vague," said my mother.

"Absolutely not!" I said grimly.

"Yes," agreed Lence, "it must not all to be so clear. The literature is one thing, and the life it is something else. If you think about it, not everything is clear in the life either. Is true, no?"

"Is true," I said.

"It's true!" Maja said energetically, putting down her ++++ knitting needles. "That's the whole point: life is one thing and literature is something else. What you can't do in life, you can do in art. That's why I love happy endings. I saw a fantastic movie once, where everyone was missing something. One character had no wife, another had no husband, another had only one leg, another stuttered, and the last one was blind. In the end they all got what they needed: the man without a leg married the blind woman, who had meanwhile regained her sight. Now that was a great movie! Do that with Steffie: she keeps on needing something and in the end you arrange to give it to her."

"But she already did!" yelped Aunt Seka. "She gave her Frndic!"

"I know," said Maja, sticking to her guns, "but in the next installment she'll need something else!"

"An apartment!" barked Aunt Seka.

"Not bad," said my mother calmly.

"You're crazy, all of you!" shouted Aunt Seka in exasperation. "A writer's not Santa Claus!"

++++ "I know," said Maja, "but here's an example from life. A friend of mine, Maria, you don't know her . . . anyway, say Frndic leaves Steffie in the next installment, like that jerk left Maria! Well, Maria lived on her own for only a few months, with her little girl, she's adorable, little Silvica. One day the little angel got measles. Maria rushed her to the hospital, and guess what happened! A young pediatrician, an intern, from Kenya. And there you are! Now she writes to me every week from Mairobi!"

"NAIrobi!" growled Aunt Seka.

"All right, Nairobi, what's the difference?"

At this point my mother realized that the whole thing was degenerating and announced a truce. "How about a little brandy? Yarmila? You, Lence?"

"Just a tiny drop, please—?" said Yarmila.

"I'll have some," said Maja.

"You bet!" said Aunt Seka.

"Oooh good idea! Is true, no?" said Lence, tapping me on the knee.

"What about you?" asked my mother.

After a longish pause I said, almost vindictively, "I'll stick to lemonade!"

My mother poured the drinks, the women sipped theirs, my mother sipped hers, I sipped my lemonade, and my mother said, "It looks like you don't like our suggestions for a second installment about Steffie's married life, or giving Frndic a mistress and Steffie a
++++ divorce, or sending Steffie on a trip to the Greek islands,

or getting her into trouble at work, or infecting her child with measles, or having her long lost parents turn up, so what now?"

"Why don't you find Steffie's aunt a lover!" Aunt Seka shouted.

"Oh, that would be awfully tasteless—?" Yarmila ++++ frowned. "Perhaps Miss Steffie starts taking German classes—?"

I abandoned myself to a careful study of the manner in which lemon seeds float in a glass of lemonade, and pretended not to have heard anything.

"Her mother-in-law!" Maja exclaimed, and put down ++++ her needles again.

"What about her?" asked Aunt Seka cautiously.

"That's the answer! A dramatic relationship! Steffie and her mother-in-law!"

"I think Frndic should have a brother!" said Aunt ++++ Seka ironically.

"What for?" asked the women with one voice.

"So Steffie could fall in love with him!"

"And Frndic would smash his face in out of jealousy!" said Maja, her eyes flashing.

"I don't know, I don't know—?" delicate Yarmila repeated meekly.

Lence, evidently with the intention of salvaging what could be salvaged, announced solemnly, "Every thing you make, a work of art too, it is like the stew. The more you put in, the better it is."

Lence stopped, took a mouthful of brandy, and looked from one woman to the next.

"What do you put into your stew?" asked Aunt Seka with interest.

"Ooooh, you like me to tell?"

"Yes, yes!" the women cried.

++++   "Potato, onions, peppers, eggplant, tomatoes, carrots, beef, rice, chili powder . . ." Lence listed.

The women all produced pens and paper from who knows where. Because of the abrupt change in the situation, I did too.

"Is very important," Lence went on, "that everything to simmer on low flame and then baked in dish of earthenware."

"Dish of earthenware," muttered the women, writing it down.

"Dish of . . ." I wrote, and then it struck me: "A new genre!" I said it half aloud and sent a coded glance toward Lence.

"It need not to be earthenware, it can be any kind," said Lence, dashing my hopes that I might at last be understood.

"Any kind . . ." muttered the women.

"Yes, so!" Lence concluded majestically, as though saying Mass.

The women put away their bits of paper contentedly. I cruelly drowned one lemon seed and swallowed another, then said in a terrible voice: "And Steffie?"

The women were silent.

"What about Steffie?" I said reproachfully.

Yarmila shrugged her shoulders and shook her head. "I don't know, I don't know—?"

The others shook their heads too.

"So none of you can think of anything? Other than clichés, I mean. Nothing from your own lives? Haven't you lived?"

"Well, in that movie with Charles Boyer," my mother began, but as she said "Charles Boyer," her neighbor,

Maja, leapt up like a scalded cat, threw down her needles yet again, and shouted, "Girls!"

The women were startled, and Maja was already on her way out of the apartment. We heard the door to the next apartment open, then shut, and in a few moments Maja came back with a large book in her hands.

"Girls, girls," Maja sang in a voice filled with promise.

On the cover was written in English in huge red letters:

HEART-THROBS!

and underneath, in slightly smaller black letters:

A COLORFUL COLLECTION OF THE WORLD'S
MOST FASCINATING MEN

It was a lost cause. I let my thoughts sink into my lemonade and absentmindedly drowned the remaining seeds with my spoon. When I raised my eyes again, I saw the lined faces of the women gradually cracking, peeling like plaster masks, and out floated the young faces of my mother, Aunt Seka, Maja the neighbor, Yarmila, and Lence.

Their voices drifted over to me.

"I'd take Boyer and Olivier, of course."

"Only two of the hundred most attractive men in the world?"

"All right, I'll take Clark Gable too. He was the love of my youth."

"I would also to sleep with Errol Flynn, Gary Cooper, and, ooooh, Burt Lancaster! Burt Lancaster! And with Marcello Mastroianni and with . . ."

"Take it easy!"

"I'd have to take Marlon!"

"And I would like it if Gerard Filippe asked me to dinner—?"

"Only dinner?"

"All right, maybe a walk—?"

"Nothing else?"

"Perhaps I would correspond with that fine young man from the cowboy films—? Ah, yes, James Stewart, with him—!?"

"She'd correspond! Ha, ha, ha . . ."

"Oooh, ladies, I would also to sleep with all the Tarzans, every one, starting with Johnny Weismuller, all of them!"

"Sold!"

"John Barrymore and Douglas Fairbanks!"

"Heavens, they're ancient history! Why them?"

"Respect for my elders!"

"Hey, girls, I used to be crazy about this one! Remember Tyrone Power?"

"I used to like Robert Mitchum!"

"I don't know, he was a terrible drinker—?"

"I would also to sleep with John Wayne!"

"You'd sleep with them all!"

"And why not? If is up to me."

"I'll stick to my three."

"I'll do Paul Newman! He's a real man!"

"Hey, girls, what about *this* one?"

I felt utterly alone. I stood up, went to the door, stopped for a moment in case the women noticed me, and muttered in a conciliatory tone: "Well, I guess I'd take . . ." (Dustin Hoffman, for sure!)—but they didn't hear me. My mother cast a distracted glance at me from within the fog of this collective hypnosis, said something like: "It'll all be all right," and sank back into the chitchat.

I left with a bitter taste in my mouth—walked straight into the elevator and then out into the indifferent street. My lips were puckered. Under my tongue I held the bitter seed of pique, in my hand the pointless recipe for the stew. In my head swirled vague thoughts, thoughts in the style of the recipe. I was thinking something to the effect that everything was a cliché, including life itself, and that I would have to think about that in more detail when the dust settled; then, that the microbes of kitsch are the most vigorous organisms on the planet; then about the melodramatic imagination and how indestructible it is; then about the imagination being like ginger, about how sensuous words with soft "g" sounds are and how I should use them more often, then something ecological about our permanent exposure to unsafe levels of kitsch, about the talk I'd have to have some time with Maja about optimistic realism; then, in connection with that, about an unexpected inheritance I would have to invent for S. C. to send her to Tahiti; my thoughts savagely crossed out Tahiti and concluded that everything should be left as it was; then I thought about how it would have been if ///////// anything had happened between my mother and Charles Boyer; something about how we are chronically infected by the fairy tale; something about whether I should leave the carrots out of the recipe or not; then about the ginger of the imagination; then about the true heart of the genre and the invincibility of the happy ending; something about eggplants, about life, and about cheap cotton fabric . . . And then the turmoil in my soul was suddenly stilled, because an old tune from a random station on a random radio in a random car driving by brushed up against me. I felt my heart skip a beat and I tapped my feet, the tune was bop-bop-bopping, I was hop-hop-hopping along . . .

FINISHING TOUCHES

1. *A Little Patchwork Novel.* The author's original intention was to introduce a "dissident" prose genre into the existing "official" typology. Specifically, the author was inspired by the diary of one Pat Patch (a pseudonym).[*] Pat Patch's engaging "diary" is an attempt to record the chatter at a tea party in London in 1888. Stimulated by her example, the author intended to reproduce the *oral* prose that women have created for centuries, *underground* prose that originated at social gatherings, feather-plucking, spinning, weaving, embroidering, washing, in harems, and in all those collective situations of women that have sprung up in various historical, geographical, national, social, traditional, and other circumstances.

2. The author wanted to reproduce the warmth that is released by the passionate friction of women's tongues, the verbal steam of their communal bath. All that remains of this intended "communal bath" are some incomplete prose fragments (verbal patches) which are to some extent the equivalent of the communicative situation of a gossip session. What is crucial in such a communicative situation is the assumption that all the participants are more or less acquainted with the object of their gossip, making explanation unnecessary and undesirable.

---

[*] Pat Patch, *Chatterbox* (London, 1888).

3. Having expressed at the outset her intention of writing a women's story, the author took into account several predominant characteristics of so-called "women's writing": the main (female) character's search for personal happiness, a feeling of isolation, love as the primary motive force, a powerful experience of the body, sensuality, passivity, an apolitical outlook, the banality of the everyday, social consciousness in the subtext, impoverished language, the impossibility of experiencing the world as a totality, etc. The author avoided all autobiographical tendencies and the predominant confessional tone. The author would like to point out that all these definitions have been taken not only from the current criticism but also from life.

4. Honesty compels the author to confess that she had greater aspirations. In the character of Steffie Cvek she secretly hoped to create a female peer of Milos Hrma, the hero of Bohumil Hrabal's *Closely Watched Trains*. However, wilting like poor Milos's lily, the author did not succeed in this by no means easy task.

5. A significant role in sewing this patchwork story was played by the residue of certain novels read in the author's adolescence. She no longer remembers any novels in particular, but she has the sense that they were mostly American. Out of this body of reading rises the outline of a poor but beautiful girl (inevitably auburn-haired) standing in front of a shop window and looking longingly at an expensive dress. It seems to the author that in these novels everything revolved around the question of who would buy the dress for the poor but beautiful auburn-haired girl, and when. The suspense electrifies the author to this

day. Because of her poor memory and the passage of time, the author may well be distorting the facts, but the image of the girl and her shop-window longings is still fresh!

6. The author took her "fabric," the advice and technical terms, from a women's fashion magazine. She did not follow the sewing logic exactly, partly because many of the technicalities remain rather opaque to her, but she took indescribable pleasure in reading, pronouncing, and copying out unfamiliar words like *gussets* and *basting* or curious collocations such as *French whipped seams*. Perhaps equally unfamiliar words like *carburetor* or *dipstick* would have had a similar charm, but poetic intuition whispered into her authorial ear that these choices would have led to quite a different story.

7. The author gave Steffie Cvek *Madame Bovary* to read simply because it is such a brilliant novel. She leaves other little semantic knots for her readers to make for themselves.

8. The author chose the character of a humble typist in search of happiness because she herself sought the charm of a *romance novel*. She copied the romance scraps from just such a novel, simply replacing the names Laura and Dirk with Steffie and Frndic, to make it match. If she had let her imagination run free, who knows where the characters might have ended up. Perhaps in an Alpine novel, where the characters leap over the mountain peaks, pick wildflowers, and like kissing almost as much as yodeling!

9. In a spirit of rapprochement, the author endeavored to stitch together *romance novels*, in which the female

characters search and search until at last they happyend-ingly find what they seek, and *women's fiction*, in which the female characters also search and search but never find what they seek—or, if they do, only with great difficulty.

10. All this relentless stitching made it possible to affix a third genre, one with a similar story line. Which *fairy tales* she had in mind her readers can see for themselves.

11. The choice of sewing as a literary device is not intended as ironic; this is, after all, "women's fiction." The author is genuinely fascinated by the profound significance of these skills. After all, are Penelope and Scheherazade not in some sense sisters?

12. The author sets great store by these finishing touches, soporific though they may be. Not only does she wish to imitate the precision of the "Instructions for Making the Garment" from the aforementioned fashion magazine, she also wishes to *iron on* the outline of the pattern as clearly as possible for others to follow. Incidentally, in the author's view, *ironing on* is the literature of the future.

13. The author has made it to point 13 at last—which she had to reach because of women's well-known compulsion to make everything symmetrical and orderly—i.e., to the aforementioned, fateful number 13 in the life of S. C. The author can finally breathe a sigh of relief, having earned the right to pick up her Hrabal and reread again the story of Milos Hrma.

1981

LIFE IS A FAIRY TALE

The power of a country road when one is walking along it is different from the power it has when one flies over it by airplane. In the same way, the power of a text when it is read is different from the power it has when it is copied out. The airplane passenger sees only how the road pushes through the landscape, how it unfolds according to the same laws as the terrain surrounding it. Only he who walks the road on foot learns of the power it commands, and of how, from the very scenery that for the flier is only the unfurled plain, it calls forth distances, belvederes, clearings, prospects at each of its turns like a commander deploying soldiers at a front. Only the copied text thus commands the soul of him who is occupied with it, whereas the mere reader never discovers the new aspects of his inner self that are opened by the text, that road cut through the interior jungle forever closing behind it: because the reader follows the movement of his mind in the free flight of daydreaming, whereas the copier submits it to command. The Chinese practice of copying books was thus an incomparable guarantee of literary culture, and the transcript a key to China's enigmas.

—Walter Benjamin, *One-Way Street*

A wonderful turnip has grown in the garden; it is more like a potato than a turnip.

—Nikolai Gogol

A Hot Dog in a Warm Bun

1.

On the twenty-fifth of March a truly unbelievable thing took place in Zagreb. Nada Matić, a young doctor specializing in plastic surgery, awoke in her room and looked at the clock. It was 6:15. Nada jumped out of bed, jumped into the shower, squatted under the stream of water, then, lighting a cigarette, jumped into a terry cloth robe. It was 6:25. She pulled on her gray spring suit, daubed some rouge on her cheeks, and grabbed her bag. It was 6:30. She locked the door, finished the cigarette in the elevator, and hurried off to catch her tram.

By the time Nada Matić stepped off the tram, it was 6:50. And just then, right in the middle of the square, Nada Matić was overcome by a sudden, unusually intense hunger. She rushed over to the Skyscraper Cafeteria, which served hot dogs in warm buns, nervously called out to the waitress, "More mustard, please!" greedily grabbed the hot dog, and impatiently threw away the napkin. (That is what Nada Matić did. That is what I do too: I always dispose of those unnecessary and shamefully tiny scraps of paper waitresses use for wrapping hot dogs.)

Then she set off across the square. She was about to bring the hot dog to her lips, when—was it some dark sense of foreboding or a ray of the March morning sun alighting on the object in question, illuminating it with its own special radiance? In either case and to make a long story short, she glanced down at the fresh pink hot dog and her face convulsed in horror. For what did she see peering through the longish bun and ocherish mustard foam but a genuine, bona fide . . . ! Nada came to a complete and utter halt. No, there could be no doubt. "Glans, corpus, radix, corpora cavernosa, corpora spongiosa, praeputium, frenulum, scrotum," our heroine, Nada Matić, thought, running through her totally useless anatomy class knowledge and still not believing her eyes. No, that thing in the bun was most definitely not a hot dog!

Utterly shaken, Nada resumed her journey to the Municipal Hospital at a much slower pace. It had all come together in a single moment: the anatomy lesson, plastic surgery, the desire to specialize in aesthetic prosthetics—it had all flashed before her eyes like a mystical sign, a warning, the finger of fate, a finger which, if we may be forgiven the crudeness of our metaphor, peered out of the bun in so tangible, firm, fresh, and pink a state as to be anything but an illusion.

Nada Matić decided to give the "hot dog" issue top priority. Taking the "hot dog" to the laboratory and dropping it in a bottle of Formalin would have been the simplest solution, of course, but what would her colleagues have said? Nada looked here and there for a litter basket; there were none in sight. As she'd thrown the napkin away and had no paper tissues, she tried to hide the "hot dog" by coaxing it into the bun with her finger, but smooth, slippery, and springy as it was, it kept sliding out, the head gleaming almost maliciously in Nada's direction.

It then occurred to Nada that she might stop off at a café and just happen to leave the "hot dog" on the lower shelf of one of the tables she often stood beside—she had said goodbye to three umbrellas that way—but in the end she lost her nerve. For the first time in her life Nada felt what it was like to be a criminal . . .

Oh, before I forget, I ought to tell you a few things about our heroine. Nada Matić is the kind of shortish, plumpish blonde that men find attractive. But her generous, amicable, amorous character kept getting in her way, and men disappeared from her life, poor thing, without her ever quite understanding why. Abandoned by no fault of her own, she naturally and periodically found herself involved in hot and heavy escapades with married medical personnel of the male sex.

Suddenly Nada felt terribly sorry for herself: her whole life seemed to have shrunk into that grotesque symbol of buncum-relay-race-baton. No, she'd better take care of it at once. She gave the bun an unconscious squeeze and the hot dog peeked out at her again, turning her self-pity to despair. And just as she noticed a broken basement window and was about to toss it away, bun and all, who should pass by with a cold nod but one of the surgeons, Otto Waldinger. Quick as lightning, Nada stuffed the "hot dog" into her pocket, smearing gooey mustard all over her fingers . . . The bastard! Scarcely even acknowledging her, while not so long ago . . . !

And then she spied a mercifully open drain. She removed the "hot dog" from her pocket with great care and flung it into the orifice. It got stuck in the grating. She nudged it with her foot, but it refused to budge. It was too fat.

At that point up sauntered a good-looking, young policeman.

"Identity papers, please."

"What for?" Nada mumbled.

"Jaywalking."

"Oh," said Nada, rummaging frenetically through her bag.

"What's the matter?" asked the policeman, looking down at the grating. "Lost your appetite?" A good inch and a half of the "hot dog" was sticking out of the bun. Nada Matić went pale . . .

But at this point everything becomes so enveloped in mist that we cannot tell what happened next.

2.

Mato Kovalić, a writer (or, to be more specific, a novelist and short story writer), awoke rather early and smacked his lips, which he always did when he awoke though he could not for the life of him explain why. Kovalić stretched, moved his hand along the floor next to the bed until it found his cigarettes, lit one, inhaled, and settled back. There was a full-length mirror on the opposite wall, and Kovalić could see his bloated gray face in it.

During his habitual morning wallow in bed he was wont to run through the events of the previous day. The thought of the evening's activities and Maja, that she-devil of an invoice clerk, called forth a blissful smile on his face, and his hand willy-nilly slid under the covers . . . Unbelievable! No, absolutely impossible!

Kovalić flung back the blanket and leaped up as if scalded. There he felt only a perfectly smooth surface. Kovalić rushed over to the mirror. He was right. There he saw only an empty, smooth space. He looked like one of those naked, plastic dummies in the shop windows. He pinched and pulled at himself several times, he slapped his face to see whether he was awake, he jumped in place once or twice; and again he placed his hand on the spot where only the night before there had been a bulge . . . No, it was gone!

But here we must say a few words about Kovalić and show the reader what sort of man our hero is. We shall not go into his character, because the moment one says something about a writer all other writers take offence. And to point out that Kovalić was a writer who divided all prose into two categories, prose with balls and prose without (he was for the former), would be quite out of place in these circumstances and might even prompt the reader to give a completely erroneous and vulgar interpretation to the whole incident. Let us therefore say instead that Kovalić greatly valued—and wished to write—novels that were true to life, down to earth. What he despised more than anything was symbols, metaphors, allusions, ambiguities, literary frills; what he admired was authenticity, a razor-edged quality where every word meant what it meant and not God knows what else! He was especially put off by intellectualizing, attitudinizing, high-blown flights of fancy, genres of all kinds (life is too varied and unpredictable to be forced into prefabricated molds, damn it!) and—naturally—critics! Who but critics, force-fed on the pap of theory, turned works of literature into paper monsters teeming with hidden meanings?

Kovalić happened to be working on a book of stories called *Meat*, the kingpin of which was going to be about his neighbor, a retired butcher positively in love with his trade. Kovalić went on frequent drinking bouts with the man for the purpose of gathering material: nouns (brisket, chuck, flank, knuckle, round, rump, saddle, shank, loin, wienerwurst, weisswurst, liverwurst, bratwurst, blood pudding, etc.), verbs (pound, hack, gash, slash, gut, etc.), and whole sentences. "You shoulda seen me go through them—the slaughterhouse ain't got nothing on me!"; "A beautiful way to live a life—and earn a pile!"; "My knives go with me to the grave." Kovalić intended to use the latter, which the old man would say with great pathos, to end the story with a wallop.

We might add that Kovalić was a good-looking man and much loved by the women, a situation he took completely for granted.

Well, dear readers, now you can judge for yourselves the state our hero was in when instead of his far from ugly bulge he found a smooth, even space.

Looking in the mirror, Kovalić saw a broken man. God, he thought, why me? And why not my arms or legs? Why not my ears or nose, unbearable as it would have been.

What good am I now? . . . Good for the dump, that's what! If somebody had chopped it off, I wouldn't have made a peep. But to up and disappear on me, vanish into thin air . . . ?! No, it's impossible! I must be dreaming, hallucinating. And in his despair he started pinching the empty space again.

Suddenly, as if recalling something important, Kovalić pulled on his shoes and ran out into the street. It was a sunny day, and he soon slowed his pace and began to stroll. In the street he saw a child peeling a banana, in a bar he saw a man pouring beer from a bottle down his gullet, in a doorway he saw a boy with a plastic pistol in his hand come running straight at him; he saw a jet cross the sky, a fountain in a park start to spurt, a blue tram come round a bend, some workers block traffic dragging long rubber pipes across the road, two men walking towards him, one of whom was saying to the other, "But for that you really need balls . . ."

God! thought Kovalić, compulsively eyeing the man's trousers. Can't life be cruel!

Queer! the cocky trousers sneered, brushing past him.

I must, I really must do something, thought Kovalić, sinking even deeper into despair. And then he had a lifesaver of a thought . . . Lidija! Of course! He'd go and see Lidija.

3.

You never know what's going to happen next, thought Vinko K., the good-looking young policeman, as he jaywalked across the square. Pausing in front of a shop window, he saw the outline of his lean figure and the shadow of his stick dangling at his side. Through the glass he saw a young woman with dark, shining eyes making hot dogs. First she pierced one half of a long roll with a heated metal stake and twisted it several times; then she poured some mustard into the hollow and stuffed a pink hot dog into it. Vinko K. was much taken with her dexterity. He went in and pretended to be waiting his turn, while in fact he was watching the girl's pudgy hands and absentmindedly twirling his stick.

"Next!" her voice rang out.

"Me?! Oh, then I might as well have one," said a flustered Vinko K., "as long as . . ."

"Twenty!" her voice rang out like a cash register.

Vinko K. moved over to the side. He subjected the bun to a close inspection: it contained a fresh hot dog. Meanwhile, two more girls had come out of a small door, and soon all three were busy piercing rolls and filling them with mustard and hot dogs.

Vinko K. polished off his hot dog with obvious relish and then walked over to the girls.

"Care to take a break, girls?" he said in a low voice. "Can we move over here?" he added, even more softly.

Squeezed together between cases of beverages and boxes of hot dogs, a sink, a bin, and a broom, Vinko K. and the waitresses could scarcely breathe.

"I want you to show me all the hot dogs you have on the premises," said a calm Vinko K.

The girl opened all the hot dog boxes without a murmur. The hot dogs were neatly packed in cellophane wrappers.

"Hm!" said Vinko K. "Tell me, are they all vacuum-packed?"

"Oh, yes!" all three voices rang out as a team. "They're all vacuum-packed!"

A long, uncomfortable silence ensued. Vinko K. was thinking. You never knew what would happen next in his line. You could never tell what human nature had in store.

Meanwhile the girls just stood there, huddled together like hot dogs in a cellophane wrapper. All at once Vinko K.'s fingers broke into a resolute riff on one of the cardboard boxes and, taking a deep breath, he said, as if giving a password, "Fellatio?"

"Aaaaah?!" the girls replied, shaking their heads, and though they did not seem to have understood the question they kept up a soft titter.

"Never heard of it?" asked Vinko K.

"Teehee! Teehee! Teehee!" they tittered on.

"Slurp, slurp?" Vinko K. tried, sounding them out as best he could.

"Teehee! Teehee! Teehee!" they laughed, pleasantly, like the Chinese.

Vinko K. was momentarily nonplussed. He thought of using another word with the same meaning, but it was so rude he decided against it.

"Hm!" he said instead.

"Hm!" said the girls, rolling their eyes and bobbing their heads.

Vinko K. realized his case was lost. He sighed. The girls sighed back compassionately.

By this time there was quite a crowd waiting for hot dogs. Vinko K. went outside. He stole one last glance at the first girl. She glanced back, tittered, and licked her lips. Vinko K. smiled and unconsciously bobbed his stick. She too smiled and vaguely nodded. Then she took a roll and resolutely rammed it onto the metal stake.

But at this point everything becomes so enveloped in mist again that we cannot tell what happened next.

4.

"Entrez!" Lidija called out unaffectedly, and Kovalić collapsed in her enormous, commodious armchair with a sigh of relief.

Lidija was Kovalić's best friend: she was completely, un-hesitatingly devoted to him. Oh, he went to bed with her all right, but out of friendship: she went to bed with him out of friendship too. They didn't do it often, but they had stuck with it for ages—ten years by now. Kovalić knew everything there was to know about Lidija; Lidija knew everything there was to know about Kovalić. And they were never jealous. But Kovalić the writer—much as he valued sincerity in life and prose—refused to admit to himself that he had once seen their kind of relationship in a film and found it highly appealing, an example (or so he thought) of a new, more humane type of rapport between a man and a woman. It was in the name of this ideal that he gave his all to her in bed even when he was not particularly up to it.

They had not seen each other for quite some time, and Lidija started in blithely about all the things that had happened since their last meeting. She had a tendency to end each sentence with a puff, as if what she had just produced was less a sentence than a hot potato.

Lidija had soon trotted out the relevant items from the pantry of her daily life, and following a short silence—and a silent signal they had hit upon long before—the two of them began to undress.

"Christ!" cried Lidija, who in other circumstances was a translator to and from the French.

"Yesterday . . ." said Kovalić, crestfallen, apologetic. "Completely disappeared . . ."

For a while Lidija simply stood there, staring wide-eyed at Kovalić's empty space; then she assumed a serious and energetic expression, went over to her bookcase, and took down the encyclopedia.

"Why bother?" asked Kovalić as she riffled the pages. "Castration, castration complex, coital trophy—it's all beside the point! It's just disappeared, understand? Dis-ap-peared!"

"Bon Dieu de Bon Dieu . . . !" Lidija muttered. "And what are you going to do now?"

"I don't know," Kovalić whimpered.

"Who were you with last?"

"Girl named Maja . . . But that's beside the point."

"Just wondering," said Lidija, and said no more.

As a literary person in her own right, Lidija had often cheered Kovalić up with her gift for the apt image. But now her sugar-sweet sugarbeet, her pickle in the middle, her poor withered mushroom, her very own Tom Thumb, her fig behind the leaf, her tingaling dingaling, her Jack-in-the-box had given way to—a blank space!

All of a sudden Lidija had a divine inspiration. She threw herself on Kovalić and for all the insulted, humiliated, oppressed, for all the ugly, impotent, and sterile, for all the poor in body, hunched in back, and ill in health—for every last one she gave him her tenderest treatment, polishing, honing him like a recalcitrant translation, fondling, caressing, her tongue as adroit as a keypunch, kneading his skin with her long, skilful fingers, moving lower and lower, seeking out her Jack's mislaid cudgel, picking and pecking at the empty space, fully expecting the firm little rod to pop out and give her cheek a love tap. Kovalić was a bit stunned by Lidija's abrupt show of passion, and even after he began to feel signs of arousal he remained prostrate, keeping close tabs on the pulsations within as they proceeded from pitapat to rat-tat-tat to boomety-boom, waiting for his Jack to jump, his Tom to thump, he didn't care who, as long as he came out into the open . . . !

Kovalić held his breath. He felt the blank space ticking off the seconds like an infernal machine; felt it about to erupt like a geyser, a volcano, an oil well; felt himself swelling like soaked peas, like a tulip bulb, like a cocoon; felt it coming, any time now, any second now, any—pow! boo-oo-oom! cra-a-a-sh-sh-sh!

Moaning with pleasure, Kovalić climaxed, climaxed to his great surprise—in the big toe of his left foot!

Utterly shaken, Kovalić gave Lidija a slight shove and peered down at his foot. Then, still refusing to believe that what happened had happened, he fingered the toe. It gave him a combination of pleasure and mild pain—and just sat there, potato-like, indifferent. Kovalić stared at it, mildly offended by its lack of response.

"Idiot!" said Lidija bilingually, and stood up, stalked out, and slammed the door.

Kovalić stretched. The smooth space was still hideously smooth. He wiggled his left toe, then his right . . . The left one struck him as perceptibly fatter and longer.

It did happen, thought Kovalić. There's no doubt about it. It actually happened. Suddenly he felt grateful to Lidija. The only thing was, did he really climax in his toe or was his mind playing tricks on him? Kovalić leaned over and felt the toe again, then went back to the smooth space, and finally, heaving a worried sigh, lit a cigarette.

"Anyone for a nice homemade sausage?" asked a conciliatory Lidija, peeking in from the kitchen.

Kovalić felt all the air go out of him: Lidija's proposition was like a blow to the solar plexus; it turned him into the butt of a dirty joke.

Kovalić was especially sensitive to clichés; he avoided them in both literature and life. And now he was terribly upset. By some absurd concatenation of events his life had assumed the contours of a well-established genre (a joke of which he was the punch line). How could life, which he had always thought of as vast—no, boundless—how could life give in

to the laws of a genre? And with nary a deviation! Kovalić
was so distressed he felt tears welling in his eyes. How he
loved—literature! It was so much better, more humane, less
predictable, more fanciful . . . In a well-written story Lidija
would have offered him nothing less than a veal cutlet; in the
low genre of life, Lidija, she gives him—a sausage!

But suddenly Kovalić felt hungry . . .

5.

On Saturday, the seventh of April, Nada Matić awoke from
a nightmare she had had for many nights. She would dream
she was working in her office at Plastic Surgery. It was
crammed with anatomical sketches, plaster moulds, and plastic models—all of "hot dogs" of the most varied dimensions.
Suddenly in trooped a band of students who tore them all
to pieces, laughing and pointing at her all the while. Nada
thought she would die of shame, and to make matters worse
she felt something sprouting on her nose—an honest to
goodness sausage! At that point the scene would shift to the
operating room, where she—Nada—and Dr. Waldinger were
performing a complex procedure. But there was a round hole
in the white sheet covering the patient, and she couldn't stop
staring through it at his hideous smooth space. Then the scene
would shift again, and she and Otto Waldinger were in a field
pulling out a gigantic beet. She was holding Otto around the
waist when suddenly she was attacked by a gigantic mouse!
She could feel its claws on her thighs.

Nada Matić was drinking her morning coffee, smoking a cigarette, and leafing through the evening paper. She
would seem to have acquired the fine habit of perusing the
Saturday classifieds. Suddenly an item in the "Lost and
Found" column caught her eye. She did a double take,
stunned by a wild but logical thought: if someone were to

lose something like that, it would only be natural for him to try to find it!

On the twenty-fifth of March, I left a collapsable umbrella in the Skyscraper Cafeteria. Would the finder please return it. No questions asked. Phone xyz and ask for Milan.

Nada jumped out of her seat. The ad was perfectly clear! The umbrella was obviously a respectable substitution for that. The fact that it was collapsible made the whole thing absolutely unambiguous!

Nada grabbed the telephone and dialed the number. The conversation was to the point: That's right. Five o'clock. See you there. Good-bye.

At five o'clock that afternoon Nada Matić rang the doorbell of a Dalmatinska Street apartment. A dark man of about thirty opened the door.

He could well be the one, thought Nada and said, "Hello, my name is Nada Matić."

"And mine is Milan Miško. Come in."

"Are you the one who lost his umbrella?"

"That's right."

"At the cafeteria?"

"The Skyscraper."

"Collapsable?"

"Yes, yes," said Milan Miško, the owner of the lost umbrella, in an amiable voice. "Do come in." Nada went in.

They sat down. The owner of the collapsable umbrella brought out a bottle of wine and two glasses.

"So, you're the one who lost it," Nada said tellingly and took a sip of the wine.

"That's right."

"God, how thick can he be?" thought Nada, beginning to feel annoyed. She took a long look at that place, but could make nothing out. She had to put it into words! But how?

"It must have been hard for you," she said, trying a more direct approach.

"With all the spring showers, you mean? I'd have picked up another one, but you do get attached to your own . . ."

"What was it like? Your umbrella, I mean," she asked its owner nonchalantly.

"Oh, nothing special . . . You mean, what color, how long?"

"Yes," said Nada, swallowing hard, "how long . . . ?"

"Oh, standard size," he said, as calm as could be. "You know—collapsible." And he looked over at Nada serenely. "The kind that goes in and out."

Now there could be no doubt. Nada resolved to take the plunge and call a spade a spade, even if it meant humiliating herself. After all, she had played her own bitter part in the affair. So she took the sort of deep breath she would have taken before a dive, half-shut her eyes, stretched out her arms in a sleepwalker's pose, and—jumped! I'm wrong, she thought as she flew mentally through the air, terribly, shamefully wrong. But it was too late to retreat.

And though at this point everything becomes enveloped in mist again, we can guess exactly what happened.

6.

The waitress switched off the light and shut the door after the other girls. For some reason she didn't feel like going with them. She sat down for a short rest and looked through the window at the passersby and the brand names atop the buildings. As she bent over to take off the slippers she wore at work, her hand happened to graze her knee. She let her hand rest on the knee and froze in that position as if listening for something. Then, heaven knows why, she thought of the dark handsome guy who'd left his umbrella in the cafeteria a week or so before and that good-looking young policeman with the funny, kinky questions—both of them so attractive and somehow connected . . . Or had she noticed them and had they registered with her mainly because they had—of that she was sure—noticed her?

Sheltered by the darkness, the cartons, and the glass, the girl sat with her legs slightly parted, relaxed, peering out of the window at the passersby, when suddenly her hands reached by themselves for one of the cardboard boxes, pulled out a few packages of hot dogs, and started tugging feverishly at the cellophane wrappers. God, what was she doing? What was she doing? What if somebody saw her . . . ? Nobody saw her.

She slowly brought a raw hot dog to her lips and quickly stuffed it into her mouth. The hot dog slid down her throat, leaving practically no taste behind. She grabbed a second and quickly chewed it up. Then a third, a fourth, a fifth . . .

There in the heart of the city, enslaved by the darkness, the cartons and the glass, sat a waitress with her legs slightly parted and her dark, shining eyes peering out at the passersby while she gobbled hot dog after hot dog. At one point the image of a gigantic, ravenous female mouse flashed through her mind, but she immediately forgot it. She was following the movements of her jaws and listening in on her gullet.

7.

In the afternoon of the seventh of April there was a nervous ring at Kovalić's door. Kovalić was a bit taken aback to see a good-looking young policeman carrying an unusual-looking bundle.

"Are you Mato Kovalić the writer? Or, rather, the novelist and short story writer?"

"I am," said Kovalić with a tremor in his voice.

"Well, this is yours. Sign here."

"But . . ." Kovalić muttered.

"Good-bye," said the policeman and, with a knowing wink, added, "and good luck!"

"But officer . . . !" Kovalić cried out. It was too late. The policeman had disappeared into the lift.

Kovalić unwrapped the bundle with trembling hands. Out of the paper fell a bottle filled with a clear liquid, and floating in that liquid was his very own . . . ! Unbelievable! Kovalić was beside himself. For several moments he stood stock still; then he went back and cautiously removed the object from the bottle and started inspecting it.

That's it, all right—the real thing! Kovalić thought aloud. He'd have recognized it anywhere! And he jumped for joy—though carefully clutching it in his hands.

Since, however, it is a well-known fact that nothing on this earth lasts for very long, our hero suddenly frowned. He had had a terrifying thought. What if it wouldn't go back on?

With indescribable terror in his heart Kovalić walked over to the mirror. His hands were trembling. He carefully returned the object to its former place. Panic! It refused to stick! He brought it up to his lips, warmed it with his breath, and tried again. No luck!

"Come on, damn you!" Kovalić grumbled. "Stick! Stick, you stupid fool!" But the object fell to the floor with a strange, dull, cork-like thud. "Why won't it take?" Kovalić wondered nervously. And though he tried again and again, his efforts were in vain.

Crushed, Kovalić was left holding his own, his very own and now, very useless part. And much as Kovalić stared at it, it clearly remained indifferent to his despair and lay there in his hand like a dead fish.

"Ba-a-a-a-astard!" Kovalić screamed in a bloodcurdling voice and flung the object into a corner and himself onto his bed. "No, I"m not dreaming," Kovalić whispered into his pillow. "This can't be a dream. This is madness, lunacy . . ." And with that he fell asleep.

8.

Lidija typed out the word malady and paused. She was still on page one. The translation of the report was due on Monday morning at the Department of Veterinary Medicine.

She stood up, stretched, and switched on the light. She glanced out of the window. It was still day, but the street was gray and empty and smooth from the rain.

She went into the kitchen and opened the refrigerator door out of habit. She peered in without interest and slammed it shut.

Then she went into the bathroom, turned on the tap, and put her wrist under a jet of cold water. It felt good. She glanced up at the mirror. All at once she felt like licking it. She moved in close to its smooth surface. Her face with tongue hanging out flashed into sight. She drew back slowly. A smooth and empty gesture. Like her life. "Smooth, empty, empty, smooth," she murmured on her way back to the kitchen.

On the kitchen table Lidija noticed a few dried-out bits of bread. She touched them. She liked the way dry crumbs pricked the pulp of her fingers. She moistened her finger with saliva, gathered up the crumbs, and went into the combined bedroom and living room. Again she looked out at the street, preoccupied, nibbling on the crumbs from her finger and on the finger itself. The street was empty.

And then she noticed a good-looking young policeman. He had a limber way about him and was crossing the smooth street, or so it seemed to Lidija, as if it were water. Suddenly she opened the window, breathed deeply, pursed her lips for a whistle, and stopped . . . What was she doing, for Heaven's sake? What had got into her . . . ?

The policeman looked up. In a well-lit window he saw an unusual-looking young woman standing stock still and staring at him. His glance came to rest on her full, slightly parted lips. He noticed a crumb on the lower one . . . Or was he just imagining it? Suddenly he had a desire to remove that real or imagined crumb with his own lips.

"What if she really . . ." flashed through his mind as he noiselessly slipped into the main door. But what happened next we really have no idea.

9.

Kovalić awoke with a vague premonition. His head felt fuzzy, his body leaden. He lay completely motionless for a while when all at once he felt an odd throbbing sensation. He tore off the blanket, and lo and behold!—it was back in place.

Kovalić couldn't believe his eyes. He reached down and fingered it—yes, it was his, all right! He gave it a tug just to make sure—yes, it popped out of his hand, straight, taut, elastic. Kovalić jumped for joy and leaped out of bed, rushing over to the mirror for a look. No doubt about it: there it stood, rosy, shiny, and erect—and just where it had been before. Kovalić cast a worried glance at the bottle. He saw a little black catfish swimming about as merrily as you please. Intent on engineering clever turns within its narrow confines, it paid him no heed.

"Oh!" Kovalić cried out in amazement.

Then he looked back down below. Situation normal: stiff and erect! Trembling with excitement, Kovalić raced to the phone.

At this point, however, the events are temporarily misted over by censorship, and the reader will have to deduce what happened from the following lines.

Exhausted and depressed, her eyes circled in black, her mouth dry, Maja the invoice clerk lay on her back apathetically staring at that horrid black fish. It was making its two-thousand-one-hundred-and-fifty-first turn in the bottle. At last she picked herself up slowly and started gathering her clothes the way an animal licks its wounds. Suddenly her eyes lit on a slip of paper lying next to her left shoe.

The paper contained a list of names in Kovalić's handwriting. Vesna, Branka, Iris, Goga, Ljerka, Višnja, Maja, Lidija. All the names but Lidija's (hers too!) had lines through them.

"Monster!" she said in a hoarse, weary voice, and slammed the door.

Kovalić stared apathetically at the lower half of his body. It was in place, sprightly and erect as ever. He flew into a rage, bounded out of bed, bolted to the bottle, and smashed it to the floor. The catfish flipped and flopped for a while, then calmed down. Kovalić gleefully watched the gill contractions subside. But it was still erect.

"Down, monster!" Kovalić shouted and gave it a mean thwack. It swayed and reddened, but then spryly, with a rubber-like elasticity, sprang back into place and raised its head at Kovalić almost sheepishly.

"Off with you, beast!" Kovalić screamed. The object refused to budge.

"I'll strangle you!" Kovalić bellowed. The object stared straight ahead, curtly indifferent.

"I wish you'd never been found," Kovalić whimpered, and flung himself onto the bed in despair. "You bastard, you! I'll get you yet . . . !" And he burst into sobs, mumbling incoherent threats into the pillow. Then, wiping his tears, he raised his fist into the air, Heaven knows why, and muttered, "I'll put you through the meat grinder!" And all of a sudden the old butcher's saying went off like an alarm in his brain: My knives go with me to the grave!

And the fear and trembling caused by this new piece of data sent Kovalić reeling—and into a dead faint.

10.

Well, dear readers, now you see the sort of thing that happens in our city! And only now, after much reflection, do I realize how much in it is unbelievable—starting from the alienation of the object in question from its rightful owner. Nor is it believable that authors should choose such things to write stories about. First, they are of no use either to literature or to the population, the reading population, and secondly, they are of no use . . . well, either. And yet, when all is said and done, there is hardly a place you won't find similar incongruities. No, say what you will, these things do happen—rarely, but they do.

For my part, I have a clear conscience. I have stuck to the plot. Had I given myself free rein, well, I don't know where things would have ended! And even so, what happened to Nada Matić? Who is Milan Miško? What became of Vinko K.? And Lidija and the waitress and the butcher? To say nothing of our hero Mato Kovalić? Is he doomed to spend his life getting it—down?!

But I repeat: I have stuck to the plot. Though if the truth be told, I did insert two nightmares from my own childhood, to wit: 1) the sausage dream ("Watch out or a sausage will sprout on your nose," my grandfather used to say when he got angry with me), and 2) the beet dream (I can recall no more terrifying story from my childhood than the one in which a whole family gathered to pull out a big, beautiful, and completely innocent beet!).

In connection with said plot may I suggest the following points as worthy of further consideration:

1. How did the object alienated from its owner, Mato Kovalić, find its way into the bun?

2. How did Vinko K. discover its owner?

3. Miscellaneous.

All that is merely by the by, of course, in passing. I myself have no intention of taking things any further . . . But if you, honored readers, decide to do so, I wish you a merry time of it and a hearty appetite!

Who Am I?

Baba Yaga hatched an egg.
—*Alexei Remizov*

I live under the covers. Dreams besiege me. Dreams suck me in, drag me down to terrible depths, spin me round like a tornado sweeping everything before it, and toss me out in a complete daze.

The night before last a man came into my apartment, made straight for my desk, snatched the typewriter, and hurried towards the door. "Hey, where do you think you're going?" I yelled. The guy got scared and ran away. I don't know who it was and why he wanted my little Olivetti. And I can't explain why that dream upset me so much. But still, ever since then I've been taking my little Olivetti to bed with me. I don't dare leave it alone.

Dreams, as I say, besiege me, devastate me like a tornado sweeping everything before it. In the morning I'm muddled, I don't know who I am, events are all mixed up, the times are confused, what's present and what's past. And the most exhausting thing of all is being afraid of falling asleep. I sit in my bed as in a train, my head falls onto my chest from exhaustion.

I keep a small bookshelf next to my bed. The books in the blue covers are the ones I keep rereading, I know them almost by heart. I never read the green ones. That's why I covered them in green, so as not to make a mistake.

I take a small blue book from the shelf and read. Thoughts like little fish in a fishbowl knock against the dome of my head. Bloop. Bloop. I've stuffed little wax balls into my ears. I live next to the highway. The noise is unbearable. That would not be a problem, the wax balls work well; the problem is that this unfortunate position makes me very vulnerable. Anyone could come wandering into my apartment at any moment. If *wandering in* describes what happens to me.

Last night, for instance, a truck turned into my apartment. It's not the first time a vehicle has turned off the main road and stopped in the middle of my room. I was lying in bed with the covers up to my chin, motionless. The driver rolled down the window, stuck his neck out like a turtle, and shouted to me.

"Hey little girl! Come up here!"

"I'd really like to know who I am. Tell me that first, and then we'll talk about it. If I like being your answer I'll come up, if not, I'll stay down here till I turn into something else!" I said.

The driver stared at me and knit his brow. He had no idea how to respond.

"Blehhh!" he said eventually, sticking his tongue out at me. He charged out of the room at full speed.

The worst thing is when someone lives in a small apartment, where one room has to serve for everything, especially if that room faces a highway. Then there is no good way for them to protect themselves from the outside world. I know what I'm talking about, I'm someone with a single room, and it faces a highway.

I take a small blue book from the shelf and try to read. My thoughts knock against the dome of my head like little fish in a fishbowl. Bloop. Bloop. I relax and feel that I'm about to fall asleep. But then through my half-closed lashes what do I suddenly see floating into my room but a streetcar! What annoys me most is the repetition. Repetition is the wicked stepmother of creation.

The streetcar driver jumped out of the cab, patted me lightly on the shoulder and said: "Sorry, Kosta, give me a glass of water and I'll move on!"

I got up obediently, went to the kitchen, turned on the tap and filled a glass with water.

"There you are! Only I'm not Kosta, you know . . ."

He wiped his mouth with his sleeve and patted me cordially on the shoulder.

"Me too, Kosta, me too!" shouted the passengers.

And what could I do, I filled the one and only glass I had and passed it up, filled it, spilled it, passed it up, repeating the actions as in a nightmare. Threatening pools were forming on the kitchen floor. "Me too, Kosta, me tooooo!" The streetcar driver looked at his watch.

"Thanks, Kosta, thanks a lot!"

"Thanks a lot, Kosta!" the passengers repeated after the driver.

"My name's not Kosta!! Will you just get lost, huh?!" I yelled. *Get lost!*, that's what I yelled, pushing the streetcar out of the room and shutting the windows.

I went back to bed, pulled the covers over my head and looked for the little hole. Whenever I feel bad, I look for the little hole in the cover and peer out through it. I peer through it for a long time until slowly, out of the depths, a little church emerges. The church is small, pot-bellied, with small round blue cupolas. I often wonder where exactly that church is. Sometimes I'm afraid it might disappear, but it's always there. That's why I never think to mend the little hole in the cover.

If I patch up the hole, I'll sew up the church as well. That's how I live, under a cover with a hole in it.

I carefully moved my eye away from the hole. I surfaced from under the cover and felt that something was wrong, as though I had pulled myself into myself, like a telescope or something.

I picked up the small blue book again. My thoughts were circling slowly and serenely like little fish in a fishbowl. And then I heard a soft tapping on the window pane. I got out of bed, went over to the window and opened it. A triple-decker chicken flew into the room.

"Hey, Chickie!" it said.

"Hey!" I replied, confused. The triple-decker chicken was a foot and a half taller than me, and I'm 5 foot 7, but I always lie about the last inch.

The chicken went straight to my fridge.

"Your fridge is empty again!"

I looked in. It was true, a few eggs, butter, milk, and some bread were all that was there.

The chicken strutted irritably around the room, its eyes checking out my books. Then she picked through an ashtray full of stubs, found one, and lit it.

"What's up, Chickie, do you not know who you are again?" the chicken asked kindly.

I didn't say anything. I looked at the chicken and blushed, wondering why I always blushed like that in front of her. I quietly took my little blue book and propped it on my chest like a prayer book.

The chicken scratched the floor, flapped her wings as though shaking dust from them, and then fluttered onto the windowsill.

"What can I say, first get rid of your inferiority complex. I could ask you which way is south from here, but I won't, because I'm afraid you wouldn't even know that!"

I smiled feebly, then went cautiously over to the window to close it but the chicken was still on the windowsill.

"And fill up that fridge, for goodness sake! Jesus, it's so boring at your place! There's nothing to talk about, and not a bite to eat."

I mumbled something like *yes, yes, of course, I certainly will*, and waved for a long time.

I waved absently, so that for a moment I forgot where I was, at a railway station or an airport? I waved for so long that I even forgot who I was actually waving to . . . When I remembered, I was overcome by fury.

I slammed the window shut, firmly resolved never to open it again.

I went back to bed. I ought to change apartments, that was it. Move to some more peaceful place. A place with a landscape. Why do people have such problems finding somewhere to live? Even a worm lives more decently. It crawls into a fresh little house, which it steadily eats up. When it's done, it looks for a new one. They say that the worms in cherries move in at the flower stage. From the very start, that is. Every worm is born with its own little house. Every cherry gives birth to its own little death. Its own little deathlet, its own little wormlet.

Under the covers my own breath warmed me. I lazily reached my hand out and felt a body. The body wriggled. I let my hand wander further and felt under my palm soft curves, smooth skin, a woolly beard. Suddenly it began to make noises.

"Don't you grunt at me!" I chided the body. "That's not at all a proper way to address me!"

"Good morning!" said the head of the Temporary Lover, pressing itself warmly against mine.

"Who are you talking to?" I asked.

"You!" said the head. You, said his hands entwining with mine. You, said his thighs rubbing against mine. You, whispered his lips pressing against mine . . .

I felt a strange pulsation. Plink! Plonk! Plank! I seemed to be growing. Where were my hands? I stretched my arms out as wide as I could and wrapped them firmly around the Temporary Lover. At the same moment I shook from a violent blow to my chin. My head had suddenly fallen, my chin struck my foot. My chin was now so closely pressed against my foot that I was hardly able to open my mouth. I wiggled my jaw. Done! My head was free. I looked along myself, seeking right and left, but there was no sign of a shoulder! All I could see was neck, long and slender, stretching endlessly up and up. Goodbye, feet! Where are you, and where am I! And where have my shoulders got to? And oh, my poor hands, where are you! How shall I find you!

As I no longer had the slightest hope of reaching my head with my hands, I worked out that I could look for my hands with my head. I saw them opening the fridge and taking out the eggs, milk, and hunk of bread, and the left hand going back for butter. Then they put it all on the kitchen table and closed up like a telescope.

I felt myself coming back to myself. I smiled at the Temporary Lover. He smiled back.

"I could eat a horse!" he said.

I went into the bathroom. I took a long shower, first with hot then with cold water. The cold water solidified my outlines. I heard the voice of the Temporary Lover coming from the kitchen.

"I'm not going to lie, I sentence you to die! Lie I shall not just, die I say you must! Just not lie. Just must die! I'll not lie! You must die! Must die!"

I went into the kitchen. Five hysterical eggs stared at me from the dish. Their empty shells gaped at me from the trash. The Temporary Lover and I sat at the table and had breakfast.

"How handsome you are!" I said.

I watched my lover

a) slice bread,

b) spread butter on the bread,

c) eat bread and butter.

I made coffee. The sun beat relentlessly on the windows. I watched as the Temporary Lover put the coffee into the cup, he put the milk into the cup of coffee, he put the sugar into the milky coffee, with the little spoon he stirred, he drank the coffee and he replaced the cup without speaking to me, he lit a cigarette, he made rings with the smoke, he put the ashes into the ashtray . . . How bright he was! Lit up from within. I moved closer to him and kissed the smooth skin of his lips. My lover grew warm and soft, softer and softer, smaller and smaller, thinner and thinner. My lover was melting. All I could hear was a whistling sound that had the tone of his voice:

"Ah, love . . . love is a sweet little sound that makes the world go round!"

All that was left of the Temporary Lover was a little pool of tepid water. I wept. My tears fell on the remains of the omelette and melted butter. Why, I thought. Who am I? If I only knew whether I had been changed in the night into something else. Was I just the same when I got up this morning? I remembered feeling a little different. But if I wasn't the same then, do I have the slightest idea who in the world I am now?

I stared for a long time at the little pool of tepid water, in which the sun was sparkling, and I wept. Then I dried my tears, took a rag and wiped the remains of the Temporary Lover from the floor. I got dressed, sat down at my desk and began to think what I was going to do that day. First I would devote myself to affairs of the mind, I thought. Maybe, as a mental exercise, I could translate some sentences from some foreign languages. And I translated one on the spot. *The magician was tall.* I liked that sentence; I liked the fact that the magician was tall. I don't like magicians of average height, and I simply can't stand small ones.

My reflections about small magicians were interrupted by the thought that I really ought to be at work, which I had completely forgotten, drained as I was by my dreams. I dialed the number of the office.

"Hello?" I said.

"Hello? Who's that?"

"That's just the trouble! If I knew, I'd come to work. But I don't, so there's no point. Doesn't that seem logical to you?"

"Who is this? Is this a joke?"

"No one. I just wanted to tell you I can't come to work today, because I don't know who I am. If I knew I'd come right away! Can't you see?"

"You're crazy!"

"Pray don't trouble yourself to say it any longer than that," I said and put down the receiver.

Then I thought that I ought to stop and think. All these recent events are devastating me like a tornado sweeping everything before it. I am completely muddle-headed, I no longer know who I am, everything is mixed up. I don't know whether I am talking in the past or the present tense any more, I don't know what has really happened and what was only a dream, I am afraid of falling asleep, I am afraid of staying awake. I ought to put things in proper order.

I took a pencil and wrote the sentence *Buy buttons* on a scrap of paper. It seemed to me that this sentence gave meaning to the day ahead of me. When you have something to do, however trivial, it means that you are not completely lost. Then I wrote *Buy thread* on the same scrap of paper. Not because I needed thread, but so that I wouldn't forget the sentence *Buy buttons*; I was doubly reinforcing my intention to buy buttons, that is, even if in a roundabout way.

Calmer now, I took the scrap of paper and put it in my purse. Then I went over to the window to open it and felt my foot knock against something.

There was a great big ugly egg on the floor. I picked it up and put it on the table. You lying triple-decker chickenshit! Whenever it visits me, it always lays an egg secretly in the hope that I'll take care of it. But no! Not this time! One of these days, you feathered con artist, one of these days I'm going to fry your offspring into an omelette! I shook my fist in the vague direction of the window.

But then I calmed down, I stroked the egg, put it to my ear. All right, I thought, I'll take care of you, I'll give you to someone as a present. I wrapped the egg in tin foil and put it in a plastic bag. Then I dialed Filip's number.

"Hello?"

"It's me,"

"Oh, it's you! What are you up to?"

"Nothing. I'm mad at an egg, or rather a chicken. Although actually I'm not mad at all any more, I've calmed down. Filip, I have to buy buttons because of the thread and I wondered if

we could meet. I think there's something wrong with me . . ."
I said all in one breath.

In a little while I saw Filip waiting at the appointed place,
outside The Golden Half-Shell restaurant. No, I thought, it
would be silly to speak to him before I saw his two ears or at
least one of them. When I saw the left one, I ran joyfully to
him.

"Your hair's outgrown you, it needs cutting," said Filip.

"Filip . . . something's happening to me, I've changed," I
burst out as soon as we had sat down.

"Hmm, so, you think you've changed?"

"Yes," I exclaimed. "I'm afraid I won't be able to explain
it to you, because I'm not me any more!"

The waiter came up. Filip ordered grilled trout and two
glasses of white wine. When the waiter left, I went on:

"It's not good, Filip," I said dejectedly. "I can't remember
lots of things I used to, and the worst of it is that I'm closing
up, like a telescope. I feel small, there's hardly enough left of
me for a human being, and a very small one at that. I've never
been as this small before, never. That's how far it's gone, Filip!
It's gone so far that I'm having eggs laid at my door!" I said,
remembering the egg in the plastic bag. "Something tells me
I'm going mad, Filip!" I burst into tears.

"It's okay, calm down," said Filip. "How do you know
you're mad?"

"I just know," I said stubbornly. "A dog growls when it's
angry and wags its tail when it's in a good mood. I growl when
I'm in a good mood, Filip, and wag my tail when I'm angry.
Wouldn't you say I was mad?"

"Hold on, slow down," Filip soothed me. "Start from the
beginning and go on to the end, and when you get to the end,
stop."

"I can't," I said, "my words have all scattered . . ."

Filip stroked my hand. "It's really not as bad as all that. Just be the way you would like to seem to others, or to put it more simply: never think of being other than it could seem to others that you are or could be were you not different from the way you were so it seems to others that you are different."

While Filip was talking, I felt myself sinking. Through a fog I saw the waiter bringing two trout on a dish. The trout were strangely flat, as though made of cardboard; the head of one was laid beside the other's tail.

"Off with their heads! Off with their heads, at once!" I heard Filip's voice. Calmly, the waiter cut the heads off the trout, and I saw Filip's left ear disappearing from his face, followed by his right ear, then his nose.

"I'm going to faint! I'm going to faint!" I whispered in a feeble voice.

"Their heads are gone, sir!" I heard the waiter's voice.

"Get me out of here, Filip!" I said feverishly.

Filip took me by the hand and led me out into the street. I breathed deeply and after a while calmed down.

"You're hungry. You haven't eaten anything," said Filip, taking a crust of bread out of his pocket. I took the crust and gnawed it. The air was soft and pink with the setting sun. I took Filip's arm, and felt that at last I was myself again and whole. And then it occurred to me that maybe the man I was walking with through streets pink with the setting sun wasn't the real Filip, but someone else, a Mock Filip.

"Filip," I burst out, "I'm in a hurry! I've still got to buy some buttons!"

I dashed off toward the streetcar stop with all the strength I could muster, leaving a flabbergasted Filip behind me.

In the streetcar I begin to think that there was really no

longer any doubt I was crazy. For if I didn't know who I was myself, how could I know that Filip was a Mock Filip?

When I got out of the streetcar, it was already dark. The stores were closed. Never mind, I thought, I'll buy buttons tomorrow. I didn't feel like going home. The very idea of finding myself in my noisy, nightmare room again appalled me. Then the comforting thought occurred to me that I could visit Marble, after all I hadn't seen her for two whole days.

When Marble appeared at the door, I said as naturally as I could:

"Happy birthday, Marble!"

"How did you know it's my birthday?" Marble asked, surprised.

"I didn't, but I've got an egg and I thought how good it would be if it was your birthday today and I could give you the egg . . . Here!"

She took the egg without much enthusiasm.

"Come in," she said. "It is my birthday."

I went in, a little put out. Marble hadn't shown much gratitude for such a big present. There were three of Marble's friends at the kitchen table. The table was large enough, but the three of them were all crowded together at one end.

"No room! No room!" they cried out when they saw me.

"There's plenty of room!" I said sulkily and sat down on the opposite side of the table.

"Have some wine!" First offered in a friendly tone.

"I don't see any wine," I said.

"There isn't any!" said First.

"Then it isn't very civil of you to offer it!"

"It isn't very civil of you to sit down at someone else's table without being invited!" says Second.

"I didn't know it was your table!"

"She's right!" said Third. "It's not our table."

"As far as I know it's Marble's table," I said.

"You don't know much," said Third brusquely, "and when you don't know one thing, you usually don't know anything else either."

"Marble!" I shouted. "These three are insulting me!"

"Which three?" Marble asked appearing from somewhere.

"These three," I said, pointing to First, Second, and Third.

"Oh leave me alone," said Marble sharply. "You know I never could abide figures!"

What's going on, I thought to myself, everything's curious today! It would be best not to open my mouth again. I'll sit here for another moment or two and then make an excuse and be off. It must be late by now.

"What's the time?" I asked politely.

"Six!" said Second. "It's always six o'clock here!"

"How come?"

"Simple. We're killing time and we began at six."

"Oh do talk sense!" I said angrily. "I don't understand what you mean by these jangling words, and I don't believe you do either!"

"Now, now, don't be cross" said Marble soothingly. "Take some more coffee."

"Mind what you're saying! I've had nothing yet, so I can't take more!"

"All right," said Marble. "I'll make some more coffee, and in the meantime have some jam."

Marble got out a jar of jam and put it on the table.

"Plum!" said First.

"Apricot . . ." said Second.

"Cherry," said Third.

I looked at them. It was really dreadful, the amount these creatures chattered, I thought.

"I think you might do something better with the time," I said, "because it really hasn't deserved to be wasted in meaningless chatter."

"If you had grown up in a house, you would have made a dreadfully ugly child, this way at least you're rather a handsome pig!" snapped First.

That was too much. I got up.

"Marble!" I asked, "which way should I go to get away from here?"

"That depends a good deal on where you want to get to," said Marble calmly.

"I don't much care where I get to . . ."

"Then it doesn't matter which way you go!"

"Just as long as I get away from here," I muttered.

"I'm prepared to bet you'll succeed in that," said Marble.

"Oh, we're prepared to bet you'll succeed in that!" guffawed the three chatterboxes.

I slammed the door of Marble's apartment and rushed down the stairs to the front door. No matter what happened to me, I'd never go there again, I thought irritatedly. That was the stupidest birthday party I was ever at in all my life, I grumbled to myself, hurrying toward the streetcar stop.

On the way home I thought about the day that had just gone by, but I couldn't remember anything. Then I remembered the egg, it all started with the egg I had taken with me. It was a good thing I'd left it with Marble. It had been horrible at Marble's. I felt as though I'd been there before, like in a hole, like in a jam jar.

I unlocked the door of my apartment with a sigh of relief. I went in and right away started looking for a pencil and paper so I wouldn't forget that tomorrow I really must *Buy buttons*. Suddenly my eyes met the two large green eyes of an unknown man who was sitting thoughtfully on my bed, smoking a cigar. I stood there stupidly holding the scrap of paper and pencil in my hand. The stranger and I stared at each other for a long time. Finally the stranger took the cigar out of his mouth and asked me in a drawl, "*Who are you?*"

For God's sake, I thought, this was really too much! Now a total stranger as well. Where am I? In someone else's apartment? In some foreign country? Who am I? And what can I tell him: that I hardly know, that I may have known when I got up this morning, but I must have changed several times since then.

"Who are you?" the stranger asked.

I waved my hands in confusion, trying to catch my breath. The words stuck in my throat . . .

"I think you ought to tell me who you are first!"

"Why?" the stranger replied calmly.

I didn't know what to say.

"Who are you?" the stranger repeated the question, puffing smoke from his cigar.

And then, all at once I felt as whole and peaceful as an egg. I walked straight to the door and locked it. I wound my alarm clock, got undressed, put on my nightgown, turned out the light, and got into bed.

In the darkness I heard my own calm and confident voice saying, "I'm Alice! Move over a bit. I'm sleepy . . ."

An ample young lady in a state of constant hunger

"There, you see!" Božica sighed sadly, reaching for a broken Pionirka cookie, popping it into her mouth, and licking her chubby fingers. "That's how it started. As soon as he slammed the door behind him and left me for good, I felt terribly, terribly hungry. And I've been eating, eating ever since. I hardly sleep at night, just so I can keep eating. It's awful!" she sobbed. Her plump shoulders shook in a brief, violent fit of weeping. Then she calmed down, wiped her tears, and bit into a Jadran wafer.

"Excuse me," said Jozo politely, taking a little calculator out of his pocket, "but when did this, how shall I put it, emotionally distressing incident occur?"

"Hmm, let me see . . ." Božica began to think, chewing an Albert cookie. "The thirteenth of June, I think it was. Yes, the thirteenth."

"And today is . . . what's today's date?"

"You can't have forgotten—Christmas Eve!"

"Oh, yes, sorry. That means you've been like this for exactly 194 days!"

"Really!"

"That is 4,656 hours!"

"Incredible!"

"Or 279,360 minutes!"

"How awful!"

"You've been, how shall I put it, in a state of constant hunger for exactly 16,761,600 seconds!"

"How dreadful! There's only one thing left for someone like me to do—kill myself!"

"Don't, Božica, don't even say it."

An incomplete personality reduced to a mouth

"Do you know how many kids he had?" Božica asked, leaning confidingly towards Jozo.

"I wouldn't know," Jozo said modestly.

"Five of his own, and three more illegitimate ones!" Božica hissed through clenched teeth and shoved a Marina cookie into her mouth to stifle a sob.

"That makes eight," Jozo said, automatically reaching for the calculator.

"But still, ever since he left me, I haven't felt really alive. I'm no longer a person, I feel empty." Božica pounded her chest. "I don't really exist. I'm an incomplete personality, that's what I am, an incomplete personality. I've turned into nothing but a mouth, a gaping mouth . . ."

"You're right, I know the feeling," said Jozo sadly, nibbling a piece of a broken cookie.

The author, who feels likewise incomplete (as an author), shyly calls attention to his presence—perhaps needed, perhaps not

Maybe shd mention that conversat'n tks plce in modstly furnishd room. Snowing outside, big flakes stick to windw, bttle of wine (red, cheap) on table, 2 glsses + piles sweet things. Door to hall half-open, tlphone in the hall—mention it for later. Clock heard tckng—

A second incomplete personality and his (the said personality's) mother

"I know the feeling. I'm, how shall I put it, an incomplete personality myself . . ." began Jozo, stammering.

"You too?" exclaimed Božica in surprise, swallowing a bite of Samo Ti chocolate.

"Yes. It all began the day father left us. That day, or maybe a day or two later, my mother made a vow that she'd never allow life's troubles to get her down, particularly loneliness and that dangerous melancholy that abandoned women so often succumb to. 'Rejected, but not dejected'—that's what my mother used to say." Then he added: "My mother is, how shall I put it, a very strong personality."

"How old is she?"

"My mother? Eighty."

"Wow, that's old!"

"You see, how shall I put it, my mother worked out a whole system for resisting melancholy, or, to put it another way, despondency, before it was too late. At this very moment, for instance," he said looking at his watch, "she is probably standing on her head, turning cartwheels, or learning Spanish. Mother thinks learning Spanish is an especially good cure for despondency . . ."

"Incredible! At her age?"

"Yes," Jozo said in a crushed tone. "And I'm the exact opposite."

An incomplete personality as the exact opposite
"But wait," Božica livened up, shoving three Speculas cookies into her mouth at the same time. "I don't see the problem. You should be glad to have a mother, and one with such a strong personality too! I haven't got anyone. Weak or strong."

"They've all passed away?"

"Uh-huh."

"I'm sorry, how can I put it, I really am . . ."

"Oh, I got over it a long time ago. Keep going."

"You said you didn't see the problem? The problem is, how shall I put it, with individuals of the opposite sex, that is to say, women," said Jozo sadly. "They've always left me. And you already know, I've twice . . ."

"What?" Božica smacked her lips and broke off a piece of a Florida cookie.

". . . been married."

"So what?"

"Well, you know, it's my despondence," said Jozo anxiously. "For instance, I never dared close the door of my room because Mother would always burst in and scream Hurraaah! You see, how shall I put it, she thought noise shock therapy was the best cure for despondency. And I was what Mother called a profound melancholic."

"Really," Božica nodded sympathetically, licking a chocolate-covered Medo cookie.

"Mother thought that shock could abruptly change a person's mood, for the better of course, that it could bring to life the vital inner forces atrophied by melancholy. Sometimes she'd be waiting for me after school around a corner, she'd suddenly jump out at me and shout Hurraaah!"

"Do you have to keep doing that?" Božica asked, coughing up a piece of Plazma biscuit which had nearly slipped down her windpipe.

"I'm so sorry," Jozo apologized politely.

"Never mind, never mind, go on. Just give me a glass of milk. There, on the counter."

"There were sudden Tarzan shrieks in the noise therapy as well," Jozo went on, pouring Božica a glass of milk. "Mother thought that this particular kind of shriek was the best way to dispel the black moods to which I, as an incomplete personality, was prone. She'd go: Aaaaauuuuaaaaa!"

"Please, not so loud!" said Božica, trawling with her finger for a piece of Domaćica cookie that had fallen to the bottom of her glass of milk.

"Oh, I'm so sorry," Jozo blushed. "Mother had other methods as well in her battle against despondence. Education, for instance. 'Education is a guiding light,' she would say, 'it dispels the darkness of the night.'"

"Really?" asked Božica, dunking a Jadranka cookie and her own finger into the milk.

"And not only that . . ."

For a healthy mind in a healthy body, knowledge is power

"Every morning we'd read the great classics," said Jozo. "How can I put it, I know the opening sentences of many great novels. 'At nine o'clock in the morning, towards the end of November, the Warsaw train was approaching Petersburg at full speed.' Do you know what that's from?"

"No idea," Božica smacked her lips.

"Dostoyevsky. *The Idiot*," said Jozo modestly. "Maybe you know this one: 'How happy I am to have come away!'" Jozo looked enquiringly at Božica.

Božica kept chewing.

"Goethe, *The Sorrows of Young Werther*," Jozo announced solemnly.

"You don't say," said Božica.

"There was only one novel we didn't dare read," said Jozo.

"Which one?"

"Camus. *The Outsider*."

"Never heard of it. Why that one?"

"Because the first sentence goes: 'Mother died today.'"

"I see."

"I'm sorry, I'm boring you . . ." Jozo said politely.

"No, but get to the point. I'm afraid I don't have a clue

about those novels of yours, I'm seriously under-read."

"Well, Mother had worked out an integrated system for fighting melancholy. She called it the H.M.H.B. system: Healthy Mind in a Healthy Body. We lifted weights repeating all the English words we had just learned, stood on our heads rattling off chemical formulae, did sit-ups to lists of unusual words from the dictionary . . . Would you have any objection to my demonstrating?"

"Please, go right ahead."

"Which letter?"

"What do you mean?"

"Which letter shall I start with?"

"Umm, how about Z!"

Jozo dropped to the floor and began mumbling—"Zabaglione, zamindar, zareba, zeitgeist, zeolite, zeugma, zibeline, ziggurat . . ."—doing sit-up after sit-up.

"Do you know what all those words mean?"

"Not all of them," said Jozo modestly, getting up from the floor and wiping his forehead with a handkerchief.

"There!" he said.

Although life bubbles like water in a pot, for the incomplete personality something is missing

"I really don't understand why you call yourself an incomplete personality," said Božica. "You're so knowledgeable, so well-rounded. Take me for instance, I'm terribly limited. My horizons go no further than a box of cookies."

"Well, how shall I put it, it has to do with individuals of the opposite sex, that is to say, with women. My wives had to practise Mother's H.M.H.B. system as well. The first stuck it out for two months, the second only five days."

"How ungrateful of them!" said Božica, opening a jar of jam.

"That's, how shall I put it, that's not all," Jozo began hesitantly.

"What do you mean?"

"Well, for instance, when I got into bed with my wife, my mother would barge into the room shouting Hurrraaaah! And I would immediately go . . . limp . . . you understand."

"You mean . . . ? Oh, you mean your whatsit? It would go, er, limp?" Božica choked.

"That's right. And in any case, it's of, how shall I put it, modest proportions . . ."

"How modest?"

"Three and a half inches."

"That's not much, I have to admit."

"There, now you know."

"Ah well, what can you do! But that last thing's certainly no tragedy," sighed Božica, scooping up jam with her finger and licking it.

"No, of course not," sighed Jozo, shrugging his shoulders. Then he added, as though he had just remembered it: "And do you know my mother doesn't sleep at all, for fear that melancholy might catch her with her eyes closed?"

"What does she do all night then? At least I eat when I'm not asleep."

"She shouts messages to me . . ."

"What sort of messages?"

"Well, the kind that can, how shall I put it, cheer a person up. For instance: 'A smile a day keeps your cares away.' Mother makes them up herself. Or: 'Life is a fairy tale!' 'La vida es fabula!' "

"What does that last one mean?"

"The same as the one before it, 'life is a fairy tale' in Spanish. What Mother liked best was sending those messages just as my wife and I were . . . you understand."

"Yes."

"Actually, it's because there weren't any other opportunities. Our little apartment was always full of people, Mother's friends from the mountaineering, cycling, and fishing clubs, amateur theater, miscellaneous hobos, card players, mother's lonely women friends, thieves . . . 'Life in our little home bubbles like water in a pot!' Mother would often say."

"Listen, why don't you move out?" asked Božica, dunking a piece of shortbread into the jar of jam.

"Why? I love my mother! Besides, I've given up all hope of becoming a complete personality. I feel most complete when I'm with her."

"So what's the problem actually?"

"Well, the problem is that . . . how shall I put it, I'm not a complete personality, that's what! Don't you see? It's like I don't have anything down below! You said so yourself, three and a half inches isn't much, especially if you never get to use them! Somehow I'm, how can I put it, sexless."

"Now I understand," said Božica compassionately, falling on a box of Frondi sugar waffles.

The author, feeling not only incomplete but superfluous (as an author), draws attention to his presence again
Outside snow is falling. Snow is falling. Outside snow is falling in large flakes. Snow is falling in large flakes. Large flakes of snow are silently falling. Outside . . .

Without rejects the ample young lady could never manage
"Tell me, how much weight have you put on?" Jozo turned back to Božica's situation.

"Over a hundred pounds."

"So per month that would be . . . Would you like me to

calculate it exactly?" said Jozo, taking the calculator out of his pocket again.

"Why do you keep calculating things?" Božica raised her voice.

"Habit. Mother bought me the calculator. For the campaign against melancholy. She said it was better for me to calculate things than to sit doing nothing and stare into space . . . How much did you weigh when this all began?"

"Average. A hundred and forty. But now, you can see for yourself. Since you've been here I've eaten at least four pounds of sweets. Luckily I work in a chocolate, candy, and cookie factory. Everyone who works there gets a discount on rejects. I bring the rejects home, shut the door, and eat, eat, eat . . . And how could I do it otherwise? I get 5,700 a week. I pay 2,500 for this room, plus electricity. And what's left for me to live on? Work it out yourself!"

"3,200, not counting electricity."

"There, you see!"

"I see."

"If it weren't for those rejects, I don't know how I'd manage, ever since this happened to me."

"You couldn't manage at all."

"Exactly! Take these cookies for instance. Do you know what they cost in the shops?"

"No."

"35."

"That's a lot."

"And the rejects are only 15!"

"Really?"

"For the same cookies."

"They certainly look the same . . ."

"The fact that they're broken means nothing."

"Of course not, you'd have broken them yourself."

"There's no difference then, is there?"

"None at all."

"There, you see!"

Some personalities unravel, others never go out—everyone has their own cross to bear

Božica got up from the table with an effort. She waddled over to the counter, took out a plastic bag full of cookies, and emptied some of them into a dish. Then she sat down, put an alarm clock on the table, and said, with a deep sigh:

"Everyone has their own cross to bear."

"That's well put," agreed Jozo.

"Take you, for instance. Or Katica and Branka, they're no better off."

"Who are Katica and Branka?"

"My friends. We work together in the filling department. I used to work in chewing gum. That's where I met my boyfriend . . . Afterwards I asked to be transferred to filling."

"Interesting," said Jozo kindly.

"Yes. Now Katica, unlike me, went down to seventy pounds. She's unraveling! It's terrible."

"What do you mean, unraveling?"

"You know why her boyfriend left her?"

"Why?"

"Because she couldn't pronounce the word Popocate-petl—imagine!"

"The volcano in Mexico?"

"Right, some volcano or other. He tormented her for days. Say *Popocatapetl*, say *Popocatapetl*. And all she could say was *Popopatecetl, Popopatecetl, Popopatecetl*—she could never get it right. So he left her. He said: 'You're an idiot, and not only that, you've got pathetically small tits.' Can you believe it? Pathetically small tits!"

"But why is this Katica 'unraveling' now?"

"Because she doesn't eat anything! And everything she wears is knitted—she's a fantastic knitter, she's knitted all sorts of things for me which don't fit me any more. It's much cheaper, you know, you buy wool by the pound and you can knit yourself everything you need. So lately Katica's just been sitting there, not talking, picking at her clothes, and fraying. The other day she was at my place, I was running my mouth off about something and didn't notice . . . the whole time she was unraveling her long wool skirt, right up to her thighs. She hadn't even noticed it herself, poor thing. She's disappearing before our eyes, just disappearing!"

"What about the other one?"

"Who, Branka?"

"Yes."

"She's almost six feet tall."

"So?"

"What do you mean 'So'? Life's not easy for a woman if she's almost six feet tall!"

"I guess not."

"That's why she never goes out with men."

"Pity."

"There, you see. That's what I'm saying. Everyone has their own cross to bear."

Closed up people can't expect anything

"It's terrible!" said Božica, suddenly banging the table with her fist. "Can I be totally honest with you, Jozo?"

"Completely," said Jozo.

"I feel just like you. Like I don't have anything down below, like I'm a plastic doll. Or like someone had bricked me shut. All closed up! And when I think about how much I want a baaaabyyyy!" Božica began to sob again.

"Don't cry, Božica, don't cry," said Jozo, patting her on the shoulder. "What can I can do, Božica?"

"Give me those cookies!" Božica said through her tears and then calmed down a little and added: "Nothing. Admit it. With my weight and your . . . three inches?"

"Three and a half."

"With my weight and your inches it's hopeless!"

Although still feeling superfluous, the author boldly interrupts the dialogue with a brief lyrical passage
Božica and Jozo sighed mournfully. Outside the window the snow was falling in large flakes. Cries of merriment reached them from the buildings next door. An unopened bottle of cheap red wine stood on the table. The clock said five minutes to midnight.

Life is not a fairy tale even when it strikes midnight
"Would you like me to tell you about filling?" Božica decided to change the subject to something more pleasant.

"What do you mean?" Jozo asked, startled out of a profound reverie.

"Filling candies, pastries, eclairs. Just a few days ago we launched a new Christmas product, Fontana snow cubes—they're chocolate, filled with white cream. Look, there are little stars, snowflakes, on the wrapping. Let's try them. I brought half a pound home from the factory." She was more cheerful now.

The clock showed one minute to midnight. Jozo opened the bottle of wine and filled their glasses. They stood up and toasted each other. It was exactly midnight.

"Merry Christmas, Božica!" said Jozo. "This is the merriest Christmas Eve I've ever spent. You know, this is the first time in my whole life I've spoken so honestly with anyone. You are, how shall I put it, the most fulfilled person I've ever met."

"Merry Christmas, Jozo! It's nice of you to say that. Still, we have to face facts. Life isn't a fairy tale after all. You still may find a decent girl, but I've lost all hope. Anyway, cheers! Come on, let's try our snow cubes!"

"No thanks. I don't like sweet things."

"Oh, go ahead, try just one . . ."

Božica and Jozo nibbled the new product, Fontana chocolate cubes filled with a mysterious snow-white cream.

The ample personality melts and the other personality is at least partially filled out / While the dialogue gets thinner, the descriptions gain weight

"They're delicious!" said Jozo. He was about to say something else, but the snow-chocolate suddenly stuck in his throat.

"What is it, Jozo?" asked Božica, alarmed. Jozo was staring at Božica in absolute disbelief as she swallowed her third chocolate.

"Božica, s-something's happening to you!"

Almost as though she knew what she would find there, Božica went to the mirror. She couldn't believe her eyes! In the mirror she saw her heavy double chin slowly melting away, her full cheeks drawing in, her eyes growing larger. Light blue eyes with almost white lashes looked back at her from an attractive face framed in angelic blond curls. For a moment she stood frozen in place. Then, forgetting Jozo, she tore off her blouse to reveal smooth shoulders, full breasts, and a slender waist. She waited to see what would happen next. Nothing happened. Božica saw a woman divided in half: the lower half belonged to the old Božica and was twice the size of the upper half.

"Jozo!" she screamed. "The chocolates! Quick!"

Completely astonished, Jozo grabbed the plate of frozen chocolates. Without taking her eyes off the image in the mirror, Božica snatched three Fontanas from the plate and stuffed them into her mouth. Her skirt slipped to the ground of its own accord. Slim hips appeared. Božica tore off her last piece of clothing and saw a triangle of fair, silky hair.

"Jozo!" Božica sobbed with emotion, flinging herself into his arms. "Jozo, Jozo!" she repeated, weeping. Suddenly she broke off. She looked at Jozo as though she had just remembered something and started undressing him.

"Quick! Quick," she mumbled, shoving a frozen chocolate into his mouth. The two of them stood naked in front of the mirror waiting to see what would happen. Nothing happened. Jozo sorrowfully contemplated his thin, pale body, the pathetic little appendage . . .

"What's this!" Božica wept. "Something's wrong . . . Why only . . . me! Something's wrong!"

Then slowly, like a timid turtle timidly stretching its neck out, the pathetic appendage began to grow. Božica ran for a ruler.

"Six and a half! Six and a half inches!" she cried, clapping joyfully. Then she turned out the light and dragged Jozo toward the bed. Stumbling in the dark, Jozo managed to find the Fontanas and surreptitiously shoved another one into his mouth.

A little later, there was a whisper in the darkness:

"Božica, you're wonderful, you smell like chocolate!"

Meanwhile, the incomplete author practises the description of a ladyfinger

—*Shape: stress particularly the handiness of its shape (like a telephone receiver, a spoon, etc.);*

—*Consistency (little sponge body): a communion wafer! just made for the cushions of fingers and tongue;*

—*Feel: a rough smoothness, barely visible floury (flowery) grains;*

—*Character: fragile, supple, unreliable (one minute it's . . . the next it's . . .): it absorbs, swells, softens, dissolves (blotting paper! ladyfinger / blotting paper . . .);*

—*Sound: ng-, that's the hard part of it; l- is the soluble part; anagrams: countless possibilites;*

—*Question: What is the opposite of a ladyfinger? A shortbread ring!*

Good things come in fours

They heard someone knocking softly at the door.

"Who is it?" asked Božica.

"It's us, Katica and Branka. We've come to wish you a Merry Christmas," came voices from behind the door.

"Come in," said Božica.

Two shapes appeared in the darkness, one small and thin, the other big and tall.

Two heads with a blanket up to their chins peeped out at them from the bed.

"You could have told us you had someone here, we wouldn't have come!" the shapes said, somewhat put out.

"Come on, don't be silly, this is Jozo," said Božica. Jozo timidly stretched his hand out from under the blanket. The shapes approached the bed, embarrassed, and shook hands.

"Katica," said the thin one, in a wool coat.

"Branka," said the tall one, in jeans and a leather jacket.

The two heads dived under the blanket for a moment.

"Let's not tell them anything," whispered one. "Maybe something will happen to them too. Okay?"

"Okay," whispered the other, giving the first one a hasty kiss on the lips. The heads reappeared above the blanket.

"Come on, girls," said Božica. "Take off your coats, sit down, pour yourselves some wine, and try the snow cubes."

"No, we're going home," they both said with one voice, frowning.

"I insist!" said Božica, in mock severity. "First a glass of wine and then a chocolate each!"

The girls sipped some wine and took a frozen chocolate each. Katica thrust hers into her mouth, while Branka just nibbled hers and then put it down.

Gradually the wool sweater Katica was wearing began to stretch, the threads snapping one after the other, and finally out leapt two magnificent breasts with big brown nipples like chocolate pralines.

"Popocatapetl!" shrieked Katica, fainting and falling off her chair. Branka hurried to catch her, but suddenly stopped, groaning, and rushed to the corner of the room. There she turned to the wall, looked down into her jeans, and gasped:

"I don't belieeeeeve it!"

Božica and Jozo threw off the blanket and got up. For some time the four of them stared at one another, astounded. Katica looked up from the floor, blinked, and cupped her huge, beautiful breasts in her hands. Branka was holding open the fly of her jeans, and Jozo had evidently forgotten about that pathetic little appendage, which now swung back and forth, suggesting a length of at least nine inches.

Božica was the first to speak.

"Keep calm, everybody. Don't panic. These seem to be some sort of magic chocolates. Neither of us knows how it all happened, why it happened, or whether the chocolates are really magic, but the fact is that tonight we've all gotten what we always wanted. Katica, you've got big, beautiful breasts and that's what you wanted, wasn't it? It looks as though you, Branka, are on your way to becoming a normal man. Jozo has acquired his desperately needed and eminently usable inches. I have a feeling that in nine months' time we're going to have a baby. I've lost weight and I'm not hungry any more. We have all gone from being incomplete personalities to being complete personalities. And now let's get dressed and throw away the rest of the chocolates, whether they're magic or not, before any of us thinks up any more wishes."

She tossed the two or three remaining Fontana chocolates into the garbage, put on her dress, and tightened her belt several holes; Katica draped a blouse of Božica's around her shoulders; Jozo pulled on his pants; Branka did up hers. They all sat down at the table.

"Hey," shouted Branka, "I've still got tits!"

"Details, details. They're small, they won't get in the way. Besides, just think, you'll grow a beard soon," said Božica sensibly. They all agreed.

"Hmm," mumbled Branka, looking at Katica with a strange new look that made Katica blush.

They all raised their glasses and clinked them.

"What a magical night," said Božica softly.

When they write, writers (complete or incomplete) feel lonely and that's why they need to be encouraged
Illuminated with a soft light they all turned their gaze towards the window. Large snowflakes softly thudded against the windowpane and burst into thousands of twinkling stars. For an instant even the old clock refused to tick, all was silent except the silken settling of the snow.

The end comes when the magic says so
"Come on," said Božica gaily, "let's finish this wine and go to bed. It's nearly morning," she added, pouring the rest of the wine. Following her old habit, she dipped her finger into her glass and licked it. Suddenly she cried out in pain. Her finger was beginning to grow with terrifying speed.

"What's this! Jesus!" Božica screamed, her face contorted with pain. Jozo, Katica, and Branka stared helplessly at the finger. When it reached the size of a melon, it suddenly turned red. Božica shrieked with pain. Her finger burst and out fell a tiny wrinkled boy.

"O my God!" They all gaped in astonishment.

"Quick! A towel!" cried Božica, regaining control of herself and snapping the invisible little umbilical cord with her teeth, as though sewing on a button.

The girls found a sheet and placed the tiny child on the table. Božica's finger abruptly shrank and flattened; the split closed up as though it had never been there.

Meanwhile, the little child began growing with the same terrifying speed as Božica's finger. Katica brought over the kitchen scales and placed the baby on it: nearly 7 lbs. Jozo picked up the ruler from the floor and measured his son.

"How shall I put it . . ." he stuttered, "twenty-six inches!"

"It's not about to grow any more, is it?" Božica asked in terror. At that moment the child began to cry loudly. Božica unbuttoned her dress and laid the baby against her breast.

"There, it's not growing any more," Božica sighed, relaxing.

"Whew!" Only now did Jozo, Katica, and Branka let out a sigh of relief.

"He's fallen asleep," whispered Božica. "Let's put him to bed."

. . . and that's why they need to be encouraged
—*Consider the simile: "The story rolls like a snowball down the snowy slope";*
—*Think about snow cubes called "Fontana"; what images does a fountain conjure up? (splashiness, delight, luxury, etc.);*
—*Check (important) whether fountains work in winter; if they*

don't, think of another name, change the name of the snow cubes?;
—Check who said: "One man's sweet is another man's poison."

Life is a fairy tale after all

"This is the last miracle we could have wished for. We don't need any more! How lovely it is not to have to wait nine months!" concluded Božica.

"Yes," said Katica and Branka a little enviously.

"Everything worked out perfectly. Jozo can get a job with us in the accounting department. With his pay of 5,000 and mine of 5,700, minus 2,500 rent, not counting electricity, we'll have . . ."

"We'll have 8,200 a month to live on!" said Jozo. And soon his deep, cheerful, confident voice could be heard from the corridor.

"Life is a fairy tale, Mother, you were right!" it said into the telephone receiver.

The author feels something is cracking inside him: changing from incomplete to complete (writer)

The author finished the last sentence with difficulty and shivered. It was cold in the room. Outside it was getting light, the snow had stopped. The author looked for a cigarette . . .

He smoked and stared sadly at the snow-covered window. No, it was all for nothing . . . everything eluded him, characters, words, rhythm, the story (the one he had in mind!) was rolling like a snowball down a snowy slope. He would never, ever be a real writer . . .

The burning cigarette reached a splinter in the tobacco and flared up. The author jumped. Suddenly he felt something within him creaking, cracking, splitting like a primeval ice floe, and then something swelling, bursting, flooding . . .

He feverishly placed a clean sheet of paper into the typewriter and energetically began to type:

A barometric low hung over the Atlantic. It moved eastward toward
a high-pressure area over Russia without as yet showing any inclination to bypass this high in a northerly direction. The isotherms and
isotheres were functioning as they should . . .

THE KHARMS CASE

2nd December 1978
To: Mr. Tvrtko Tvrtković, Editor:

Dear Mr. Tvrtković,

As I am most impressed by your publishing program, which displays surprisingly fresh and unconventional editorial taste, I am taking the liberty of offering you the work of a virtually unknown writer, equally unknown in his own country—in short, a writer as yet to be discovered. I am speaking of the Russian writer Daniil Ivanovič Kharms (1905–1942).

Daniil Kharms (real name: Daniil Ivanovič Juvačev) made his literary debut in 1926 with a volume of poems. In the autumn of that year, the Institute of Visual Art (*Institut hudozhestvennoi kul'tury*), run by Kazimir Malević, founded a theatrical group called Radix. Their production *My Mom Is All Decked Out in Watches* (*Moya mama vsja v časah*), consisting of a collage of poems by Kharms and Vvedenski, was unfortunately never performed. The Oberiu group (*Ob'edinenie real'nogo iskusstva*), or Association for Real Art, was founded at the end of 1927. Its members were Daniil Kharms, Nikolaj Zabolocki, Alexander Vvedenski, Konstantin Vaginov, Igor Behterev, and Boris Levin. At their first joint appearance (in January 1928), under the title *Three Left Hours* (*Tri levykh chasa*), the members of Oberiu read their texts, published a manifesto, and performed Kharms's play *Jelizaveta Bam*. They later made several more appearances. After a vicious attack on them in the periodical *Shift* (*Smena*) they disbanded and the miscellany they had planned, *Archimedes' Bath* (*Vanna Arhimeda*), failed to appear.

In their manifesto they declared themselves "a new detachment of left revolutionary art." Kharms himself is portrayed as follows: "Daniil Kharms, poet and playwright, is concerned less with the static figure than with the collision of a series of objects and their mutual relations. At the moment of action the object acquires new, concrete contours, full of authentic meaning. The action, now altered, contains both a classical stamp and at the same time the broad sweep of the Oberiu worldview."

It is hard to speak of Kharms and the Oberiu writers outside the context of Russian literature. The "Oberiu" are the last avant-garde grouping, in many ways similar to European Dadaism and Surrealism. Their artistic vision belongs to the trajectory that begins with the poet Kozma Prutkov, the Russian popular theater, and Gogol, and continues with the work of the writers Khlebnikov, Kruchonykh, and Tufanov, the painters Malević, Filonov, and Sokolov, the theater director Terentjev and others. Vvedenski and Kharms, in their absurdism, illogicality, and black humor, are the most radical Oberiu artists. Nikolaj Zabolotsky subscribes briefly to their worldview only in his first collection of poems, *Proofs* (*Stolbcy*), while Konstantin Vaginov, both in his prose and particularly in his verse, follows a rather different stylistic model.

Kharms and Vvedenski worked on the periodicals *Hedgehog* (*Jež*) and *Siskin* (*Čiž*), and it is only as children's writers that both of them are known in the Soviet Union today. Working with Maršak, Švarc and Olejnikov fuelled Kharms's avant-gardist infantilism. It was during this period that he wrote *Cases* (*Slučaj*).

Kharms perished in a Leningrad prison in 1942 and his work was forgotten. His slow rehabilitation began in the sixties, when unpublished texts began sporadically appearing, arousing great interest among Russian scholars.

This is a brief introduction to Kharms. I am convinced that his short, absurdist, black-humorous prose with its numerous parodic elements is more in tune with the sensibility of the modern reader than any other recently discovered work of Russian avant-garde literature.

I leave you now to read the manuscript, with warmest good wishes,

Vavka Ušić

P.S. You may remember, we met several months ago at the launch of Krleža's *Collected Works*. I very much hope we shall meet soon in connection with Kharms.

5th May 1979
Dear Mr. Tvrtković,

I should like most respectfully to remind you of Kharms, and should be interested to know whether you have read my manuscript. Please let me know by phone or postcard. I have given my translation of Kharms's story "The Old Woman" ("Staruha") to the magazine *Off* and sent some of his short pieces to *The Literary Word*. All this will be good advance publicity (I'm thinking on Kharms's behalf, of course) should you decide to publish him.

As I write these lines I recall a dream I had last night. I dreamed I was in Leningrad, on the corner of Nadeždinske and Kovenske Streets, looking up at a house. And there, leaning his elbows on a window sill, was Kharms. He had a round cap on his head and a small green dog drawn on his cheek. From time to time he would pick up a book, place it on his head, put it down, and then, with unusual seriousness, pick his nose. Although the distance was considerable, I could clearly see the title of the book. It was Knut Hamsun's *Mysteries*. "Yes," said Kharms, "I wish I could be like Goethe!" I remember being astonished, in my dream, by the fact that I could hear perfectly although the distance would have made it impossible.

I am eagerly looking forward to your reply.

Best wishes,
Vavka Ušić

1st June 1980
Dear Mr. Tvrtković,

You have now had my translation of Daniil Kharms in your possession for more than a year and a half, and I have yet to receive any response from you.

I hope I shall soon have the opportunity of learning your decision in connection with Kharms.

Regards,
Vavka Ušić

17th June 1981
Mr. Tvrtković,

I am truly shocked that my manuscript of Kharms has been with you (I assume untouched) since December 1978 (!) and you do not find it fitting to inform me about its status. Such behavior is totally unacceptable. Incidentally, several of my translations have been published in the journal *Scope*. It is interesting that others seem to have a feeling for Kharms's

irresistible charm. If I were you, I would give this matter some
serious thought.

V. Ušić

21st February 1982

I received your message informing me that you are reading my translation of Kharms. Am I supposed to be grateful?! . . .

V. Ušić

25th May 1982
Dear Mr. Tvrtković,

I had a strange dream: I was lying in bed and beside me
(with a cap on his head) lay Daniil Kharms, smoking a pipe.
"Okay," I thought in my dream, "he smoked a pipe in life as
well."

"Pleased to meet you, Garfunkel," said Kharms, offering
me his hand politely.

I remember feeling rather uncomfortable about the fact
that he was smoking in bed, that he had got into bed in his
climbing boots, and that he had been dead for forty years.
Somehow I didn't feel like shaking hands with him. Sensitive as he was (in my dream I realized that he was sensitive, although everything pointed to the contrary), Kharms
understood that I didn't like the situation so he took off his
cap and, clearly hoping to amuse me, began to pull out white
rabbits, which were actually little Pushkins (!), pigeons
which were actually Gogols, and silk handkerchiefs, which
were actually—silk handkerchiefs. I remember clearly that
one of them fell to the floor, crumpled up, and began to
cough. I didn't know who it was and that frightened me.

And then I realized that Kharms wasn't lying beside me, he wasn't lying at all but sitting, and that it wasn't Kharms at all but you!

You were sitting on the bed (mine!), thumbing your nose at me!

I am still waiting to hear what you think of my manuscript.

Warm regards,
Vavka U.

P.S. I wonder what the dream means and how I should interpret that nose-thumbing.

28th June 1982
Mr. Tvrtković,

A new book about Kharms and Vvedenski, *Laughter in the Void*, has recently been published, and translations of several Kharms prose pieces just appeared in the student periodical *Junk*, accompanied by an exhaustive introduction and translator's notes.

It is quite clear that I directed all my efforts over Kharms to the wrong person. I hope that you will at least have the decency to return my manuscript.

V. U.

21st October 1983

I hope that you have seen *The Book*, a translation of Kharms's short stories, in the bookstores. I no longer even know how much time has elapsed since I asked you to return my manuscript. If you fail to do so immediately, I shall be obliged to seek the assistance of a lawyer.

Vavka Ušić

25th November 1983

Hideous, sweaty monster! Sniveler! Idiot! Bonehead! Cur! Pig! Loathsome, shameless creature! Insolent fool! Peasant! Dolt! Turd! Filthy beast! Nonentity! Lunatic! Wash your feet!

As you see, the number of insults Kharms uses in his fiction is not very extensive. I would like to point out that some of them, such as *idiot*, *fool*, and *pig*, recur quite often, and would also like to remind you that you have still not returned my manuscript!!!

Vavka U.

28th November 1983

Dear Mr. Tvrtković,

I was extremely surprised to receive your letter informing me that you have included Kharms in your list for 1984. I must admit that I am surprised at your decision to publish what will now be the third volume of Kharms in our small literary market. Of course, I would be delighted to add to my selection and write an afterword. I must also say that your letter has rather thrown me, because I had quite reconciled myself to the fact that Kharms was not going to appear.

Still, I am glad that you too have finally come to admire and love the unique charm of Kharms's humour.

Sincerely Yours,
Vavka U.

P.S. My apologies for the ugly physical incident that occurred in your office. But if we knew each other better you would have known that you simply cannot use *that word* in an argument with me.

P.P.S. How is your ear? I hope it has healed. Once again, my apologies, really.

15th December 1983

Mr. Tvrtković,

I don't know whether you keep up with the contemporary journals? I was recently flipping through the literary section of *Off* and was furious to discover that 50% of the contributions were directly copied from Kharms, 20% were crude imitations, and 30% were more or less attempts to write in his style. As a translator and, I might say, a close follower of the literary scene, I am most surprised at the resurrection of a writer who belonged to quite a different age and literary milieu. I wonder whether the young are imitating Kharms simply because he lends himself to imitation (short stories similar in structure to the joke) or because they like his destructive attitude (with respect to traditional literature). Or could it be that our own everyday life (I hardly dare think it) has begun to resemble the "life" in Kharms's stories? If our grocery stores are selling the same big cucumbers as in Kharms's stories, then . . . See what I mean?

Perhaps the theme of Kharms and the "Kharmsians" would make an interesting afterword?

Best wishes,

Vavka U.

14th January 1984

Dear Mr. Tvrtković,

Once, among friends, Kharms suggested that everyone there should write down on a scrap of paper "What I Really

Like and What I Can't Stand." Kharms's piece of paper
looked like this:

I REALLY LIKE: Gogol, Chekhov, Rabelais, Bach, Mozart,
Kozma Prutkov, Zoščenko, alley cats, Grosz, walnuts, the colors
of Konaševič and Vasnecov, roast potatoes, long-haired dogs, old
books.

I CAN'T STAND: the statue of Laocoön, Wagner's loud music,
soy sausages, Mayakovsky's paintings, fake bowties, the smell of
carbolic acid, playing cards, Balmont's and Ščepkin-Kupernik's
poetry, rattlesnakes, vegetarian cooking, and, worst of all, record
players.

All the best,
V. U.

P.S. I absolutely agree with Kharms's opinion of vegetarian
cooking and in passing would like to remind you that we need
to discuss the afterword.

24th February 1984
Dear Tvrtko Tvrtković,
I recently read an article claiming that Russian avant-
garde art, which challenges all aesthetic conventions and
thematic taboos, did not break down erotic limits. More
than that, it seems that Russian avant-garde was not particularly interested in sex. In this sense, Kharms himself is
a real puritan. In a letter to friends in 1932 he writes that he
has read a "very interesting book about a young man who fell
in love with a young person, and that young person was another young man, and that young man loved another young
person, who loved another young man, who did not love

him but another young person. One day that young person slipped and fell through the opening of a sewer and broke his back, and just as he fully recovered, he caught a chill and died. Then the young man who was in love with him shot himself and the young person who loved that young man threw himself under a train. Then, in despair, the young man who was in love with that young man climbed up a pole and was electrocuted by a streetcar cable. Then the young person who loved that young man swallowed powdered glass and died of damage to his intestines. Then the young man who loved that young person ran away to America, but there he took to drink and had to sell all his clothes, and as he had no clothes he was obliged to stay in bed, where he developed bed sores and died."

Kharms clearly invented the book, but the description of its contents represents the peak of his connection with the theme of love. If we were to consider the psychopoetics of Kharms's opus, we could confirm that certain discoveries connected with his attitude to sexuality could be discussed on the anal-oral level. Namely, it is striking how often Kharms mentions food, particularly porridge. Coarsely ground, especially. Having no intention of bothering you further with porridge and the possible symbolism thereof, I send you my best wishes.

Vavka U.

1st March 1984
Dear Mr. Tvrtković,

May I respectfully remind you that we have not yet come to any agreement. At the same time I am sending two little stories. Read them and answer the question: who is the author?

1.

Once upon a time, in the town of Leningrad, there lived a most ordinary Ivan Ivanovič who drank beer, worked as a cashier, and knew how to walk through walls. He didn't make much of a fuss about it, he just knew how to do it, that's all . . . He often used to make bets that he could, and his friends in the bar would say, "Bullshit, Vanya, you can't," and he would go ahead and do it. Once he had an accident; walking through a wall, he got stuck, or his leg did, and they had to call the chairman of the Residents' Council and the police, put together a file, and break down the wall. Ivan Ivanovič came to a very bad end. He walked through a wall without taking account of what floor he was on, fell, and smashed himself to bits.

2.

Once upon a time in the town of Leningrad there lived a very learned dog. It knew how to turn itself into anything and everything. Once its master had company.

"Turn yourself into central heating," said its master, and the dog obediently turned itself into a heater.

"It's warm," said the guests, not at all surprised.

Answer: I knew I wouldn't be able to fool you. The author of these two stories is obviously not Kharms but his friend and collaborator, the children's writer Jurij Vladimirov.

14th May 1984

Mr. Tvrtković,

You have still not contacted me about Kharms. I keep wondering about what would make a sufficiently attractive afterword, or indeed foreword. The most interesting thing for the general public would certainly be anecdotes connected with Kharms's life. In his novel *The Harpagoniad*, Konstantin Vaginov describes a German who doffs his hat politely and bows whenever he meets a dog. I am convinced that the prototype of that German was Kharms, because Kharms included his own person in his concept of artistic action. The person as work of art, the transformation of everyday life into an artistic concept, is not rare in the art of avant-garde groups in the twentieth century. Kharms played above all with the notion of authorship, signing his works with various pseudonyms: Daniel Khaarmst, Khkh-arms, Daniil Dandan, Čarms, Harmonius, Ivan Toporiškin, Kharms-Šardam, the writer Kolpakov, Karl Ivanovič Šchusterling, etc. The same concept governed his strange clothes, the numerous strange letters he sent his friends, the way he greeted telegraph poles in the street, and the like. We must take into account not only literary influences but also the group in which Kharms was active and which inspired him.

The children's writer Nikolaj Olejnikov, who used the pseudonym "Makar the Brutal," was no less inventive. There was a jokey rivalry between Olejnikov and Kharms. Olejnikov parodied Kharms, but Kharms paid him back in kind. There's an anecdote about Olejnikov: he is supposed to have appeared in Leningrad with a genuine certified declaration stating that Nikolaj Olejnikov is a handsome man. In her *Epilogues*, Lydia Žukova writes that she once went into a shop on Nevsky Prospect with Olejnikov and he said, "Give me something blue. I need something blue to eat." The salesman replied in some confusion, "I'm sorry, but we're out of blue at the moment." Olejnikov wrote numerous occasional poems and letters (attacking the wearing of suits or long skirts, approving haircuts, wishing his typist well on the occasion of her buying a new shawl, etc.). He wrote these epistles and dedicated them to his friends, taking no account of their artistic value. The poems were published relatively recently and they show Olejnikov to be an excellent, even inspired poet and confirm the thesis of the individual as a living artistic concept.

One of my favorite poems is entitled "Benevobelly," a comic account of the dramatic struggle between two passions: love of the body and love of food. "Without bread and butter / I can no longer love / Lest my ardor stutter / Put some stew on the stove!" And so forth . . .

Forgive me for getting carried away with Olejnikov. It is only because I find him closest to the Oberiu spirit and feel that he influenced Kharms far more than can be proved today.

I do not intend to bother you any further so I'll stop now. If you think that the above-mentioned theme could make an interesting afterword to Kharms, let me know in good time.

Yours,

Vavka Ušić

1st November 1984

Mr. Tvrtković,

Now it's November, and I still don't know where I am with Kharms! A few days ago I was thinking about a (possible) afterword again. Namely, as I am reading the novels of Konstantin Vaginov for a third time, it occurred to me that one could draw a nice parallel between Vaginov and Kharms. I do not intend, of course, to burden you with excess information. So, I have translated a very short vignette of the kind Vaginov likes to interpolate into his novels, this one is from the novel *The Life and Work of Svistonov* (*Trudy i dni Svistonova*).

At the same time may I remind you that I am eagerly awaiting your reply.

Best wishes,

Vavka U.

The Experimental Novelist

"Before I put anything on paper, I must experience the phenomenon I am describing."

Such was the principle of the tailor Dmitrij Ščelin. For two years now he has been writing a "novel of everyday life" with all its horrors.

Two months ago Ščelin intended to complete a chapter of his novel with the main character's attempted suicide by poison. Naturally, Ščelin wanted to experience the sufferings of a suicide who tries to poison himself. He got hold of some poison, drank it, and lost consciousness. He was taken to the Mary Magdalene Hospital where he spent two months.

As soon as he recovered, he started working on the novel. Now he had to experience the sufferings of a suicide who tries to drown himself. Just after midnight the following night, Ščelin jumped from Tučkov Bridge into the Little Neva. Guards from the bridge saw him in time, rowed out to him, and dragged him out of the water.

The experimental novelist was taken back to the Mary Magdalene Hospital in an unconscious state. In the morning he came round but that was not all. Now he had to experience the sufferings of suicides who fling themselves under trains.

"Only thus will all the phenomena in my novel be real and deeply permeated with emotion . . ."

The life of the novelist-tailor is a difficult one.

1st December 1984

Dear Tvrtko Tvrtković,

I am sending you an extract from Nilvich's article "Reactionary Juggling." The article was published in the newspaper *Smena* in 1930 after an Oberiu reading. The article did its job: the group held no more readings. By the way, what news is there of Kharms?

. . . All the discussants, to the wild applause of the audience, unanimously and resolutely rejected the Oberiu. It was observed, with disapproval, that in the period of the most strenuous efforts of the proletariat in the forefront of socialist renewal, in the period of decisive class struggles, the Oberiu stand outside social life, outside the social reality of the Soviet Union. They seem to feel one should bury oneself as far away as possible from that tedious reality, from unbearabable politics, and indulge in one's own crude insolence and hooliganism!

The Oberiu are remote from renewal. They hate the struggle being waged by the proletariat. Their rejection of life, their senseless poetry, their artificial juggling is a protest against the dictatorship of the proletariat. Theirs is a poetry alien to us, the poetry of the class enemy, as the student proletariat has declared.

What could the Oberiu say to that?

With unheard-of temerity Vladimirov likened the assembled company to a bunch of primitives who, on their first visit to a European city, had seen their first motor car.

Levin announced that "for the time being" (!) few people understood them, but that they were the only representatives (!) of a genuinely new art and were constructing a great new edifice.

"Who are you building it for?" he was asked.

"The whole of Russia," came the classic reply.

The student proletariat responded to the provocation of the famous Oberiu in a dignified manner. They decided to record their opinion in the form of a resolution and send it to the writers' union.

Incidentally, why does the writers' union tolerate such trash in its ranks? Is it not a gathering of *Soviet* writers?

6th January 1985

Mr. Tvrtković,

Leafing through Kharms again, I am struck for the first time by the fact that nowhere are there so many deaths as among the Oberiu. Vvedenski's play *Christmas at the Ivanovs* (*Jelka kod Ivanovyh*), for example, is surely unique in Russian literature: in the last scene alone nine characters die!

Death in Kharms's texts may be divided into two categories: *intentional* (70% of the cases) and *unintentional* (the remaining 30%). Unintentional (chance, accidental) death (or injury) generally results from unusual circumstances. One may divide the causes by frequency into three groups:

a) *falls*; b) *food*; c) *other*. One may further divide *falls* as a
cause of death according to frequency into:

  falling through windows (5)
  falling from cupboards (2)
  falling under a car (1)
  falling under a train (1)
  falling into a sewer (1)

Food as a cause of accidental death occurs on three occasions:

  excessive intake of peas
  tomatoes
  powdered glass

The *other* causes of accidental death are the following:

  drowning in a lake
  receiving an electric shock
  suffocating in garbage
  overextending the neck as a result of throwing the head
    backwards
  bedsores
  tetanus
  chill

I have noted only two cases of sudden *physical distress* af-
fecting Kharms's characters: sudden hair loss and sudden
blindness.

Far more frequent is *intentional death* (sometimes it's a
matter merely of mutilation, causing physical injury, etc.).
Intentional death (or physical injury) in Kharms's fiction is
generally carried out:

a) by mechanical means
b) by nonmechanical means
c) by a combination of the two

Mechanical means include a poker, a sugar bowl, a beer tankard, an iron (or bone) rod, a primus stove, an iron, a branch, a croquet mallet, a hammer, a chisel, tongs, a trough, a crutch, a spade, a stone, a table leg. Kharms also introduces into literature two highly original instruments for physically injuring one's adversary: a set of false teeth (!) and a cucumber (!).

Nonmechanical means of mutilation or killing are confined to brute strength, that is, roughly the following repertoire of actions: punching (the head, body); tearing off (limbs: arms, legs, head, etc.); spitting (on the victim); blowing one's nose (into the victim); beating up; breaking (jaws); chopping off (ears, head, arms); trampling; raping; throwing (the victim against a wall, live people into a pit); rubbing (a child's face against a wall); standing (on the victim's stomach with one's full weight); banging (a head against a wall); wrenching (a live child from its mother's womb).

Particularly perverse actions include the act of licking blood stains (belonging to the victim) from the floor. Burning as a means of death is mentioned only once in Kharms's writings.

It is interesting to note that animals are never hurt (he liked them); indeed, they are rarely mentioned at all. Only in one text do we find a character rubbing a dead dog over the floor with his foot. It is also indicative that Kharms's most frequent victims are old women and children. The dead are mentioned for the purpose of terrorizing others on several occasions.

Mr. Tvrtković, I have made this brief statistical analysis of death, crime, and perversion in Kharms's writings as I reflect on a possible afterword for his works. The title could be roughly: "The Relationship of Murderer to Victim: A Typology of Black Humor in Kharms's Work." In fact, a great deal could be written about Kharms's black humor in connection with Freud, the European tradition (Jarry, de Sade, Swift, and others), the Russian tradition (Gogol, Dostoevsky), and the poetics of Surrealism or the avant-garde's negation of the rationality of the world.

However, this all seems to me like dragging out the problem artificially, and in my approach I would stress two other key features. The first would be the influence of the *chastushka*, or street ditty, a traditional form of Russian oral literature and certainly the largest and most vital storehouse of black humor. Olejnikov's blackly humorous poems are nothing but "literary" *chastushki* (cf. *Kunstmärchen*). There are various kinds of *chastushka*: political, labor-camp, erotic, pornographic, Young Pioneer . . .

Here's what a Young Pioneer one looks like, to give you an idea of the genre:

> The child whines "Mommy, my teddy bear!"
> "You see that socket? Take a look in there."
> The child's bones fry, the guests smell smoke
> And they laugh loud and long at the wonderful joke.

The other important point as I see it is what might be called the humor of the "gang." Kharms, Vvedenski, and Olejnikov were children's writers, meeting day after day in the editorial offices of *Hedgehog* and *Siskin*, and you can imagine that together they developed the same black humour sensibility.

Kharms's famous children's poem, written for the first issue of *Siskin*, looks like this in Olejnikov's parodic version:

In a flat there lived
Forty four
Forty four sad siskins
A siskin with paralysis
A siskin with syphilis
A siskin who was paranoid
A siskin who had adenoids

What I want to suggest is that Kharms's black humour (hatred of children, etc.) results more from the fact that he was a children's writer than from a desire to parody Dostoevsky!

I shan't bore you. I'm simply throwing out ideas, leaving you to decide for yourself what will best suit the afterword to the Kharms book.

I look forward to hearing from you.

Warm regards,
Vavka U.

1st February 1985

Dear Mr. Tvrtković,

I called on you at your office today, but was told you had just gone to a Workers' Council meeting. I was going to wait for you, but when your secretary said you had a meeting after that with the Commission for Systematizing Posts, I gave up. Let me know how things stand with Kharms.

Vavka U.

2nd March 1985

Mr. Tvrtković,

Kharms is evidently not coming out although it is now 1985. I am also surprised not to have heard from you, although

I have written you a considerable number of letters. Let me know once and for all what is happening with Kharms and the afterword; in fact, it is the afterword that concerns me most at the moment. I really do want to come to an arrangement in good time, not at the last minute.

Thinking about the afterword, I have been leafing through the existing literature on Kharms again. As early as 1981, Jovanović's article "Daniil Kharms as Parodist" analyzes Kharms's story "The Old Woman" as a parody of Dostoevsky's *Crime and Punishment* and in a way anticipates all the articles which examine the parodic aspect of Kharms's insubstantial opus. Thus, Jovanović is joined by Ellen B. Chances, who analyzes Kharms's "Old Woman" as a parody of Pushkin's "The Queen of Spades" and finds obvious parallels, without of course ignoring Dostoevsky who referred to "The Queen of Spades" in *Crime and Punishment*. Chances also links Kharms with Gogol and Chekhov.

A second line of research in Kharms scholarship points towards the European drama of the absurd (Jarry, Beckett, Ionesco, Genet), and a third towards the Russian avant-garde context (Khlebnikov, Malević, Tufanov, Kruchonykh).

I have found nothing in the existing research on the structure of Kharms's short story (which closely resembles the anecdote, the joke) that does not recur in a surprising way in relation to the work of all short story writers. Have you read Kafka and Borges? Have you read Michaux's stories about Plim? Have you read Cortázar? If you have, and I don't doubt you have, you will know what I mean.

I won't bore you any longer. Please let me know whether to concentrate on these suggestions or on some other theme for the afterword to the forthcoming Kharms book.

Best wishes,
Vavka U.

15th August 1985
The fur iron

. . . To accuse me of having displayed in my earliest youth an inclination to sadism because I wrung the necks of chickens is really stupid. That just goes to show that the accusation is devoid of elementary investigative precision. Apart from anything else it's banal. And banality, dear judges, is the mother of all crimes. Wringing chicken's necks is just another of your policemen's sado-infantile fantasies. I did wring necks, as you say, but of rabbits, not hens. And those two actions cannot be compared. The difference is great, like between the music of Mozart and Wagner. But to understand such things you have to have an ear.

My childhood fascination with soft and above all silent death profoundly shaped the whole of my rich and passionate life. The investigators omitted to notice that fact. From that first omission onward the accusation abounds in unbelievable mistakes.

The accusation includes the sentence that I drank blood from the slit throats of my countless victims. That's simply insultingly inaccurate! Can victims be "countless"? What you ought to know is that, unlike all of you, I loved my victims. I know their names and their exact number. Ninety-nine, dear judges! Ninety-nine, no more, no less. And they were all wonderful, interesting people, full of life.

Secondly, I am nauseated by blood! I killed my victims highly hygienically, with great tenderness and respect. In my apartment, had you been attentive, you could have observed an object, a fur iron. That iron is a work of art! It is more than that, it is a chef d'oeuvre of mercy! It was with that object, which I made with my own hands, it was with that "rabbit" that I gave my victims the last, merciful blow.

Thirdly, I cannot stand shrill noises. If you have ever had the opportunity to observe the way rabbits die, you would know that those small, soft, charming animals have a special talent of dying submissively, decently, and without a sound. My victims died like rabbits. If one was on the point of screaming, I would tenderly thrust a rabbit-skin glove into its mouth.

In the charges against me you burden me with cannibalism. Here too things need to be clarified. What pains me most is the false accusation that I drank blood from the slit throats of my victims. How many times must I repeat the notorious fact that blood nauseates me! I boiled my victims, and, as you can see, that is dramatically different. And I ate them because I loved them. And is it not the most natural thing in the world to consume the object that attracts you most passionately? It never occurred to me to eat a pig. You, who have never tasted fresh human brain steamed and covered with almond sauce really have no right to judge my culinary tastes.

Nor should you neglect the ideological nature of things, which, in fact, is not mentioned anywhere in the charges. All those sick, criminal brains that kill in the name of something are truly unbearable and I state here that I have nothing in common with them. All those Raskolnikovs who kill in the name of an idea—whether it be revolution, war, the homeland, injustice, defence or self-defence—are deeply repugnant to me. That cannibal from Suzdal with whom you have the effrontery to compare me, that animal who polished off some fifty people, justifying himself by the horrors of communism and sexual dysfunction, has nothing in common with me. Communism is really not my problem. I killed people for the beauty of killing, and not in the name of vulgar ideas. I ate my victims because I loved them, and not out of hunger. My sexual life was entirely normal. If they were alive, all my male and female partners would be able to confirm that. For only passionate and deeply affectionate natures, such as mine, are capable of bringing the act of love to its legitimate end, to death, to total bodily unity . . .

P.S. I wrote this exercise for you inspired by Kharms. I think he would be proud of me. What about you?

1st September 1985
Dear T. T.,

I came to look for you again today. Your secretary told me you were at the dentist, so I decided not to wait. For some reason I have the feeling you are avoiding me. If that is the case I don't see why.

V. U.

23rd January 1986

My dear Mr. Tvrtković,

I went to the hospital today, but they wouldn't let me see you, though they were kind enough (only after my fervent insistence, I must admit) to show me your diagnosis. Terrible, really terrible, I'm extremely sorry . . .

I must say I find it simply unbelievable that, after at last finding the folder with my Kharms translations in the cabinet, you pulled down a pile of other manuscripts, which then brought the whole cupboard down with them, which, as far as I could judge, was in any case wobbly and had weak, or, rather, non-existent legs. My God, so that old worm-eaten cabinet could cause contusions of the head (*contusio capitis*), a concussion (*commotio cerebri*), and a fracture in the parietal bone of the skull (*fractura ossis parietalis lat. sin.*), which is certainly dreadful, but logical since the cabinet did hit your head first. All the rest, *fractura claviculae lat. sin.*, *ruptura lienis*, and *fractura femoris sin cum dilocationem*, occurred when the cupboard had already fallen onto you with its full weight. The contusions of the rib cage and the rib fractures (*contusio thoracis cum fracturam costarum IV-VII lat. sin., fractura costae V lat. dex.*) probably also resulted from the cupboard's fall, although I do not rule out the possibility that their cause was the understandable clumsiness your secretary and I displayed as we lifted the cupboard off you, trying to drag you out as fast as possible. Only the *vulnera icta manus dex.* is an inexplicable riddle. What was the cause of the gaping wound in your right hand when all the objects with which you came into contact may be said to be blunt, or at least far from sharp? There's no way a cupboard can make a wound so deep, anyone can see that!

I can't tell you how sorry I am that it all happened just as you were extracting the Kharms manuscript. Believe me, I would feel far better had it been any other manuscript.

I send my very best wishes, trusting in medicine which can do wonders these days, and hoping you will make a very speedy recovery.

Yours truly,
Vavka Ušić

25th February 1986
Dear Tvrtko,

I telephoned the hospital today, and the nurse's kindly voice told me you are much better, so I'm writing this letter to drag you out of the gloomy hospital atmosphere and bring you back at least for a moment to your job, which you enjoy so much and where your return is impatiently awaited, as I had the opportunity to verify yesterday, when I made a brief visit to your office.

Your secretary told me that the unfortunate Kharms had been sent to the printer with the speed of a torpedo, which made me feel really awkward, because I had gone to the office with the intention of withdrawing the manuscript! This will come as a surprise to you, I imagine. How can it be, you are surely wondering, that someone who has waited patiently for **EIGHT** years should give up just like that? I hasten to answer your question, though I am not sure that you will approve of my reasons.

The whole thing came about, as always, by the ill-fated worm of doubt. Whether it was the old editorial cabinet which so unexpectedly collapsed on your body that was to blame or something else, I don't know. I only know that that day (the day the cabinet fell) I began to be preoccupied with the evil and intrusive thought that Kharms's texts, which various people had published in various periodicals, might all have been falsifications or semi-falsifications, or, at best, badly copied.

Let me recount, by way of example, the fate of the writings of A. Vvedenski, Kharms's inseparable friend, so you will understand the basis of my conviction.

Druskin, a musicologist and close friend of Kharms and Vvedenski, records having seen in the early thirties a notebook of Vvedenski's poems written before 1922. Today we have only two poems from that period. Another notebook, of poems written between 1925–27, shared a similar fate. The contents of that notebook were copied down by Kharms himself. Of 36 poems only five have been preserved in toto, and a further five in fragments. In 1928 the painter Pavel Mansurov emigrated to the West taking with him a few sheets of Vvedenski's writings. It is not known where they ended up. In 1926 Kharms and Vvedenski sent Pasternak a selection of poems with a covering letter. The letter has been preserved; the poems have disappeared! Vvedenski's poems, which otherwise ended up in the official garbage, were kept by Hardžiev until the beginning of the war, but at the request of the author himself he returned them in 1940. They too disappeared without trace! The manuscripts from the mid-thirties were burnt: Vvedenski's wife at the time set fire to the existing manuscripts when she learned of her husband's imprisonment. The manuscript of the play *My Mom Is Decked Out in Watches*, though written out in multiple copies for the actors, has not come down to us. When Kharms was arrested, Druskin went to Kharms's apartment with the intention of hiding the manuscript archive. Since he was unable to take all the manuscripts at once, they left Kharms's *Grass* (*Trava*), Vvedenski's novel *Murderers, You are Fools* (*Ubyci vy duraki*), and certain other papers for later.

When they returned to the apartment, all they found were ashes: the remaining manuscripts had been "successfully" burnt.

How is it possible now—after this story about Vvedenski, whose literary destiny and life are inextricably linked with Kharms—to believe without a vestige of doubt in texts that have risen to the literary surface after so many years?

A few days ago I received a letter from a friend in Moscow including a short piece by Kharms:

I was born among rushes. Like a mouse. My mother gave birth to me and placed me in the water. I began to swim. There was a fish with four whiskers on his nose circling round me. I began to cry. The fish cried too. Suddenly we noticed some porridge floating on the water. We ate it and began to laugh. We thought it was very funny . . .

I've been troubled for several days now by the question of whether that is an original Kharms or not. Everything would suggest that it is. It's his style, his kind of subject. The mouse (it's a play on words: Russian *kamish* means rushes; *kak mish*—like a mouse) is the key word, because it is also used by Vvedenski in the fragment "The Gray Notebook" ("The mouse began to twinkle. Turn round: the world is twinkling like a mouse."). Still . . . My suspicions are fanned by the fact that Kharms's short story model lends itself to imitation. Recall the whole crowd of young short story writers who are now mercilessly imitating Kharms.

Once this thought strikes you it doesn't let you go. It goes further and deeper, finds more and more reasons, even broaches the ultimate question: what if KHARMS is everything and nothing? And what if he was completely invented as a collective game, designed to add one more absurdity to all the existing absurdities of totalitarianism? What if there were, and still there are, secret ghostwriters prolonging his life?? What if Kharms is anonymous collective work in progress, an ultimate literary fabrication?? What if Kharms clones are appearing, disappearing, and reappearing in literatures around the world just to make fun of us devoted and hardworking men and women of letters??? No, it can't be. All I know is that YOU MUST stop the printing! RIGHT AWAY!!

Yours, as ever,
Vavka U.

P.S. I have discovered that your secretary is intending to visit you tomorrow. Incidentally, I have been reconstructing the fall of the cabinet again in my memory and have worked out where you got that inexplicable *vulnera icta manus dex.* As your secretary was lifting the cabinet, she must have stepped on your arm with her high-heeled shoe. The pressure of the stiletto (combined with that weight!) could easily have caused a deep wound. I wear flat-soled shoes, by the way.

25th March 1986

My dear love, my world-twinkling-like-a-mouse, my own little mousey,

I just got back and sat down at my desk at once. I want you to get this letter tomorrow. In the bus I kept thinking about the sweet blindness we've been living in (like two stupid mice) for eight (is it really eight?) years, I persistently clutching Kharms in my hands (like a compass, yet with no idea where he would lead me) and you persistently rejecting the same, not knowing yourself why (for God's sake, it was only a book after all). And all the time Fate, wearing Kharms's mischievous mask, was toying with us. For I am certain it was fate that raised your hand from the armrest of the hospital wheelchair and placed it on my knee . . .

My love . . .
Your Vavka. Vav-ka. Your Ka
(Ka—like kamish, like rushes, like a mouse)

3rd May 1986

Dear Love,

Yesterday when I saw you in the front hall of the convalescent home, I felt my heart leap with joy for the first time in ages. You've made a wonderful recovery, you are getting better before my very eyes, day by day. That slight limp you're so worried about—it won't last. I'm sure it won't. If nothing else, we'll do the same as in Kharms's "Incredible Cat." In that poem a cat hurts its paw, so they tie a balloon to it and then the little cat half-walks, half-floats above the ground. My love, I imagine you floating above me, you come close, you kiss me tenderly and lift off like a balloon, and I have to reach out my hands to catch you.

I'll see you on Wednesday, I can't wait.

Yours always,
Ka

20th November 1986

Mousey,

Lift up the cloth, your breakfast is under it. The roll is fresh. Don't dream of skipping breakfast and just giving yourself a shot of coffee, as usual! I love you.

Don't forget to phone Ivek the plumber about the washing machine. I'm at the university library. See you at lunchtime.

Luv, Ka

31st December 1986

My dear love, Happy New Year! Dear Mousey, I'm giving you this gold fountain pen so that you have something for correcting "stupid" texts. I love you, Ka

2nd February 1987

Mousey,

I've taken the meat out of the fridge to thaw. We've got company tonight, sorry I didn't mention it before, but I didn't know myself. I met Lars S., a Swedish Slavist (and "Kharmsologist," imagine!), in the University Library. He's at the summer school here, and I've invited him and his wife to dinner. I just popped home to change. I'm going out now to show them some of the sights. If you get home before me, as you probably will, please peel the potatoes and wash the lettuce. I'll buy some wine. And give the apartment a once-over, if you have time. Luv, Ka.

Munich, 3rd May 1987

Mousey, it's wonderful here! I've met some new, really interesting people. Lars is here as well. (Remember that Swede and his wife, who got hiccups at dinner?) Lars gave a paper yesterday on the meaning of numbers and especially zero in Kharms's opus. It was a great success. My own "Kharms's Mask" didn't go down badly either. (Why? Because my mouse copied my paper beautifully and neatly, my mouse, whom I love more than anything in the world!)

I ran into an acquaintance from Moscow, too, Maša M. She told me that some wonderful people I met long ago in Leningrad are no longer among the living. G. G., who talked to me about Kharms, has died, that was the most upsetting news.

I've bought you a wonderful cashmere scarf at a sale.

Hugs 'n' kisses,

Ka (as in "kashmere"!)

15th August 1987

Mousey,

I'll stay at Mother's for another few days. Work on my article "Totalitarianism and Sadomasochistic Fantasies" is going well.

I hope the builders have finished the work. Don't forget to remind them to paint those pipes in the bathroom as well. Details like that are easily overlooked.

Hugs 'n' kisses. And another big sloppy one!

Stockholm, 3rd December 1987

Fifty years ago (31 October 1937) Daniil Kharms wrote:

The only thing I care about is what is senseless, what has no practical sense. I care about life in its absurd form. Heroism, pathos, courage, refinement, hygiene, morality, charm, and risk—these are words and feelings I despise. On the other hand I fully understand and respect thrill and rapture, inspiration and despair, passion and timidity, debauchery and modesty, sadness and misery, joy and laughter.

I hope that this quotation will tell you more than I can myself. Our life together has lost its spark. That's why I've decided to stay here. Lars has left his wife, we've decided to live together. We have lots in common, if that even matters in relationships.

As for practical matters, you take care of everything as you think best for both of us. You know yourself that I really don't care about that kind of thing. "Life must be useless, like a gift," said Kharms.

I wish you all the best,

Ka

P.S. The only thing I'd like to keep is that portrait of Kharms, and anyway Vladek did it for me. Send it to my mother.

Moscow, 10th November 1988

I'm writing from Moscow, from the International Slavists' Congress, where Lars and I are at the moment. Starting next year we'll be in the States, Lars has been invited to the University of Connecticut to give a course on Kharms. I'm working on my book, *Totalitarianism and Sadomasochistic Fantasies*.

This year an edition of Kharms's works was published here, for the first time. I thought you'd like to have the first Soviet edition, so I'm sending you a copy. I think the editor chose a fine title for the collection: *Flight to the Skies* (*Polet v nebesa*).

Regards, Ka

The Kreutzer Sonata

Arise, O Sophocles, and recount my tragedy, my conjugal woes!

From Zagreb to Dugo Selo

One day in October I was waiting for the Belgrade train to start—the express was full, so I had to take the local—when a man carrying several nylon bags and an enormous wooden cannon joined me in the compartment. He hoisted the bags into the net above the seat by the door—I had a window seat—and placed the cannon carefully in his lap. Shortly thereafter a restless-looking man with disheveled hair and unusually luminous eyes burst in. He scanned the compartment, then mumbled a few words and took the seat opposite me, fixing his gaze on a point outside the window.

The train was under way when a fourth passenger entered. She was a blonde. She had messy, oily hair and was wearing a loose jacket and jeans. She plonked herself into a seat, dropped her plastic British Airways bag on the floor, and, stuffing a stick of gum in her mouth, settled in to chew.

The man sitting opposite me emitted occasional noises that sounded like a throat being cleared or a laugh sputtering on and off. At first their strange quality attracted our attention, but we soon grew as used to it as to the tedious clatter of the train. Since I had forgotten to buy a newspaper before boarding, I didn't know what to do with myself and alternated between staring out of the window and staring at my fellow travelers. But eventually, true to genre (train, four basic characters, length of action unknown, because one never does know with our trains), I opened a conversation with a gambit that struck me as exemplary.

"Nice cannon you've got there," I said to the fellow in the corner.

"Bought it in Germany," said the fellow, clearly relieved the silence had been broken.

"What is it anyway? A toy?"

"Hell no . . . See this hole here? Well, you stick a bottle in the hole. You know, when you have people over? It gives some class to the drinks and all. Looks great too . . . I always bring back a gadget or two from Germany. For the missus. Hell, you know the ladies, how they go for those things!"

"Right . . ."

"Damn right I'm right!" said the cannon man, getting into the swing of things.

The blonde pulled the gum out of her mouth, pushed it back in, made a smacking sound, scratched her thigh, and looked the man up and down.

"Damn right!" the man repeated, but mildly enough to keep the conversation going.

"How about your other cannon?" the blonde inserted. "You keep that for the missus too?" Her leer revealed a gap in the upper jaw.

The cannon man perked up and was about to respond when the man sitting opposite me said pompously, "Disgusting!"

"What was that?" the blonde asked, tugging at her gum.

"I said, Disgusting!" the man repeated nervously.

"Well!" the blonde snapped, and, grabbing her bag, stalked out of the compartment. The nervous man came out with a noise like hysterical laughter, then gave me a questioning look and said softly, "Please accept my apologies."

"But I really don't . . ."

"It's just that I . . ."

"Yes?"

"Nothing," he said with a wave of the hand and went back to gazing out of the window.

An uneasy silence descended upon the compartment.

"Keep an eye on my cannon, will you?" the cannon man said to me.

"Fine," I said willingly.

The man laid his cannon on the seat and stumbled out of the compartment in a fog.

As soon as the door closed behind him, the nervous man glanced over at me and said thoughtfully, "Women . . ."

"Hm . . ."

"Women are awful. They don't understand a thing."

"What do you mean?"

"Don't you see? That woman can't understand a man's going all that distance to bring his wife a nice gift; all she can do is make fun of him and allude to something completely irrelevant."

"But she didn't mean anything . . ."

"Oh, yes she did," the nervous man interrupted. "That's exactly what she meant. Women have a one-track mind."

"But . . ."

"But me no buts! Women! If you knew what one did to me . . . But why am I telling you this?" And with another wave of the hand he went back to his window.

"No, go ahead, really," I said. "I'm interested."

"Well, one of them did me in completely, made a total wreck out of me."

"You don't look like a . . ."

"True, it doesn't show. You can't understand unless I tell you the whole story."

"Well then, do," I said.

Out of the corner of my eye I saw Dugo Selo fly by. By the time I'd made myself comfortable and lit a cigarette, my nervous neighbor had embarked upon his tale.

From Dugo Selo to Ivanić Grad

"My initial encounter with what at first glance seemed merely a pleasant girl produced so enigmatic a reaction within me that—walking down a side street and going against my custom and the rules of propriety—I turned for a second glance. You can imagine my consternation when I saw her standing and gazing at me, and I moved on immediately, yet I admit I was glad, because there was something vaguely attractive and sensitive about the girl, something spiritual, something to do with the soul. That was what made me notice her, I who till then had deemed women the least important part of my life.

"Several months went by before I saw her again, but then I began to run into her on the outskirts of town walking arm in arm with soldiers of varying rank. Clearly she felt the predilection for the uniform so common among women of inferior upbringing, the sort that forms attachments on the basis of clothes, faces, and elegance, and ignores a person's privileges and intellectual capabilities. Thus, like many others of her sex, she calibrated the intelligence of a man by the cut of his suit or the last of his boot, excluding the possibility of a dandy being a snob or a pretty-boy an idiot.

"One day we met. Her name was Anka. We met under the boughs of a chestnut grove with the sun setting and autumn rustling all around us—it was, if I do say so myself, a perfectly splendid setting. From then on we saw each other every day, always in the lap of nature, preferably by a pond or a stream.

"Unfolding one by one the events of her wretched life, Anka told me she had become the object of everyone's hatred after her mother died and she was forced to live with her step-

mother. The trials that woman put the poor girl through! Here
is one example for many. When as a young girl she called her
stepmother 'mother,' the cruel woman would stuff her mouth
with hot peppers, beat her black and blue, and throw her into
the cellar, threatening to bury her there if she dared repeat
her crime. Uneducated and unfeeling, she would torture the
poor, defenceless Anka at every opportunity.

"The child was thus continuously and systematically mis-
treated until one day she ran away from home and slashed her
wrists in a park. A week later she was found in the bushes by
some soldiers, who took her home, half dead. They are to be
commended.

"In any case, Anka and I met regularly at dusk. I would see
her home. She listened to my theories with delight, laughed
wholeheartedly at my burlesques. As an orphan she had never
known a parent's love, and I tried to fill the gap with my
own.

"Before long I came to feel that Anka was as much a part
of me as the church was of the Middle Ages. I loved her as a
bedouin his oasis or a nightingale its freedom. I was, I admit,
so intoxicated by my purely Platonic and profound feelings
that I would kneel before her at her door like a slave and beg
her to stamp upon my heart and shatter it to pieces.

"I must also mention that even though the most outlandish
things were said about her—that she suffered from a number
of venereal diseases, for example—I never stopped loving her;
I maintained my own, autonomous view.

"And then she confessed the terrible, painful truth. In
Dubrovnik, where she had gone for her apparently frail
health, she spent an evening in the company of a certain
heartless young man, a cynic—or, as she called him, a student—who in his unbridled profligacy held forth frivolously
on the low incidence of virginity in the modern woman. The

lewd discussion, revolving entirely around bestial sexuality, dragged on late into the night. At one point Anka stood and returned to her hotel room, leaving the door unlocked. Before long there was a knock on it, and a voice from within bade the visitor enter. It was the frivolous profligate! He sat on her bed, and she, looking him straight in the eye, said, 'I give you leave to verify my virginity.'

"On the morning following that cursed night of defloration she came to me with a disingenuous announcement of the fact and implored my noble heart to bear her no malice. In a frenzied rush of love I forgave her her sin and begged her to be my lawfully wedded wife. I forgave her for the sake of my love and her bitter fate, forgave the orphan who sought protection in me and lived in the belief she had found it. How could I shatter her hopes, how could I dash her on the grave of her ideals!

"And how it pains me that the name of that perfidious seaside profligate will ever remain a mystery to me, the Dubrovnik caper being nothing but a fairy tale begotten of false naïveté, fabricated to hide her early depravities, for as I have said: the most outlandish things were said about her!"

From Ivanić Grad to Kutina

My nervous neighbor again came out with his strange hybrid of throat clearing and sputter.

"A deplorable fate," I muttered, but he convulsively clenched his fist, pounded his chest, and cried, "And what about mine! What about mine!"

"You *will* tell me the whole story, won't you?" I said compassionately, fearing he would go back on his word.

"Do you mind if I eat some sunflower seeds?" he asked, taking a small newspaper packet of them out of his pocket. "Here, have a few. I find them calming."

I declined the offer and lit up again. He continued his tale.

"In any case, Anka and I were married. I recall a minor detail that will show how much I loved her. Not long after our wedding there was a terrible epidemic of influenza in our town. Even many doctors were afflicted. When Anka fell ill, I took fright and moved from my bed to hers so that I might contract the strain and we might die together. What was life to me without my Anka, after all? For eight days I rubbed her with garlic and wine vinegar and poured Jamaican rum down her throat; for eight days she lay at my right hand. On the ninth day she rose. Life was like the sun on a spring morning. And there was a child on the way . . .

"To make a long story short, one morning I woke to find Anka gone! Yes. Here today, gone tomorrow. She took everything I owned and left me with a newborn baby. Next day she returned to demand we sever all relations. I was terribly hurt by the sudden, inscrutable announcement, I was cut to the quick. Then, of course, came the tears. On all sides. She wept, I wept, the child wept. A madhouse, an inferno, a purgatory.

"Whereupon life took up where it had left off. Though not for long. One morning I woke, still weary with woes and obligations, to find her gone yet again! And with her the bed-clothes, my new suit, my shoes, socks, hat, and numerous other items. There I was in a state of nature with only my baby to cover my shame. For Anka had taken what even the man who robbed jolly Demosthenes left behind!

"I somehow managed to procure a suit of clothes, though even then I had to drag myself to work. The outside world meant nothing to me. All I cared about was my child. I was like a dog whose brain has been removed for experimentation. And suddenly there she was again, lips trembling, eyes shining. 'Tell me, Anka,' I said gently, compassionately, 'how long will things go on like this?' She vouchsafed no reply. I pleaded with her to tell me the cause of her repeated decampments, but all she could do was shrug her shoulders and weep.

"Of course within a few days she was gone. And this time for a much longer interval. Thinking she had perhaps paid for her inconstancy with her life, I wept like a child over its mother's grave; I lamented more than Orpheus when he lost his Eurydice, because he was not alone in his grief—he had animals standing over him, he had Furies crying over him—while I was completely and utterly alone!

"For days and nights I roamed the streets half-naked, half-insane, scouring the gutters and streams, the parks and bushes. In the end I locked myself in my room and mourned for two whole weeks. My neighbors were afraid of me: my eyes had something terrifying in them; they made people's blood run cold. At last I ran across her in the street; I fell before her as if she were the Madonna. 'Come with me, Anka, come home,' I said to her. 'Think of the baby! You haven't forgotten our little angel, have you?' Whereupon she looked me up and down and answered, 'I have.'

"The moment I heard her sarcastic reply—the reply of a mother and a wife—my legs buckled, my temperature plummeted, and my soul, invisible yet in pain, sobbed as only a soul knows how. I thought I would kill myself. For two days I prayed for her and wept at her psycho-intellectual savagery, her moral decadence, but in the end she relented and we went on together."

From Kutina to Banova Jaruga

"Unbelievable," I said.

"What was that?" asked my nervous neighbor, clearly chagrined at having been interrupted. He spat out a sun-flower seed; it stuck to the top of my left shoe.

"Oh, nothing. Nothing at all," I said apologetically. "Do go on." And I lit up again.

"Our life together was less than stable," he continued. "Anka made friends with a washerwoman, a frivolous blonde who thought of her maidenhead in terms of this or that popular ballad, and although her disgusting blather turned my stomach and made my gorge rise, I was forced to countenance her so as not to offend my Anka.

"Then one day Anka's father died and she had to leave me for several days. Just before she set off, I said to her, 'Be careful, son (I always called her "son"). Avoid all strangers, have a good night's rest when you arrive, and remember that your baby and your husband are awaiting you here at home.' Such were the words I chose to send her on her way.

"She did not return. Not after a week, not after two. I would go to the station and wait for her train, but she was never on it. I went to five different stations, waited for days on end, but in vain; in my desperation I even waited for goods trains, but in vain . . ."

Suddenly silent, my nervous neighbor stared mournfully out of the window, recalling those days of frustration.

"And did you ever find her?" I asked.

"Did I ever find her?" he repeated, coming to.

"Anka. Did you ever find her?"

"Oh, of course," he said with a frown. "One day I collected my wits and went to see Milica the washerwoman. And there she was, asleep in a hovel, without a care in the world, as if she had no husband, no child, no heart, no soul. I woke her charily. What could I do? When honor and sincerity fail, one turns to diplomacy. But she responded with stories from the streets and ditties from the cafés. I invited her home with me, but her eyes clouded over and she refused. I cursed her heart and soul with what was left of mine. We parted for good. I did not know then what I later learnt, namely, that the fellow from Dubrovnik was behind the door all the time. Though as a man of intelligence and experience I should have known, for while the sun takes only ten minutes to set in nature, it takes ten years in a woman's heart. Or as the Germans say, '*Schwer ist die Vergangenheit der alten Liebe.*' Yes, I should have known that the twentieth century would give us no new Lucrece!"

From Banova Jaruga to Novska

My nervous neighbor gave a theatrical wave of the hand and turned his mournful gaze to the yellow-gray fields gliding past. When after a time he emerged from his meditation, he fixed the gaze back on me and asked, "Forgive me, but what do you do?"

"What do I do?"

"For a living, I mean."

"I'm a . . . typist."

"Strange occupation for a man."

He was right. Mine *was* a strange occupation, though I had lied about it—well, fibbed. I was embarrassed to admit I was—a writer. Amazed at the ease with which my chance companion, my perfectly ordinary fellow traveler had told his story, I suddenly felt terribly inferior. The time it would have taken me (a professional!) to invent such a story or even imitate the manner in which he told it! Was it merely a matter of chance that I'd ended up in this compartment, or was the encounter with my nervous neighbor preordained by an ironic muse to rub my nose in business I had refused to face? Being creative is no easy matter. I was sick of the anemic, lifeless prose I kept chewing and rechewing. It had lost its pleasant, indefinable sweetness the way a fresh stick of chewing gum loses its flavor, but I chewed on, lacking the courage to spit it out, on and on, the same old stick, pushing, pulling, blowing bubbles, always the same, rewriting myself. And the saddest part of it was that my colleagues did no better! Though they knew how to make virtues of their faults, and I kept losing ground because of my old-fashioned feeling that the whole undertaking was simply behind the times. I had discovered the rules dishonest. I was simply behind the times. I had discovered the rules of the game, but could no longer bring myself to join the senseless, third-division heat around the literary track. That's why I told my nervous neighbor I was a typist. It wasn't even a fib, really. It was the way I felt.

From Novska to Nova Gradiška

"Maybe that's why you're so depressed!" said my nervous neighbor. "Believe me, it's not what a man *does*, it's what he is that counts!" He took another packet of sunflower seeds from his pocket. "Anka certainly proves that."

"Yes, well, tell me how things turned out," I said.

"Whenever I thought of that cursed night in Dubrovnik when she so frivolously, so improvidently gambled and lost the lily of her valley, her *virgo intacta* virtue, I knew she was doomed to a life of erotic excess. The moral anguish of it all! To think that while I slept the sleep of the just with my innocent child, that inveterate sinner and her latest cretin flame were indulging in orgiastic practices in my nuptial bed, perverting the psychic functions of sexual behavior!

"I was on the point of taking poison, killing myself, for I was no longer a human being, I was all *fluidum amoris* and emotion, all pain as deadly as arsenic and my fallen wife's phariseeism. Wandering in the regions of ardent love and despair, my diseased soul would keen in paroxysms of melancholy and compose epistles to Anka, epistles in which I did not choose my thoughts or formulate them, give them words, as I was wont, but simply stated with no poetic frills that I loved her and wished her to return. She sent them back unopened. Insulted and injured, I suffered a bout of melancholia and like René Descartes I took to doubting everything but doubt itself, everything but the doubt that my wife lay in the unbridled embrace of an idiot, cynic, or swine, who by dint of his status or wealth had engaged her for a single, callous, sinful night. That I could not doubt, for she had an absolute prerogative on moral depravity! Yet much as she tortured me and tortures me still, vivisecting my soul, resecting my brain, I could not forget her. I had all but breathed my last for her, for that dissolute, degenerate woman. "Take me to the madhouse!" I felt like shouting with Friedrich Nietzsche. "Let me forget what she was to me and I to her!" Yet I swallowed my pride and hid my subjectivity beneath the pathological emotions born of love spurned and clinically dangerous depression. I, a child of logical thought, sent her one last missive to the effect that I was fed up with everything but most of all with life, which missive, though she refused to read it, I wrote out of unspeakable pain: I still loved her, loved her with a love that bordered on fetishism, no, went beyond it, for in the frenzy of that love I spoke of the no-more-than-average intelligence of a basically coarse woman in absurdly inflated, hyperbolic terms—an egregious error on my part, because she began to believe me. Psychologists agree that praise spoils a woman, inflames her vanity, and produces a highly deleterious effect on her psychic and emotional make-up. Supremely confident of my clearly unnatural love, Anka trampled on her duties as a mother and on the feelings of a sensitive soul. Only now do I see how sterile her conception of maternal and uxorial obligations actually was. What love she felt for her child and me was more coercive than noble or sincere. In her petty, sick, feminine mind she assumed that the prodigious love and burning heart of a demigod would mask her crass cruelty and that in my despair I would stain our barren nuptial bed with my blood and the blood of our offspring! But as a child of reason and light, a Gnostic, and a self-respecting human being, I was far from giving in to the perverse instincts of a woman. I sensed from the outset that she was vain enough to hope our marriage would end in the obituary column. Well then, her will be done: I would raise the veil of my married life and show it in all its Edenic state of nature, though minus the sensational blood-spattered tragic incidents she might have wished to see included."

From Nova Gradiška to Slavonski Brod

"I'm not boring you, am I?" my nervous neighbor asked, interrupting his monologue.

"Not in the least."

"I've got to see a man about a dog," he said and left the compartment.

I opened the window and took a breath of fresh air. My neighbor hadn't bored me; he'd worn me out. Without realizing it, he'd been a constant stimulus. As he sat there embellishing his sad, bare tale with verbiage, I conceived a desire to write a story about him. That's right—about him. So I wasn't washed up after all. And this time I'd avoid the trap we contemporary writers had fallen into. How right our predecessors were to let their curiosity run wild and put life down on paper! But then copying from life lost its appeal, came to be seen as shameful, passé. Literature was drowning in itself, when in fact it was as easy as pie. All you had to do was take the first train and wait for a story to come your way. Putting it down on paper was like copying from life. The way our predecessors did. All you needed was a decent memory . . .

My nervous neighbor returned. The compartment was quite cold and I tried to close the window, but it was stuck and he jumped up to help me. Just then the train jerked to a halt and we flew into each other's arms.

"Terribly sorry," said my neighbor.

"It's nothing really," I said.

We took our seats. The train started up again, and my neighbor went on with his story.

"You know, those five years my wife kept me in her thrall with addictive love and fictive fidelity left a gaping wound in my life. Her dark past and general debauched nature left no room for doubt about her promiscuity, though I didn't receive proof positive of it until the end of those five purblind years, when she revealed the secret of her sinful night in Dubrovnik and the fee she earned not only from that bon vivant but from his brother as well.

"And that wasn't all. Her depravity demanded ever new sacrifices of me. Among the myriad vices she harbored within her much tarnished soul was the perverse pleasure she took in making me jealous. Did you know that when the wife of none other than Fyodor Dostoevsky told him she had deceived him he leapt at her like a madman, tore the chain from her throat, and drew a gun on her. And when he learnt it was merely a bad joke, he said coldly but sternly, 'Never do that again! Do you hear me? I won't vouch for myself.' If that is how the great philosopher of the steppes reacted, how could I react otherwise?

"Only now do I see that Anka did not even deserve a normal intelligent man, to say nothing of a man like me! She certainly did not deserve a man who lives a pure, spiritual life and lacks all contact with brutal reality. That is why she took such parasitic advantage of my mind and my soul. That is why I was both 'god' and 'louse' to her. Even Napoleon, whose genius is beyond dispute, was a 'louse' vis-à-vis the sexual imperative of his wife, Marie-Louise. Why, had I been Socrates, John Chrysostom, or Kant, to say nothing of Edgar Allan Poe, Oscar Wilde, Byron, Baudelaire, and Knut Hamsun, she would have despised me still, because she lacked intelligence of the soul and wallowed in moral and intellectual decadence.

"Anka so underestimated the ideal and reduced everything to the most material of bases, her platform for human existence, that she would rather I sold shoelaces, padlocks, or candles than took to market the loftiest commodity man can produce: his literary efforts, that is, his intellect plus bits and pieces of his heart, drops of his tears! I bitterly regret that my wife cared more for the coin of the realm, that she preferred *Wienerschnitzel* to the music of my pen and *Schweineschnitzel* to my *exercises de style*."

"Excuse me," I broke in.

"What is it?" he said, frowning again at the interruption.

"Excuse me, but what do you do?"

"What do I do?"

"For a living, I mean."

"I'm a writer," he shot back, "or rather I plan to be one."

"Ah," I said, my mouth falling open.

"Now where did I leave off?" he said without a smile.

"At the point where your Anka preferred *Wienerschnitzel* to the music of your pen."

"Oh, yes . . . How was she to know that laurel wreaths are only for the deceased and that Spinoza lived for fifty years on a few farthings a day? That is why Nietzsche says, 'One pays dearly for immortality.' That is why one dies many times in a life.

"By the way, vice had put down such deep roots in her soul that she lost her self-image as both woman and mother. Not that she had ever been impressed by moral adages. If I had told her what Nietzsche said about woman being a riddle whose answer is motherhood, she would surely have stuck out her tongue at me. Even the sage of Yasnaya Polyana would have wept at the moral dissipation and maternal dereliction of my very derelict wife.

"I feel certain she will pay for indulging in debauchery and jeopardizing the sanctity of her womanhood. She is a beast and deserves only derision! I feel that every woman who falls into erotic excess should be deprived of her civil rights and, if she is a mother, of the right to bring up her children. For how can a morally impaired mother bring up a morally healthy child? Her behavior is bound to stimulate a kind of erotic hemotropism, and she will fall victim to her own flirtations.

"Psychologists assure us that forgiving one's wife her sins requires true heroism. Well, I say that if our society continues to tolerate current moral practices, every bachelor will need to turn hero the day after he marries. Thus I would, with Lenin, legalize free love—as long as legitimate marriage was punishable by fine or imprisonment. It would make for a good deal less pain and tragedy.

"And even though, following Nietzsche, I wash my hands after coming into contact with people who consider themselves believers, I heartily subscribe to at least one tenet of Christianity: Thou shalt not commit adultery! I would, however, propound and propagate the Platonic concept of love and apply it to marital relations, for is it not Plato who says, 'Woman exercises such an influence on man that she determines his character'? Yes, I agree with Plato and admit that with her I was no better than a rake. But now that she is gone, I am a new man. A sure sign that Plato was right."

From Slavonski Brod to Vinkovci
My nervous neighbor raised a finger as if to make a point, and I took advantage of the pause to rise and say, "I've got to see a man about a dog."

"Go on, then. I'll be here."

I was glad I had to wait for the toilet. My fellow traveler was tired: his story had lost its rhythm. I wished the blonde would come back, and the cannon man. My nervous neighbor was getting on my nerves, smothering me with his palaver. I dawdled as long as I could. I took an aspirin for my headache, but in the end I had to return to the compartment.

"Here I am," I mumbled.

"You certainly took long enough."

I didn't like his tone. My plan to write a story about him popped like a balloon. In fact, I couldn't wait to get rid of him. "How far are you going?" I asked, lighting another cigarette.

"To Šid."

"Well, what happened next?" I asked gingerly, wondering whether I could withstand the verbal torture as far as Sid.

"Where did I leave off?"

"At Plato, if I'm not mistaken."

"Yes, well, if you really want to know what happened next, all I can say is—nothing. While I was struggling body and soul to find my way out of the labyrinth of thoughts and obligations arising from her departure, I received a letter from her announcing that she had been proposed to by a butcher! Unable to find spiritual sustenance in my literary endeavours, she sought it in pigs' entrails and cows' hoofs. Et tu, Brute? You too, Anka?

"Only now do I realize that instead of raising a savage woman from the depths of crime and depravity I should have followed Maestro Paganini's precedent and used a stiletto on her, my *amata*. I should have done so regardless of whether the darkest of dungeons awaited me as the galleys of Genoa awaited him. I should have done so to rid society of a hotbed of crime.

"On the other hand, poor Byron did not become Byron until he broke with his cynical and hypocritical wife, and Oscar Wilde did not become the demiurge of style and sensitivity until his sinner woman left him as my Anka left me. So no matter how unbearable, how abhorrent—abhorrent to the point of banality—I found the sufferings that resulted from her deed, no matter how they deadened my ambition and my will to indulge in any sort of creative labor, I resolved nonetheless to write, to offer the public 'pieces of my heart, drops of my tears.' And given the fact that, as Lorand has pointed out, brilliant people are not always lucky in love, indeed, are often unhappily married (that is, they can impress the world but not their wives), I resolved to take up my pen and write the death notice of my once beloved bride and pride of my heart, who, though still very much alive and well, was now dead for me. The only way I could quell my blistering, agonizing emotions was to lay my love in its grave and tell the world to scorn the mother who abandons her own flesh and blood!

"Oh, I know that a cynic will come forth and say that the sincerity with which I profess my marital problems is abnormal. Well, what do you expect from literary pigmies or, rather, literary idiots, morons, moral robbers and confidence men! For a cool-headed Gnostic, however, any attempt at concealment is a vice, and he says what he must from a position far above the mentally incompetent attacks of your literary 'Praetorians' (read 'ignoramuses').

"No, I thought, that *femme fatale* is not going to turn a Gnostic into a mental patient. And my heart, my feelings gave way to common sense. Hard, cold reason told me Anka was now dead for me, and I, like a lion, who never looks back at a victim it has missed, I can say once and for all, 'Get thee gone, and never darken my door again!' "

From Vinkovci to Šid

At that, my nervous neighbor stood up and gave me his hand. He took me by surprise.

"Good-bye. I must be on my way."

"But we haven't come to your station."

"I've got to get my things ready."

I took his hand. He cleared his throat one last time and left the compartment. I didn't know what to think. He'd left so quickly, unexpectedly. Now that he was gone, I started toying again with the idea of writing a story about him. I liked the old-fashioned device of the train setting. I'd have to find ways of breaking up the long monologues, giving it a rhythm of its own. Maybe I should come up with a social angle as well. It's not a particularly attractive topic, but if I brought in a few more characters, chance passengers, I could hold a mini-symposium on marriage. Right there in the compartment. Yes, I might be able to make something of my nervous neighbor after all. As material. Raw material.

When the train stopped in Šid, I opened the window to catch one last glance of him. He looked up at me as he stepped off the train, and waved. I waved back, lit a cigarette, and sat down. When I stood up to close the window, I saw his arms fluttering in the air. He was rushing towards the exit with—no! the blonde at his heels! Well, well. I certainly never thought it would end like that! The train lurched forward, and I sat and stared at the picture postcard in the frame just above the place where my nervous neighbor had sat. It might as well have read "Greetings from the Back of Beyond." Now there was a story for you! The kind you'd pick up at a railway kiosk.

From Šid to Stara Pazova

Suddenly the door opened and in came the man who had left his cannon with me.

"Where'd she go?" he growled.

"Who?" I asked.

"The blonde, damn it!"

"I think she got out at Šid. Why?"

The cannon man collapsed on the seat. He was breathing hard, plainly drunk.

"Fleeced me, the bitch."

"Really? How much did she get?"

"I don't want to talk about it. Everything I had on me."

He spread his arms, shrugged his shoulders, and shook his head. I didn't know what to say.

"You should have known! You should have known by the looks of her."

He kept shaking his head and breathing hard.

"It—how shall I say—it comes with the image. It had to happen."

Judging from the look he gave me, he did not take well to my attempt at consolation.

"So it had to happen, eh? It had to happen. Five hundred deutschmarks! Five hundred fucking marks! Not counting the drinks I bought her at the bar."

His eyes bored into me.

"And a ham omelette."

I no longer tried to comfort him. I just made a sober suggestion.

"Why not go to the police?"

"Oh, come off it. It's a lost cause."

We didn't exchange a word until Stara Pazova, when he stood up and I said, "Good luck."

"Oh, come off it," he said, slamming the door.

I was alone again. Only then did I notice he'd forgotten his cannon. The train was under way, but I tried to stick it out of the window. It wouldn't go.

"Your caaannon!" I shouted. "Your forgot your caaan-non!"

He turned, paused, then said something and made a dismissive gesture.

"What was that?" I shouted, still trying to shove the cannon through the window. As luck would have it, the window got stuck.

"Fuck the cannon!" I heard my second neighbor's angry voice cry out, but by then I could no longer see him. The train clattered on towards Belgrade.

From Stara Pazova to Belgrade

I was upset. I felt sorry for the man who'd lost not only his five hundred marks but his cannon as well. I needed a cigarette, but the pack was empty. I reached into my pocket—my left pocket, my right pocket, my left breast pocket . . . My wallet was gone! I checked again: left pocket, right pocket, breast pockets . . . No, not a sign of it! Then I came upon a scrap of paper in the left breast pocket and removed it as if it were a dead mouse. It contained the following typed (I seemed to have received the fifth carbon copy) message:

Dear Fellow Traveler,

I take the liberty of charging whatever sum you may have had in your wallet for my free interpretation of excerpts from the as yet to be published novel *The Sinner Woman*. Do not worry about your personal documents: I shall return them to you C.O.D. Many thanks for your lyrical understanding. As a prospective member of the literary community I found our trip, *inter alia*, an artistically rewarding experience.

Yours sincerely,
"Tolstoy"

And so, satisfying one of the givens of the railway novel, I sat in an empty compartment staring at the black husks decorating my left shoe. When I raised my foot in the direction of the window, the shoe took the form of a shiny, phantasmagoric fossil. One hand held the scrap of paper—the proof of my active participation in the journey genre, third class—while the other inadvertently stroked the cannon. Suddenly someone in the neighboring compartment struck up a folk song . . .

There I sat—clattering on to Belgrade one fine October day, with a cannon, a spotted shoe, a scrap of paper, and an empty cigarette packet—freshly fleeced of all my documents and three hundred and fifty dinars, my eyes fixed on the view of "The Back of Beyond," and suddenly I was overcome by a vague feeling of ecstasy: The world was full of fellow writers!

LEND ME YOUR CHARACTER

Is a pen a symbolic penis?

Relations between Writers

You should never have anything to do with writers. But I'm afraid I did. One day I ran into Petar, a writer. He gave me a friendly thump on the shoulder and invited me for a coffee.

"By the way, I read that story of yours," he said.

"Really?"

"It's good."

"You like it?"

"Yeah. Especially the main character. I was wondering . . ."

"Yes?"

"She's a great character, and I thought . . ."

"You thought what?"

"I'm writing a story, you know, and . . ."

"What is it, for heaven's sake!" I burst out.

"Can you lend her to me?"

"What?!" I was dumbfounded.

"I need her for my story," he went on.

"What does my character have to do with your story?"

"I need her, well . . . for coital purposes," Petar said stupidly.

"Wait, you want my character for some character of yours to screw, is that what you mean?"

"Right," said Petar.

"Who is he?"

"Who?"

"What do you mean *Who*? That character of yours!"

"No big deal, just a guy who likes sex."

I took a deep breath and said decisively:

"No!"

"Why not?"

"Because I'm not going to have my character screwed by some maniac!"

"Actually," Petar dug in his heels, "a published literary work, whether yours or Shakespeare's, is public property. Everyone has the right to draw on it. It's called intertextual relations, you know what intertextual relations are, don't you? Besides, what I'm writing isn't erotic really, it's more fantastic, kind of magic realism."

"Absolutely not!"

I drank my coffee in a huff, lit a cigarette, and looked at Petar. He was looking back at me with a calm, open face, as if his proposal were the most natural thing in the world.

"Listen," I said, more gently, "why doesn't your character get it on with Anna Karenina? What's my ordinary little character compared to someone like her?"

"Come on now, you're not as ordinary as all that," the flatterer replied.

"Okay, it doesn't have to be Anna Karenina. Why doesn't he go to bed with Joan of Arc, that would be much more fantastic."

"I don't write historical novels," Petar observed.

"Well, let him screw Mother Goose then!" I snorted.

"Why can't you understand," said Petar. "A normal, basic character is just what I need. Besides, if you don't mind my saying so, in your story she's a bit, how should I put it, neglected?"

"What do you mean?"

"Just that, sexually neglected. You must know what I mean . . ."

"Huh! And your little hero's the one to put that right!" I snorted again.

"Naturally," Petar said with complete self-assurance.

I said nothing. Perhaps I should have noticed the signal: the little red light that always comes on when I meet certain members of the opposite sex. This time the light on the display panel was warning me that *this guy has potential.* But as usual I failed to notice it.

"Alright, pal, you can have her," I blurted out so quickly that I surprised myself. That's exactly what I said, "pal," thumping Petar on the shoulder. I never do that and I have no idea why I did it then. But there we were, thumping each other.

And then we parted. It was quite an idea, I had to admit. I was sorry I hadn't thought of it myself. On the way home I considered possible boyfriends for my heroine. Tom Sawyer? The Scarecrow? Winnie the Pooh? No serious writer would ever have names like this pop into her head. But I had often dreamed of a boyfriend like Winnie the Pooh myself, so I must not be a serious woman either—no serious woman would consider a brainless bear as boyfriend material. A serious woman would think of James Joyce.

Clearly I wasn't a serious writer. I had written a little book called *Alice Comes Home to Ozalj* and the only thing I really liked about it was the title. I was proud of that title, I kept pestering people to guess how many other titles it contained. Things might have been better if I was a serious woman but that, as I say, was by no means certain.

The Writer and Life's Roadblocks
On Saturday I ran out to the nearest kiosk and bought the *Evening News.* I could hardly wait to get home, settle down, and read Petar's story.

His story had a promising title: "The Hot Tongue." Its

main characters were named Peter and Ulla. I read the story straight through and it took my breath away. I called Petar immediately.

"Terrible!" I hissed into the receiver.

"You've read the story?"

"Yes. Crap!" I said telegraphically.

"You don't like it?"

"Total shit."

"Can I come and see you?"

"Yes, urk," I gargled into the receiver, and hung up.

Still in shock, I hurried to straighten up my offended appearance a bit. I put on a respectable little black dress, as though dressing for the theater, and placed the *Evening News* into my left hand, rolled up into a truncheon. Petar appeared at the door with a bunch of flowers. I deliberately didn't put the flowers in a vase of water, but I did offer Petar a drink and sat down, still holding the *Evening News* in my hand.

"You didn't need to borrow her for a piece of trash like this," I said.

"Why are you using such vulgar language to describe my work?" asked Petar calmly, like an elementary school grammar teacher, not a writer.

"Because my character gives herself to yours after a single . . ."

I opened the *Evening News* and announced, as though reading out a verdict: " 'After a single moist glance . . .' Please! Talk about male fantasy! Who ever heard of such a thing? And the hero's name is *Peter*! Come on, we're not children."

"Wait a second," Petar tried to interrupt.

"Why should I wait! Male writers always take some female character just so their male character can end up on the floor with her, behind the counter, rolling in a pool of beer! And all they need is one moist glance!"

"What book does that happen in again?"

"It doesn't matter which book! You'd all like to roll around in pools of beer, that's what you'd like!" I shouted, waving the *Evening News* and taking a gulp of Petar's drink by mistake.

"All this fuss over a simple erotic story," said Petar in a conciliatory tone.

"You mean pornographic," I specified.

"Why pornographic?"

I opened the *Evening News* again, as evidence.

"In just five pages Peter and Ulla *moan* fifteen times, they are *flushed* three times, he *cries out with passion* twice, she *shrieks with pleasure* twice. He *enters* her three times, while she *surrenders to his caresses* once. *Hardness* is mentioned four times, *moist* or *moistening* three times, *sweat* eight times, eight times!, *gushing* and *flowing* three times, *animal* is mentioned only once but in connection with *biting*. Then *ecstasy* twice, *salivate* twice, *pleasure* eight more times, and parts of the body—*lips, thighs, loins, armpit, belly, belly button, breasts, tongue, moles,* and *little hairs*—thirty-five times in all!"

I looked at Petar triumphantly, folding the *Evening News* into a truncheon again.

"I'm the author, I do whatever I want with my characters," Petar flared up.

"No, you can't, not where my character is concerned. I lent her to you! And I expected at least a minimal sense of responsibility on your part . . . By the way, how come she has two pairs of tits?"

"I told you my story has fantastic elements. Anyway, I have the right to exaggerate as much as I want!" Petar blustered again.

"It's because of that male exaggeration of yours that sex is what it is!" I said, sweeping the truncheon through the air, in a gesture of accusation towards my non-existent male audience.

LEND ME YOUR CHARACTER

"And what is it?" Petar asked, offended.

"Shabby, that's what," I said, thumping the bed dramatically with the *Evening News*. Petar stared at the spot I had indicated with the paper, as though expecting to find some solution there. I followed Petar's gaze myself. Then I felt something catch in my throat.

"My character deserved something better than *panting* and *heaving* under yours," I said, barely holding back my tears.

"What's the matter?" said Petar gently, sitting down beside me. "You're not going to cry, are you? Just because of an ordinary piece of fiction? Besides, she's not even your character. Didn't you notice that her name is Ulla?"

"That's true," I said, looking for a tissue.

"Yours isn't named Ulla, is she?"

"No," I sniffed.

"There, you see . . . she's not your character," whispered Petar, embracing me tenderly.

"That's not the point, I'm not crying over an individual case, I'm crying for all the female characters in the world! I'm crying generally, literary-historically, and globally, don't you understand?" I began to sob.

When Petar wiped my tears with his lips, I cried harder and harder and felt warmer and warmer and saltier and moister and softer and . . .

"Come here . . ." whispered Ulla, giving Peter a moist glance.

The Writer's Work Ethic

Two days later Petar moved in with me. There were a few more love scenes between Peter and Ulla and then Petar gave up.

"I'm not writing any more erotic stories. They're so boring, so limited."

We put away the Peter and Ulla masks before we had had much chance to play with them. I was left with a little stick in my hand—I stood there like a child who was given a lollipop stick without a lollipop, but nobody notices, they just think she's eaten the lollipop already. I gazed longingly at my imaginary stick. It was over too soon, like a bad story where the happy ending comes so fast that the reader hasn't had a chance to really want it.

Petar turned from erotic stories to a novel called *Anxieties*, something about the relationship between a certain individual and a certain social structure. He soon abandoned that idea and moved on to a novel called *Sufferings*, something about the relationship between a certain individual and himself.

Unlike Petar, I turned into an emotional pudding. In other words, I fell in love. My creative life developed according to a strange rhythm whose meaning I could never quite grasp. So for the first few days of our shared life I was always cooking something. I would get up early, while Petar was still asleep, and in the morning quiet I would carry out the little ritual of preparing breakfast with almost holy fervor. In the gray light of dawn I wrote a mysterious letter on the white lace tablecloth. Every morning I dyed boiled eggs a different color and painted love notes on them with a fine brush. I made thin, delicate fingers of butter and arranged them a different way every morning. I wrote hieroglyphs of love for Petar, without understanding them myself. I cut bread into thin slices shaped like hearts. Once I even tried to bake the bread myself, writing a love poem on the dough. The poem emerged from the oven as a bumpy, illegible mass: I could press my real language into the dough but it wouldn't take.

After that I threw myself with the same creative zeal into cleaning, washing, ironing. I spent hours and hours ironing.

I liked sheets most of all, white sheets—my unwritten pages. I ironed all my desires into them, pressing secret messages into the white linen.

Then I took to knitting and knitted Petar a quite pointless scarf several yards long.

Without knowing it, I was retracing in miniature the whole history of female literacy. Petar didn't notice the creative whirlpool spinning behind him. He was calmly developing his third idea for a novel, called *Doubts*, something about the relationship between a certain individual and certain other individuals.

Then I switched my strong but vague creative urges to food, again without understanding what was happening to me. I ate alone, hiding from Petar, because I was ashamed of that terrible, treacherous hunger. Sometimes, pretending I had an errand to run, I would sneak into the nearest pastry shop. At night, while Petar slept, I would get up and tiptoe into the kitchen in the dark. There, by the narrow strip of light from the open fridge, I would crouch and eat, sending out my desperate signals from that sad position.

One day, as Petar sat at his desk working on his new novel, I summoned up my courage, went into the room and said:

"Peter, I've been thinking about that story of yours in the *Evening News*. It wasn't such a bad story, you know . . ."

"Why do you say that all of a sudden?" Petar was surprised.

"It doesn't matter. I just think it was good, actually it was very good . . ." I stroked his hair and gave him a moist glance.

"No. You were right the first time. Pornography, it was bad pornography," he said, not noticing my subtly dropped metaphorical handkerchief. I picked it up myself and wiped my nose with it.

Weaving Life into Writing

Yes, I was an emotional pudding.

"Why don't you do some of your women's writing?" suggested Petar.

What could I tell him? That there is nothing a pitiful pudding can do but hope that someone will eat it?

Once, when I went to the pantry to get something and turned back to the kitchen to fiddle with something there, I happened to notice my smiling face in a mirror. That senseless smile shook me. I stood there confused, with an onion in my hand, trying to rewind the film. I had gone to the pantry to fetch an onion; when I bent down to take it from the basket, a little net hanging from a nail on the wall had grazed my cheek. My cheek interpreted the graze of the net as a caress and I had smiled!

And now, standing transfixed in front of the mirror, Ulla became aware of a silent film running in her consciousness. For the first time she saw, perfectly clear and sharp, those innumerable tiny actions which she performed each day without noticing. She saw herself stroking the edge of an armchair, then, holding a tomato in her hand, she saw the dramatic instant when she broke off the stalk, she saw herself gazing at the pinkish hollow where the stalk had just been like a child who spends hours peeling a scab on its knee, intrigued by the new pinkish skin underneath. She saw herself rubbing her hand on the jagged edges of metal bottlecaps, running the tips of her fingers around the edges, squirming her fingers into the hollow spaces. She saw herself in the bathroom, under a jet of warm water, collecting the drops on her lips, bending her head, pressing her lips to the back of her hand and staring for a long time at the indifferent white tiles. She saw herself rinsing cherries, taking one, licking off the drops of water, breaking off the stalk, putting the cherry in her mouth, tensely anticipating the sound of the sweet flesh bursting, caressing the stone with her tongue, rolling it around in the hollow of her lip before spitting it out into the soft pillow of her palm. She saw herself touching the wrinkled skin on warm milk, and in the same way tenderly drawing an imaginary line with her finger from the root of her own nose to its tip, holding an egg in the hollow of her hand for a long time before lowering it into boiling water, stroking her index finger with her thumb or her thumb with her index finger, stroking the edges of things, sharp, wooden edges, stroking her lower lip for hours, as though numb, thinking of who knows what . . .

The onion fell to the floor with a dull thud, the images dispersed, and all at once Ulla saw in the mirror her own solitude, her terrifying desire for touch.

"Peter!" she cried out.

Peter sat at his desk, buried in papers.

"Peter!"

She began to kiss him, touching all the edges he had on him; she rubbed the tips of her fingers around his buttons, undoing them; she stroked the edge of his ears, the edge of his nose, the edge of his wrists, lips, chin, eyebrows, then slipped further down until she came to that swollen, finger-like edge . . .

Writing as a Method of Investigating Life

Petar and I were spending an afternoon in so-called conjugal bliss. In other words, I lay reading while Petar sat at his desk writing. Eventually I put down my book.

"I had a strange dream last night," I said.

Petar pushed his chair away from the desk, took off his glasses, and looked at me inquiringly.

"I dreamed about something like a horn."

"Oh?"

"I don't know how to describe it to you. I had a little horn growing down there . . ."

"It's obvious! A phallic symbol. You're just jealous because you haven't got one. In your dream, your envy, or rather your sense of inferiority, took on the shape of a little horn, a phallic symbol," said Petar, in the tone of a gym teacher.

"It wasn't a symbol, it was a little horn," I insisted.

Petar was not very interested in my dream, but he got up from the desk, yawned, stretched, and sat down next to me.

"What are you reading?"

"A novel."

"By?"

"Stanislav."

"Stanislav's written a novel? When did it come out?"

"A few days ago."

"I didn't know that," said Petar, trying to conceal his envy. "How is it?" he asked, pretending not to care and yawning.

"The first part was something about a certain individual and a certain social structure and the second part was something about the relationship of that same individual to himself."

"Sounds boring."

"Not at all. It's got pace, it's got everything you could ask for."

"Even a plot?"

"Yes."

"Lemme see."

Petar leafed through the book, idly yawned again, and tossed it into a corner.

"Garbage," he said briefly. He suddenly came to some inner decision and put his hand on my breasts. He began to unbutton my shirt, slowly, to undo the zipper on my jeans . . . "I'll write you something better," he murmured, kissing me. "Come here . . . ."

I felt uneasy. I closed my eyes and when I opened them again they met Petar's cold, interrogating gaze.

"Everything's like a horn," said Ulla. I pulled down the zipper on her jeans. The sound split the air, hovered for a moment, then burst like a soap bubble. I unbuttoned her shirt and began running my fingers around her nipples. Ulla suddenly seemed thin and small. I didn't know how to approach her and enter her. Then she turned her back and her shoulder blade leapt out in front of me, covered with a thin layer of soft fur. I flinched a little, but then I began to nibble the tender protuberance. Still, I was afraid, because it didn't belong to Ulla. I moistened it a bit with my saliva and bit it. She cried out. Like a horn, everything's like a horn.

Suddenly Ulla began to grow. Now she was too big and again I didn't know how to approach her. She was like a gigantic whale, I even thought I smelled a strong, dark, fishy smell in my nostrils. I was frightened. But at last Ulla returned to her natural size. I touched her breast. I felt a strange stickiness on my palm. I wanted to take my hand away but her breast came with it. I kissed her lips, but our mouths stretched like chewing gum. I heard her say something but couldn't make out what it was. Strange, I thought, it doesn't hurt at all, how is it that we can breathe . . . Like a horn, everything's like a horn.

I began to need to put it into her, but I was afraid of remaining in her forever. Finally I gathered my courage and felt myself melting inside her like a tablet in a glass of water. Little bubbles tickled me, it felt good, only what should I do now, I thought, what will I do without it? I withdrew from Ulla and in its place I saw a little horn sheathed in soft, grayish deer skin . . .

"Let's stop," I said, extricating myself from Petar's embrace and lighting a cigarette. Petar and I were silent for a time, and then he said in a dull tone:

"I want to write a novel about a man who spent his life without living it. Just idling, like a car! That's what I'll call it: *Idling.*"

Who Is a Writer and Who Isn't

With time I developed a crust (just like a pudding), but still I couldn't embark on any real prose. So I directed all my creative energy to scholarly work. My articles—"A Revisionist Analysis of 'Beauty and the Beast,'" "Pinocchio: Archetype of the Male Erotic Imagination," "Why Did Anna Karenina and Emma Bovary Kill Themselves?" "The Czar's New Clothes: Mythmaking and Historical Denial in Eastern Europe," "Toad-Men and Snake-Women in the Slavic Folk Tale," "The Treatment of Woman in Contemporary Balkan Literature"—were simply preparations for my great secret project: *A Lexicon of Female Literary Characters*. And when I rushed over to my mother's one day to read her my entry on "La Dame aux Camélias," in a scholarly fervor, and when my mother cried for a full five minutes without stopping, I knew I was on the right scholarly track.

I had reached the letter L and was writing an entry on "The Little Match Girl" when I ran out of paper. Petar had gone out to buy cigarettes and I reached into the drawer of his desk . . .

Peter stood up and stretched. His back ached from sitting at his desk. His writing hadn't gone well today either. He looked around for Ulla and saw her through the half-open door of the kitchen, bathed in a shaft of light coming from the window. A slight chill ran down his spine. It was as though he were seeing her for the first time. She was bent over the kitchen table, mangling a piece of calf's liver on a cutting board. She was removing the skin and it kept sticking to her fingers. She angrily shook the bloody membrane from her fingers and cut the liver into thin strips. Sharp, hard lines appeared on her face. Peter saw Ulla clearly now: slightly sweaty, with a double chin from bending her head, slightly hunched back . . . Peter felt ashamed, because of his unintentional spying, the pitiful spectacle, the treacherous light. He suddenly saw a stranger, an unknown woman who was not Ulla. He felt a powerful sense of revulsion well up in him, and, with a vague sense of relief, he felt his love for Ulla slowly dissolve, like a tablet in a glass of water. He sat there for a long time. And then he wished that someone would quietly close the door and Ulla would disappear, fade like an overdeveloped photograph, vanish quietly, painlessly, as though she had never even existed.

"What's this?" I asked when Petar appeared at the door.

Petar calmly took off his coat and asked innocently:

"What?"

"This!" I shrieked furiously, thrusting the treacherous page into his face.

"You can see for yourself, it's a piece of fiction," replied Petar, reddening slightly.

"I presume it's the opening of a new novel about a certain writer and his relationship with . . ."

"Shut up!" said Petar roughly.

I held back my tears.

Petar said nothing, smoking, with bowed head.

"Can't you see how awful this is, Petar? We're not living, we spend all our time describing each other," I said in a husky voice and dropped the page onto the floor.

"Whoever said life is for living! And what does living mean anyway?" Petar shot back bitterly.

"So why don't you dissolve once and for all like your stupid metaphorical Alka-Seltzers!" I shouted.

"Shut up," Petar shouted.

"Pitiful pen pusher!" I screamed.

"Pathetic literary housewife!" he screamed.

"Third-rate literary thief!"

"Functionary!"

"Hack!"

"Loser!"

"No-talent con artist!"

"Piss-poor poetess!"

"Impotent plagiarist!"

"Female scribbler!"

"Short-story jerk-off!"

"Hormonal ink spiller!"

"Stupid metaphorist!"

"I hate you!"

"And I hate you!"

"I hate you the most!"

1.

"The game goes on! Come here!" Ulla said in a husky voice, licking her upper lip with the tip of her tongue, and giving Peter a moist glance.

2.

"The game goes on!" Ulla said and opened the door with a powerful kick. Ulla entered the room with a tan, broad-shouldered man in a black leather jacket and leather pants tightly hugging his body. Ulla tossed a cascade of her long blonde hair with a cold gleam in her eyes.

Peter turned pale and squinted fearfully through his glasses.

"Tie him up!" Ulla ordered the young man. The young man leapt, like a panther, found a clothesline, and tied Peter tightly to a chair.

"Ulla! What are you doing?" cried Peter. "Have you gone crazy!?"

"The grinder!" Ulla ordered. The young man appeared at once with a meat grinder in his hand.

"Right!" said Ulla, paying no heed to Peter's horrified stare. "And now for a little game with this pig . . ."

3.
The game goes on, Ulla thought bitterly, rolling a jagged metal bottlecap between her fingers. Then she put down the bottlecap thoughtfully, rolled a sheet of paper into the typewriter, and began to type:

"You should never have anything to do with writers. But I'm afraid I did . . ."

Fluid, Ash, and Literature

Towards five o'clock the day grew cooler; I shut my windows and went back to my writing.

At six o'clock in came my great friend Neno; he was on his way to the Writers' Club.

He said: "I say! Are you working?"

I replied: "I am writing."

"And what is it?"

"A story."

"Would I like it?"

"No."

"Too clever?"

"Too boring."

"Why write it, then?"

"If I didn't, who would?"

"Still more confessions?"

"Hardly any."

"What then?"

"Sit down," I said.

And when he sat down, I went to pull the page out of the typewriter and read him what I had just written. A strange thing happened: I pulled out white silk handkerchiefs as though from a magician's hat, one after another, each one discreetly perfumed with despair.

De l'horrible danger de la lecture

(author's notes)

Katica Rodeš spat into her dried up and dusty inkwell and mixed it with the other end of her pen as though mixing a roux in a saucepan, and then spent the whole of the following week copying some expressions out of her Miscellany of Love, and in the end she wove into that whole gingerbread hodgepodge a little truth, bitter as wormwood.
—Miroslav Krleža, "The Battle at Bistrica Lesna"

The collection of stories *Life Is a Fairy Tale* was first published in Zagreb in 1983. In this edition, I freshened up the author's notes and added a story, "The Kharms Case," but the rest is more or less the same. The rest of the book, I mean; everything else has changed. The country where the book was first published no longer exists: it has split into five new countries. The author of the book no longer lives in Zagreb, but in Amsterdam, where, surrounded by the Dutch language, I continue to write in my mother tongue. But my mother tongue too has divided, in three. The changes that have taken place sometimes strike me as more fantastic than the metamorphoses that happen in my stories, and they may help explain my newly acquired passion for afterwords and footnotes. I am haunted by a constant sense of needing to explain things, because Time revises faster than I do. Some things seem much older than they are, and some much younger. This afterword is an attempt, albeit a vain attempt, to keep up with the speed around me.

When my stories were first published, the word *post-modernism*, uncertain of its meaning, was gaining currency in literary-critical circles. The concept had penetrated into my native literary environment from haphazardly translated foreign articles. For the local critics, postmodernism was something like gossip from a distant literary world, and so instead of adopting the concept itself they adopted *gossip* about it. Using my own "Author's Notes" as the only relevant source, critics concluded that this collection was a typical "postmodern construct," which at the time was merely a polite phrase for plagiarism. Very few critics troubled themselves to investigate the relationships between the original models and the "constructs." That would have required them to read, and nothing irritates critics more than an author inviting them to remember texts they are assumed to have read. In short, in a literary milieu that takes for granted that literature grows out of real life it was not easy to drive home the simple idea that literature grows out of literature. Books have always had their roots in other books, and they still do. If life had to write novels, there wouldn't be any.

As far as the subject matter is concerned, it seemed to me at the time that I was writing an erotic book. Leafing through my native literature, I discovered to my astonishment that the only writers who spontaneously touch on erotic themes are children's writers.[1] So I bravely took on

---

[1] Here is a passage from the fairy tale "Stribor's Wood" by Ivana Brlić Mažuranić: "The old woman was amazed that things were like this at night, and she went into the kitchen. When she got there, the kindling in the hearth burst into flame, and a crowd of Little People—tiny men barely a foot high—started dancing around the fire. They wore sheepskin coats and peasant shoes as red as the blaze, their hair and beards were gray as ash, and their eyes were bright as the glowing coals. More and more of them emerged from the flames, each from his own piece of kindling. As they emerged, they laughed and shrieked, they flung themselves round the fireplace, squealing with merriment and joining the dance. And dance they did—on the hearth, in the ashes, on the chair, round the jug, over the bench! Fast! Faster! Squealing, shrieking, pushing, shoving. They spilt the ash, tipped over the yeast, scattered the flour—all

the literary task of cultivating a new genre. I wrote six stories by altering other stories: copying someone else's story and interpolating my own text, or writing my own story and interpolating someone else's text, or writing someone else's text and interpolating my own story, or letting someone else's text write me.

Today I still think that the act of repeating or copying is a deeply erotic one. This idea of the erotic is, admittedly, a bit eccentric, but that does not make it any less erotic. How would the history of literature have developed over the centuries, after all, if it did not give pleasure?

A more well-known type of eroticism is in play as well. My book was written in the language of a minor literature, in an environment which sees writing as an unnatural activity, and all the literary "-isms" which have wandered into my native literature have come from outside, including postmodernism. The only authentic "-ism" which grows naturally, like a weed, and thanks to which this minor literature still survives, is sadomasochism.[2]

As far as narrative strategy is concerned, I would rather to invoke the unwitting postmodernism of my distant forebear, the literary heroine Katica Rodeš, than any acknowledged

---

for sheer joy. The fire in the hearth flared and glowed, crackled and leaped, and the old woman watched in wonder. She did not regret the spilled salt or the yeast, but rejoiced in the merriment God had sent to console her."

[2] So as not to get bogged down in grim national examples, I shall quote a positive instance of the link between culture and sadomasochism, and one which is not Croatian but Chinese. I once met a Chinese poet who suffered from a terrible toothache but stubbornly refused to go to a dentist out of profound respect for Wittgenstein. He was convinced that the spirit of Wittgenstein had moved into his tooth, and he preferred to endure the pain rather than disturb the great philosopher with a dentist's drill.

postmodern models. In what follows, I shall acquaint my readers with the ingredients which I mixed together in my literary saucepan, with the caveat that ingredients do not, of course, make the dish.

A Hot Dog in a Warm Bun

This story was directly inspired by Gogol's story "The Nose," just as Gogol's story was directly inspired by the literary and extraliterary "noseology" of his time. Truly interested readers may refer to V. V. Vinogradov's exhaustive and movingly intriguing study, "The Theme and Composition of Gogol's *The Nose.*"

It is true that I used the most vulgar form of substitution. It was really not difficult to make the connection, nor, indeed, was it difficult for Gogol's numerous interpreters to find all sorts of things in the vanished nose of Major Kovaljov. I decided on this crude substitution neither to hold myself up as Gogol's equal nor, heaven forbid, to hold anything against him. My story is an attempt to turn psychoanalytical-interpretative gossip about Gogol's "The Nose" into literature, in an indirect defense of the great Russian writer. The story also expresses my attitude toward a categorization of writers which was popular in my literary milieu at the time, into *writers with balls* and *writers without balls.* Unbelievably, this division is still equally popular there today.

I could, actually, have settled for a story from real life. I knew an individual of the male sex who suffered from an awkward and unusual fixation. This individual of the male sex used to appear in public with a handkerchief covering his nose, convinced that instead of a nose he had a penis. I don't know whether he also thought that instead of a penis he had a nose. Fortunately, this individual of the male sex was successfully cured. I couldn't use this incident because one mustn't try to transform life so directly into literature.

That is to say, I did not know then what I was to discover later: that life imitates literature and not the other way
round. The proof came into my hands fourteen years after
the story was published. In a weekly magazine I came across
an article about the case of the forty-seven-year-old Prayoon
Eklang from the little town of Korat in Thailand, whose wife
cruelly punished his unfaithfulness by cutting off his penis
with a kitchen knife. The article suggested that this custom
of amputation had reached almost epidemic proportions in
Thailand. According to some data, between 1980 and the
present day at least a hundred cases of amputation had been
reported. Thai people enjoy telling the story of the woman
who fed her husband's unfaithful penis to her ducks. In the
Thai language there is a saying: *Be good or I'll feed the ducks.*
Incidents of penis-chopping-off are usually not reported, so
it is hard to confirm the real dimensions of this cruel custom.
Experts in the Department of Microsurgery at the Siriraj
Hospital in Bangkok have perfected the technique of suc-
cessful transplantation of the estranged member; Dr. Surasak Muangsombut, head of plastic surgery, has personally
succeeded in reattaching nine decapitated organs. "Never-
theless, we are working under great pressure," Dr. Surasak
stated. "If we don't succeed in transplanting a finger, the
patient has four left. With a penis we have only one chance."
If the amputated organ is found in time, the chances of a suc-
cessful transplantation are great, say the Bangkok surgeons.
One wife threw the amputated member into the toilet and
flushed it, but her husband immediately called the plumbers,
who fortunately found it. The transplantation was a complete
success.

As for Prayoon Eklang, he did not find his member. He
became a monk in a Buddhist monastery. "The Buddha has

taught us that the pleasures of life are the cause of much un-happiness," said Prayoon for the newspapers.

There is another detail connected with the story "A Hot Dog in a Warm Bun" that I would like to mention, this one of native origin. The destiny of a fellow writer hooked itself to my story like a burr. Maybe it was thanks to my indirect liter-ary influence that he became a fellow writer at all. The ways of creativity are often mysterious and the muses capricious.

In 1983, when my book was first published, I received an unpleasant letter from an unknown correspondent, a certain Ante Matić. This Matić attacked me violently for having sullied his noble name by giving the surname Matić to my *vulgar* heroine (the one who only cared about "hot dog dicks," as the writer of the letter formulated my heroine's activity). Soon afterwards I met the sender of the letter, which was not difficult to arrange since he was a mail clerk in the publishing house which brought out my book. I tried to explain to Ante, a bony, bearded, and angry fellow countryman, that I had chosen the surname Matić precisely because it was so ordinary.

"Why didn't you call her Nada Dimić?"[3]

"Because that's the name of a textile factory," I said.

"You have sullied my honorable surname!" he insisted.

"How could I, the name Matić takes up half the Zagreb phone book," I defended myself.

This mention of the phone book nearly earned me a slap from the living relative of my fictional heroine. I soon forgot

---

[3] Nada Dimić was a young communist tortured and murdered by Croatian fascists during the Second World War. From 1945 to 1991, she had a posthumous life as a "national hero." In 1991, with the coming of the new government and sudden unpopularity of anti-fascist heroes, her name was erased from the collective memory.

the incident, although not entirely: not a single one of my subsequent characters has the surname Matić.

Exactly seven years after this incident (in 1990, therefore), I stumbled over the surname Matić again. That was a year of great political changes. In the heap of names of fervent Croatian nationalists hurling themselves in a euphoric stampede towards positions of power, the name of Ante Matić happened to catch my eye. As a zealous member of the ruling party, Ante Matić had clawed his way up to the office of cultural advisor in Podsused, a small village outside Zagreb. There was an interview in the paper under the title "The Vaclav Havel of Podsused" (in Croatia back then self-styled Havels were springing up like mushrooms!). It turned out that, in addition to his regular cultural and political activities, Matić had found the time to publish a novel called *Mounting the Motherland*. The novel received positive reviews and the full attention of the literary community, the sort of attention deserved by a writer with such (national) *balls*.

Let me finally add a detail that will give scholarly weight to my otherwise rather light story. Anthropologists who are concerned with culture-bound syndromes have discovered an unusual phenomenon, which has various names, including the medical name GRS (genital retraction syndrome), but which is still best known by the Malaysian name *koro*. Chinese versions of koro are usually translated as "shrinking penis" or "turtle." The person suffering from koro (always male; the syndrome has not been observed among women) believes that he has lost his genitals. Episodes of koro are individual, but they occasionally occur as epidemics, as for example the great koro epidemic which began in Singapore in 1967 and then spread to Hainan Island and the Leizhou

Peninsula in the Guandong Province of China. The most recent epidemic of koro was in India. Although the koro phenomenon is geographically confined to China, Indonesia, and India, the anthropologist James Edwards reports "the strange case of a Russian man whose penis spontaneously retracted into his abdomen, but it reemerged by the next day, and did not repeat its disappearing act."

Who Am I?

This story is an example of the widespread literary exploitation of Lewis Carroll's *Alice in Wonderland*. Some 20% of the text is taken from that book. The sentence "The magician was tall" is taken from "The Old Woman," by Daniil Kharms. Kharms's story is in turn an example of the literary exploitation of Dostoevsky's *Crime and Punishment*.

Life is a Fairy Tale

Two chance newspaper texts were particularly influential in making this story: an amusing little news item[4] and a letter to a columnist.[5]

---

[4] "Love and the emotions it arouses cause the secretion of endorphines, substances similar to the amphetamines that stimulate the central nervous system. It has been established that this substance is found in large quantities in chocolate. Experts from the New York State Institute of Psychiatry have concluded that the majority of people who treat the pains of love with chocolate in fact do so instinctively in order to compensate for the reduced amount of endorphines in their systems." ("Love and Chocolate," *Vecernji list*, 12 December 1979)

[5] "Dear Doctor, I am writing for advice about a serious problem. I have noticed that my member has begun to grow, leading to unforeseen complications. I hope you can help me. Will it keep growing? And what exactly is the matter with it? The current length of my member is 15 ins. I hope that this situation will not get any worse. —Josko" (*Zum-Reporter*, 21 March 1979)

The thought that writers are lonely beings who need to be encouraged belongs to Jorge Luis Borges.

"The Story of a Complete Gentleman" by the Nigerian writer Amos Tutuola is one of my favorite stories.

"A barometric low hung over the Atlantic. It moved eastward . . ." is the opening of *The Man Without Qualities* by Robert Musil.

Pionirka, Jadran, Albert, Marina, Samo Ti (Only You), Medo, Plazma, Domaćica, Florida, Frondi, and Fontana were the names of cookies and sweets produced in Yugoslavia at the time when the story was written. Many of these products no longer exist today, because the country, like Božica's cookies, has been broken and thrown into the pile of historical rejects. I am leaving in the names out of personal nostalgia.

The Christmas story is my favorite genre, increasingly so, I confess, with time. And, as the years pass, I like the idea of the writer as a literary Father Christmas more and more.

As I reread this story I was astounded by my own far-sightedness. For example, the story contains several monetary figures—salaries, rent, and so on—and in the first edition I did not state the currency. At the time, it would have been Yugoslav dinars; today, the currency in use is the Croatian kuna; but I can simply leave the numbers as they were. Because you never can tell with money—or, for that matter, countries.

I also experienced the effect of dislocated reading, an experience I had previously had when reading other people's writing. As I read, there came into my head for some quite unknown reason the image of "socialist apartments," although there is no mention of them in the story. I felt a lump in my throat, and suddenly saw before me the exciting image of those dusty ficus plants, little curtains, crocheted doilies, embroidered throws, knickknacks on the TV set, three-cushion settees (ah, yes, *settees*!), sectional cabinets (a wooden "composition" against the wall, 9' x 8'6"), kitchens in the shape of the letter L (*L-shaped kitchens*!), climbing plants on the walls whose journeys the tenants defined with nails and strings, songbirds in cages, plastic rugs, synthetic bearskin rugs whose static electricity fills the air, ah, that heavy sweet air of little socialist apartments . . . I saw the people sitting squeezed into their *L-shaped kitchens*: each male with a cigarette in his mouth, wearing navy-blue pants with two white stripes down each leg (*tracksuits*!), each female with round wire rolls woven into their hair (*curlers*!). Male and female, the socialist Adam and Eve, sit like that, surrounded by green ivy, rubber plants, rumpled fake bearskin, they sit lost as if in a jungle, as though they had died out, as though time had stopped, as though it were always six o'clock and there was no need whatsoever for things to be different . . .

Finally, I copied the idea of reject cookies as a nutritional product from real life. I knew a woman who worked at the Kraš chocolate factory. She fed herself and her pale, numerous children with rejected cookies that she brought from the factory in plastic bags. "We can afford meat once a week," she told me. I myself got a little bag as a Christmas present. Rejected cookies taste just as good as non-rejects.

The Kharms Case

For the requirements of this story I adopted the narrative mask of an overexcited translator of Daniil Kharms. Kharms, a Russian avant-garde writer, was first published in the Soviet Union in 1989, after this story was written. In the same year, a collection of Kharms's stories appeared in Croatian, entitled *Noughts and Zeroes* and translated by none other than myself.

Also in that same year, a certain Mr Z., an expert on Kharms's work, spent a short time in Zagreb. This Kharms expert had spent several years in a Soviet prison. A literarily inclined providence had thrust him into the same prison in which Kharms had spent his last days. While serving out his sentence, with the permission of the prison authorities, the assiduous Z. undertook the noble task of studying the dossiers of notable prisoners. That is how Z. came across the fact that the accepted date of Kharms's death—4 February 1942—is incorrect. On that day the prison authorities returned an unopened food parcel to Kharms's wife Marina Malich, while Kharms himself died somewhat later, in the prison insane asylum. In the asylum he is said to have selflessly distributed medals from the Society for the Philosophy of Balance and walked around with his head bandaged because if he took off the bandages his ideas would escape. Daniil Kharms really had founded the Society for the Philosophy of Balance, together with his Leningrad friend the philosopher Druskin. Druskin's brother, a composer, whom I met while in Leningrad, confirmed the existence of this unusual society.

During his stay in Zagreb, Z. contacted me twice: once unselfishly to tell me of his necrologico-historico-literary discovery, and a second time by telephone, asking me to lend him a hundred dollars, claiming that he had just been mugged near the main post office. I did not lend him the money, although that wasn't very nice of me.

Whether there is any secret equilibrium between these events is not yet clear.

The Kreutzer Sonata

This story stems from the old idea that certain well-known stories should be written again. Closing the pages of a book, passionate readers often wonder what would have happened if it had been different. I am just such a passionate reader. It usually occurs to me to fight for the neglected rights of female characters, but while reading *Anna Karenina* I wondered what the novel would have been like if Tolstoy had written it from the perspective of Anna's husband. Seeing as he had not, I took on the modest project myself. However, the great Russian writer would not be so great if he had not foreseen such things, and he did in fact write something similar himself, under the title "The Kreutzer Sonata." I therefore abandoned my intention. But one day, browsing through a second-hand bookstore, I came across a little book with the exciting title *The Sinner Woman*. Leafing through it, I realized that every great idea has probably already been used by some other writer, and that consequently a wise writer should avoid great ideas altogether. At the crucial moment, however, I lacked that wisdom.

Today, after so many years, it is some consolation that my rewriting inspired some similar performances from my countrymen, although no one ever gave me credit for it. Several years after my book was published, a Croatian writer—envisioning world literature as a big piece of Swiss cheese—published a book called *A Hundred Big Holes* and felt called upon to fill those literary holes himself. And some ten years after that another compatriot of mine wrote a book about Vronski. By the sheer force of this Croatian novelist's will, Vronski was catapulted into the distant future and the Croatian recent past, into war-torn Vukovar in 1991. In the Serbo-Croatian war, Vronski fights on the side of the Serbs, of course. The novel is not remotely funny, and it may have less to do with postmodernism, as local critics and the author himself enthusiastically maintained, than with a belief in reincarnation. This thesis is confirmed by an interview with the Croatian colonel Theo Ljubić who fought at Vukovar. Ljubić said:

"In my previous life, I was born in Germany and died in the Balkans in World War II, as a soldier in the Princ Eugen division. I even found a picture in a book of a Lieutenant Fischer, who I think was me."

Opting for romantic patriotism, many of my fellow writers went a hundred years back in time and became "avant-garde" anticipators of the end of postmodernism. On the other hand, in a charming little book for children about postmodernism, it is maintained that "the only cure for postmodernism is the incurable sickness of romanticism"!

Finally, I should add that the Zagreb–Belgrade trains really did run, then for a few years they didn't, and at the moment they are running again, although nothing else is the same as it was before. Luckily, the transportational reality with which the first edition of my book scrupulously corresponded has made sure to reflect the route described, unchanged, in the second edition, more than twenty years later.

Lend Me Your Character

This story was inspired by the simple idea that people are mortal while literary characters are immortal. This means that literary characters, if they earn tickets to eternal life, become free and, loosed from the chains of their creators, they can choose whom to befriend, to love, to strangle, to bore to death. I myself imagine the eternal literary hunting grounds as an arena of joyful promiscuity, where Peter Pan and Mephistopheles exchange kisses, or Winnie the Pooh and Nikolaj Kavalerov, or Heathcliff and Anna Karenina. Although this idea is exceptionally powerful, I remembered that a real writer should avoid overpowering effects and thus abandoned the theme of literary-historical promiscuity. I relied instead on life, which itself copies literary ideas!

I should mention that this story has its "feminist" side which readers from other literary backgrounds may find a bit old-fashioned today. In the literary world back home, however, it is just as relevant as it ever was. My native literary community still maintains the deeply rooted conviction that men's literary talent comes from God and women's from the Devil.

That is to say, in the literary scene the men respect each other, polemicize with each other, test and measure themselves against each other, enthuse about each other, pat each other on the back, write each other lengthy open letters, and dedicate their literary creations to each other. They never dedicate anything to women, even when they write love letters—at most, they dedicate a poem to a female initial. They do not quote women writers, even famous foreign women (except, for some reason, Hannah Arendt), but they always refer to famous foreign men.

Men are everywhere. They are editors, jury members, members of editorial boards, critics, reviewers, members of literary societies, and presidents of those same societies. They direct the publishing houses, compile anthologies and textbooks, edit literary journals and magazines, lecture on the national literature at universities, and write histories of those literatures. If a woman does take on some function in literary life, then the reason must be sought in her loyalty to a world ordered by the male.

The first and only writer's manual published in the former Yugoslavia, *How To Become a Writer* by Petar Mitić, moved me so deeply that I could not resist using some of its chapter titles as the subtitles in my story. And Andre Gide's little book *Marshlands* is one of the few books I would rewrite word for word as my own, if I could; I contented myself with stealing a few lines from it.

Finally, I am not sure whether my story has answered the question posed in the epigraph: "Is a pen a symbolic penis?" But perhaps an answer has been provided in a verse by the Croatian poet Ivan Slamnig:

> I used to be a mouse and a hero,
>
> Now I am nobody, no, and zero.

Here the end of this book, like a snake which bites its own tail, rejoins the beginning.

Amsterdam, 2003

SELECTED DALKEY ARCHIVE PAPERBACKS

FOR A FULL LIST OF PUBLICATIONS, VISIT:
www.dalkeyarchive.com

SELECTED DALKEY ARCHIVE PAPERBACKS

FOR A FULL LIST OF PUBLICATIONS, VISIT:
www.dalkeyarchive.com